FRUIT OF THE LAND

OF THE GODS - BOOK ONE

GINA STURINO

D1517795

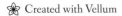 Created with Vellum

For my husband, who said it'd be a funky adventure and delivered. For my parents, who are inspirations in love and life. And for my daughter, who made me a mama, which is the best job in the world!

PROLOGUE

Little hands tugged at my chin as soft breaths tickled my cheek. I rolled over, blinking awake to find Calla's sea-green eyes inches from my own.

"Wake up, Mama! Look, it's sun-shiny outside!" She bounced to her knees, clasping her hands together and tilting her chin toward the bright, arched window. "Can we go now?"

I heard the same plea every morning for the last two rainy weeks, even on the day when a hailstorm pinged against the windowpanes.

"You need a haircut," I said, brushing a tangled lock off Calla's face. Her thick, dark hair tumbled down her back, clashing with the bubblegum-pink pajamas she had insisted on wearing the last three nights. According to my five-year-old daughter, fairies had long flowy hair that didn't require combing or brushing, and they only wore pink.

"Right now?" Her shoulders slumped.

"No, silly. It's too early for a haircut. Let's watch cartoons in bed. When we get up, we'll make muffins for Mrs. Cooper."

"And *then* the park?"

"Yes, and then the park." I couldn't help but grin as I patted Calla's pillow. She flopped down, settling into her usual space on the left side of the bed.

Most nights after I'd fallen asleep, Calla would sneak into my bed, carrying her favorite stuffed animal, Leon the Lion, and her pink ruffled pillow. I didn't mind her kicks and prods through the night. Waking to find Calla snuggled next to me offered reassurance, a sense of security.

Clicking the television remote, I sunk back into bed and willed a few more minutes of precious sleep.

"Mama?" Calla interrupted, just as I drifted off. "Will Mrs. Cooper ever see Jasper again?"

Our elderly neighbor had burst into tears when we bumped into her the previous day. Her precious kitty, Jasper, would not be returning from the veterinarian. We knew he'd been sick—we'd gotten updates every afternoon when we dropped off her mail—but his terminal prognosis came as a surprise. Homemade muffins were the least we could do, even if my last batch looked and tasted like hockey pucks.

"Yes, sweetheart." I stroked her cheek and smiled. "Mrs. Cooper will get to cuddle Jasper again someday. When we die, we move to a better place. Remember?"

"Like Daddy, right?"

My smile faded, but Calla didn't notice. Her eyes were on the cartoon, oblivious to my lower lip which drooped for a second. She rarely asked questions or talked about Nick. No one did. All but forgotten by everyone but me, as if he never existed.

Almost six years later, Nick's loss still left me breathless.

"Can we make muffins now?" Calla asked, still staring

at the screen, oblivious to my pounding pulse. "My belly's starving."

"Sure, baby." Plastering the smile on my face again, I tugged her into my arms. I wouldn't have fallen back asleep anyway.

PART ONE

There is no fear in love,
but perfect love casts out fear.
(1 John 4:18)

ONE

The screech of tires. The smell of burning rubber.

My eyes popped open and my head twisted side-to-side, searching for Calla. Instead, a bright, blinding overhead light came into focus.

This can't be happening. It's a dream. No, it's a nightmare.

Nausea churned in my stomach. I dug my elbows into the stiff mattress, attempting to push up, but my heavy limbs could only groan in response. I slumped back against the pillow.

"You're awake." A nurse hovered under the doorframe before coming to me and silencing the beeping machines.

Fat, hot tears rolled down my cheek. It wasn't a dream or a nightmare.

"Can I see her?" My raspy voice escaped in a low plea. "Please, I need to see Calla."

"You..." She considered her words, taking a long, deliberate breath. As she exhaled, her calm eyes met mine. "You collapsed. You had a nasty fall."

I lifted my hand, the one unencumbered by an IV, to rub my temple.

Milwaukee General Hospital. Dr. Lisle's clammy hands. Tubes and gauze. Calla's prognosis.

The nurse placed her hand over my shoulder and gave a gentle squeeze. "Let me get Dr. Shanahan. He may want you to rest longer."

I met her eyes, recognizing the sympathetic face and tender tone. I was no stranger to loss. After people learned of Nick's death, of my situation, I became accustomed to sad stares and pitying nods.

"Please, *please* let me see her."

"I'll do my best." She gave a limp smile before slipping back through the door.

That morning, any glimmer of hope disintegrated with two simple words—brain dead. There was nothing more they could do.

Days of exhaustion, dehydration, and wrecked nerves cumulated with Calla's devastating prognosis, shattering every last bit of my composure. I had collapsed, hitting my head against the edge of her ventilator.

The machine keeping my daughter alive had knocked me unconscious.

HOURS LATER, Dr. Shanahan allowed me to leave the ER and return to the trauma center where Calla remained in critical care. Since I'd been pumped with fluids and a strong sedative, the discharge nurse guided me through the hospital's sterile halls.

My unwilling feet moved like concrete blocks as she led me into the elevator. We ascended in acute silence, the machine creeping slower than a snail. With each passing floor and announcing ping, my heart pounded faster. I held my breath until the door squeaked open.

The trauma center's main nursing station, the gateway to the most critical cases, buzzed with activity. Flashes of white coats and pale-blue scrubs whirred past. An orderly I'd met earlier in the day stopped when he noticed me, his face softening in recognition.

There's nothing more we can do. I am so sorry. She is brain dead.

Dr. Lisle's solemn words echoed in my head, rapidly intensifying from slight whispers to deafening rumbles. I took a wobbly step backward, reaching for the nurse by my side, only to catch air.

I was falling again, plummeting into the same dark hole that swallowed me earlier. Only now, nothing caught me as I succumbed to my grief.

Thickening and churning into a black fog, air rolled against my cheeks. It wrapped around my throat and clouded my vision, roaring in my ears like an angry animal, a beast built from my despair. We wailed in unison, tumbling and twisting into a blur, until we became one, and I was the animal, the beast. I pinched my eyes shut and begged for it to stop, but somewhere deep within my core, I understood. Nothing more could be done. Calla was gone.

With a final cry of defeat, I whispered my sweet child's name into the air.

And it stopped.

No lingering sounds or vibrating sensations. The fog and my body went still. I squinted, and the dense air quickly cleared, turning from black to grey to white. It dissipated like steam. I blinked the final puffs away.

I hadn't blacked out. I was standing on two feet, bent

over gasping and heaving, but on steady ground. My dried lungs burned as they expanded with stinging air.

As my breathing slowed, I peeked around, realizing I was no longer in the trauma center. Despair had swept me outside, far from the hospital. In awe, I absorbed my surroundings. Everything seemed familiar, yet it took me a moment to place myself.

Our park, but not our park.

Brighter, crisper. Familiar... yet different. I looked up to a vibrant sky—blue, pink, yellow, white, purple. Unearthly.

The air around me quivered again. Without the fog, it looked like a wave in water. Softly, it settled to absolute stillness. Everything paused—the breeze, clouds, sun—every simple show of life ceased. I blinked, and nature—*life*— woke again. Trees rustled, grass swayed, wind whistled. Rays of golden sunshine brushed my shoulders while white clouds floated in a clear sky.

It was a new world. In it, I was changed. Like a weight lifting, my body felt lighter and brighter.

As I raised an unsteady hand to rub my eyes, a faint noise came from behind, growing louder until I could distinguish the various sounds. A baby crying, squealing, laughing, babbling, all at once. Sweet, familiar sounds. I turned deliberately, as in a dream, not wanting to startle myself awake.

There she was. My little girl.

She appeared everywhere and in every phase of her short life. Flashes of her spun around me. I'd forgotten how tiny she was at birth and how quickly she grew. But instantly, memories of her washed over me.

A newborn baby with a dark crop of hair. A slightly older infant, cooing. Melodic laughter, delicate skin. The baby-powder scent of infancy. Another wave of her sitting and clapping. She grew before my eyes, crawling and exploring as a curious toddler, then a preschooler dancing and jumping. *My baby*.

Her essence flashed faster until she became a blur. I squinted, trying to focus, and as my vision adjusted, she became one. Whole, healed. No longer the little girl with the broken body I had seen earlier in the trauma center. No gauze or tubes. Only her perfect face peering back at me.

Silky black hair spilled down her back, obliterating the image of tangled hair matted with blood. Her pink and white floral sundress flowed around like a cloud. All tatters and stains from the accident miraculously mended, all signs of the accident seemingly erased.

Calla's bright eyes, almost twinkling, met mine.

"Mama! You came!" she squealed, running to me. I dropped to my knees to embrace her. "Isn't it beautiful? The most beautiful place ever!" She let go to twirl around, then her arms were back around my waist, squeezing me.

"Baby?" I asked, not believing I was hearing or touching her again. "Baby?"

"Yes, Mama?" Calla asked, her eyes wide and bright. I hadn't heard her precious voice in three long days, not since the accident, on the morning we set out to the park after visiting Mrs. Cooper.

I pressed my nose into her hair, breathing in the floral scent of her shampoo, and then pulled back to run my fingers through her hair and stroke her cheek. I needed her to fill every bit of my senses.

"It's you. I can't believe it's you!" I cried, smashing her against me. "I've missed you."

"I missed you too, but now you're here, and I get to show you everything!" She leaned away, and I saw that the world had changed again. Plush grass, so thick and green, it didn't appear real, but I could smell it. The earthy, clean scent of freshly mowed grass, a perfect combination of plant and soil. Calla broke from my embrace. "I live here now."

Fanciful trees bloomed around us while emerald bushes shined under a glowing sun. Was that *our* bench behind us? Yes, the fountain too. Our park, but... different. Better.

"What do you mean, you live here?" Calla's statement should've startled me, but instead my racing heart settled. She came to my side again, resting her head on my shoulder. Beauty and peace blanketed the park.

"After I got hurt, I came here." Calla looked up with a goofy grin. "And look, I can do cartwheels now!" She skipped away to display her new skill, maneuvering with the ease of a seasoned gymnast. Her legs and arms moved in perfect alignment, her sundress fanning as she showed off the trick.

"Cal, that's amazing!" I clapped, and she beamed with pride. She'd started gymnastics classes a few weeks before the accident. Then she'd been clumsy and shy with inexperience.

"Uh-oh, Mama. I don't think you're supposed to be here." Calla's eyes darted and darkened, not scared but mischievous.

The temperature dropped, as if air conditioning had kicked on in the great outdoors. I turned slowly toward her stare, meeting a set of stunned eyes.

Nick.

Not taking his eyes off me, he moved closer and asked quietly, "Calla, did you bring her here?" His tone was not angry, but direct and commanding.

"No, Daddy!" Calla exclaimed, not noticing the strange tension that had built an immediate barrier between her parents. "I was playing, and poof! Mama was here!"

"Poof, she was here?" he asked in a low, incredulous voice. He shook his head. "Not possible."

Too taken aback to reply, I allowed the incredibility to sink in. My daughter, my little girl, who days earlier had the breath of life knocked from her in a horrific car accident, stood before me, healthy and beautiful. Nick, Calla's father, who I hadn't seen since before she was born, towered beside her.

The magnitude of the situation settled, and I repeated, "Poof! I was here."

Then I staggered, and the air quivered. Nick held out his arm, too far away to touch me, yet the gesture steadied my footing.

"Not possible," he said again, and the breeze stalled.

The three of us stood in silence, assessing one another.

"Am I dead?" I whispered. "No, I'm dreaming." Assured, I repeated louder, "I'm dreaming."

But Calla is real. And the grass tickling my toes, the wind stroking my cheeks—that was real too. Too real to be a dream. Every sensation within me tingled with life.

"What the *hell* is going on?" Panic lumped in my throat.

"Mama, bad word!" Calla exclaimed. She giggled and skipped away to turn cartwheels, bored with us. Her laugh and carefree essence set me at ease, but seeing Nick and Calla, I knew something was terribly wrong.

"Am I dreaming?"

"No." Nick offered no further explanation. We stood silent as I considered the possibilities.

"What's going on, Nick?"

"I don't know."

"Where am I?" Desperate now, my chest tightened. I tried to take long, calming breaths, but the air seemed so thick I could hardly choke it down. I needed something, anything, to make sense of what was happening. "Really, you can tell me. Am I dead? Is this heaven?" My head shook slightly, until I inhaled at the one plausible option.

With a firm voice I declared, "It must be heaven, because you're dead."

TWO

Six Years Ago

A sticky breeze rolled through the loft, carrying the sweet scent of fresh buds and damp earth. I had waited months for this moment, when I could prop open the windows and wipe away winter.

I sank into the couch, dust rag still in hand, and gulped ice water. Spring cleaning sucked up the morning, but at least it kept my mind off Hank.

Our breakup wasn't what stung. That was inevitable. But catching him with my longtime friend Elisa, canoodling over coffee, *that* was two simultaneous slaps to the face.

So, with a change in the seasons came a change in my relationship status.

"Out with the old, and in with the new," my best friend Novalee had proclaimed. She cheered when I told her Hank and I were over. I could practically see her doing a victory jig through the phone. She never liked him, but then again, she never liked anyone I dated.

The text message she sent that morning offered a new twist on her relationship advice, though I'd hardly call her an expert on the subject. *Best way to get over the old is to get it on with someone new. We're going out tonight, no ifs, ands, or buts. Wear something that'd make "Hank the Skank" drool.*

At least it made me giggle.

Shrugging off thoughts of Hank, I got up from the sofa and tossed the dust rag into the trash. Novalee was right. Just like spring cleaning, out with the old.

~

AFTER A MORNING SPENT ORGANIZING and tidying, I'd somehow misplaced my grocery list. I gave up searching after checking the obvious places—the coffee table, my nightstand, the trash bin. It seemed to have disappeared into thin air.

I lived by checklists and Post-Its, going so far as categorizing grocery items in order of aisle and shelf location. Without my meticulous list, I wandered the produce department feeling more than a little lost.

Bananas and eggs. And don't forget bread.

My rickety cart came to a screeching halt as I stopped at a tower of mangos. Nope. They weren't on the original list, but after walking three blocks in the sweltering heat to the Metro Mart, nothing sounded more refreshing than a tropical smoothie. I might struggle following a simple recipe or baking a boxed dessert, but I worked magic with a blender.

I reached to pluck the best-looking mango, toward the bottom of the pile, when my hand collided with another.

"Excuse me," I muttered, reflexively snatching my arm away. Glancing at the offending fingers, my eyes traveled along to a thick, muscled forearm, a solid chest, and finally rested on the face of a man. *A stunning man.* Unusual green eyes, a strong chin, and glossy dark hair. Not inky black like mine, but more the color of wet sand.

Tall, dark, and handsome with a rugged edge. He looked like one of those models you'd see in a cologne ad, the kind who never had a shirt on.

The thought flashed across my face, and I blinked, awkwardly averting my stare back to his hand, which now held my fruit, and then again to his eyes. I knew I'd never seen him before, yet the words tumbled out. "Have we met?"

This man, mango in hand like a prize, shook his head. The corner of his lip twisted upward, softening the sharp angles of his jaw. "No."

The certainty in his voice made me laugh. "Okay." I nodded, embarrassed. "Right." It did sound like a pick-up line. Heat crept into my cheeks.

"I'm not from here," he explained, holding the mango out as an offering. He placed it in my cart. "Here, you have it."

"Okay, well, thank you." My eyes moved from the fruit in my cart back to him. Gorgeous. A strong body, like granite cut into the form of a man. I flushed, the heat now traveling to the back of my neck. As his grin widened, deep dimples dotted each cheek, and I reddened more. With a little shake of my head, I moved my cart, backing away with a whispered groan. I always embarrassed easily, but this was silly.

Have we met? I cringed and continued down the produce aisle, stopping next at the tomatoes. As I picked one up, I couldn't help but again peer over to the stranger. Why did he seem so familiar? With his back to me, I assessed the plain black T-shirt, pulled tautly over broad shoulders. Khaki shorts, flip-flops. Nothing special, yet his presence dominated the room. I couldn't look away.

He turned, and once again our eyes connected. This time, despite his knowing smile, I did not break contact. I could not. We stood motionless, gazing across the rows of produce, as if captivated by some unnatural force.

An immeasurable amount of time passed—minutes or mere seconds—before the spell dissipated. Perhaps I blinked, but whatever rendered us frozen melted away, and we were again two strangers staring at one another.

I realized I'd been holding my breath and blew out through pursed lips. His smile widened, again flashing those dimples. The heat at the back of my neck notched up a few degrees as he walked the few steps to me.

"I'd try to steal your tomato too, but that might be too obvious," he said, now close enough that I could catch his cologne. He smelled of sweat and woodsy aftershave.

"Oh?" I asked dumbly, and then realized he was flirting. "Oh."

"I'm going to just ask because I prefer to be direct." He took the tomato from my hand. "Would you like to get coffee?"

"Coffee?"

He laughed and nodded. "Yes, coffee."

"Where?" Could I give more than one word answers?

"Anywhere."

And with that, we left his basket and my cart orphaned next to the tomatoes and mangos.

~

WE WERE steps out of the store when several things struck me. *Which coffee shop? Is this safe? How do I look? Is this crazy?*

He answered the first question by pointing toward Dark Beans, a trendy coffee shop in my neighborhood. "How's this place?"

"Great, it's great. I go there all the time." That was a little white lie. I hadn't been to Dark Beans since the incident with Hank. "I live just a couple blocks away, so this is my go-to place."

If the answer to question two was *no*, I gave away that I live in the area. But I realized I wasn't afraid, in fact the opposite. This man, whose name I didn't yet know, somehow made sense.

I am walking to get coffee with a friend, not a stranger.

But... he was a stranger, and I didn't know his name.

We walked in silence, stopping at the corner of Ogden and Van Buren to wait for the streetlight.

"What's your name?" he asked.

Turning toward him, I looked up, momentarily awestruck by his intense green eyes. Blinking back to reality, I extended my hand, then breathily introduced myself. "I'm Mirabel. Mira."

"Nice to meet you, Mira. I'm Nicholas." Clasping my hand, he gave a gentle shake.

He released his hold, but my hand remained mid-air. I turned my palm upward, studying it as if I'd just shaken hands with a celebrity.

I giggled then, a short, high-pitched, girly snort, finding the absurdity of the afternoon's events too amusing to contain. Popping out to buy a few groceries and now, here I was, on a possible first date. Stuff like this happened to Novalee, not me.

Attempting to collect myself, I dropped my hand to my side and paused for a breath. Looking up, I channeled Novalee and coolly asked, "Nicholas. Do you go by Nick?"

"Sure, I'll go by whatever you want to call me." He flashed a smile, the kind that can reduce a woman to a giddy, starry-eyed teenager.

Careful to keep my composure, I gave a nod. I'd outgrown the silly, awkward stage years ago, coming into my own, and even appreciating the features I used to despise. The black hair that clashed with my porcelain complexion. My full lips that stretched nearly ear to ear when I smiled. *Fish lips.* That's what Tim Teeters called me in the seventh grade. While it stung then, I now had the confidence to recognize my beauty.

I just wished I would've checked a mirror before leaving home, maybe worn something other than running shorts. And my hair—my hands flew to my head to pat back loose strands. First thing I'd do is excuse myself to the bathroom for damage control.

Nick chuckled. "Unexpected, huh?" He didn't wait for a reply. Instead, he held open the door to Dark Beans. "Well, shall we?"

As we walked in, I nearly choked at my luck, which ended as I spotted Hank, occupying the same table he'd shared with Elisa just a few weeks before.

Hank perked up in his chair across the room, then drew back as he realized I was with the large guy dominating the entryway. Both men took note of one another. I smiled meekly and gave a little wave.

Nick glanced toward Hank then back to me. "So, what'll it be? Shall we take it outside?"

"Yes, outside. Coffee, black. Please," I stuttered, turning my back on Hank.

The barista handed two cups to Nick, and I excused myself to the restroom. Thankfully it was an individual room which offered privacy to fix my hair and assess my makeup-less face.

Novalee's nagging beauty lectures whispered in my ears like the little devil that sometimes sits on your shoulder and gives you unwanted advice. We were nearing thirty, and she admonished me about the fact that I still didn't use moisturizer, let alone mascara and lipstick. As a horticulturist, it didn't seem necessary to get dolled up for the plants and flowers that dominated my day-to-day life.

Inwardly groaning, I realized I did appear dressed for a day working in the garden or a workout at the gym. At least my hair was still in place, pulled back into my signature ponytail.

Under the fluorescent lighting of the bathroom vanity, I figured I was presentable. Regardless, I swiped shiny clear gloss over my lips and then headed out to meet Nick.

When I emerged, Hank blocked my way. He must've stationed himself outside of the bathroom to wait for my exit.

"Who's that?" he asked, crossing his arms over his chest.

"Who?" I replied in an innocent tone. "My friend?"

"Right, a friend. Guess you move on quick."

I bit my tongue. He was out of line, but there was no use poking the bear. "Let's talk later, okay?" I suggested and moved past him. Then I caught Nick closing in.

"Everything okay?" Nick cocked his head, looking from me to Hank.

Hank visibly shrank. He gave a nod, then sauntered off. As a polished professional, he cared more about his appearance and the appearance of who he was with than anything else. His ego might be bruised, seeing me with another man so soon after our break-up, but he wouldn't get into a public spat. Not at a coffee shop where people he knew might witness it, and definitely not with a man who looked as fierce as Nick.

"Ex-boyfriend?" Nick asked.

"Yep, he's just surprised to see me." Hank might've seemed a bit aggressive, stalking me outside the bathroom, but underneath the insecurities, he was harmless. A fool, but harmless.

"Recent?"

"A couple weeks ago." I shrugged.

"Sorry. Must be kind of awkward." Nick noted a change of topic was in order. "So, tell me about yourself, Miss Mirabel."

From there, we sat for hours and talked. And talked. The magic that rendered us frozen over produce now kept us captivated over coffee. We refilled our cups until my fingers tingled from caffeine. Neither of us was willing to make the first move to leave. Neither of us wanted our time together to come to an end.

THREE

The Present

"We're not dead, Mama, we're gods," Calla answered, stopping her gymnastics to rejoin the conversation. "We don't die."

I took an inadvertent step back, my head shaking as I looked from Nick, who'd been buried over five years ago, to Calla, who'd just been declared brain dead.

Nick's eyes shifted from Calla to the ground and then met mine. She followed suit, looking from Nick to me.

"Something wrong?" She arched a brow.

My head continued to bob, which Calla took as an answer. The crease above her brows softened.

"Mira." Hearing Nick say my name again for the first time in years sent a shiver through me. Simple yet seductive, his voice evoked sweet memories and intimate moments that were long buried.

My heart pounded, the tension palpable. He must have felt it too, because he said again, but stronger, pushing away the intimacy, "Mira." He took his eyes off me for a second, just a quick glance to Calla, before blinking back to me. She shrugged and turned away, again doing cartwheels, oblivious to her parents' nerves.

"Is this heaven?" I whispered.

"No." Nick breathed in deeply and looked to the sky as if asking for an explanation.

But what was happening could not have an explanation. It was surreal. Unreal.

"It's not heaven. And I don't know if what I can tell you will make sense... to you... for you." He exhaled.

A fat tear slipped from my eye, rolling down my cheek and landing into the corner of my mouth. I swiped it away with the back of my hand, leaving a wet glaze on my cheeks.

"Calla and I are gods. It's true."

"Gods?" I whispered. Truth mingled with the humid breeze, covering me like a blanket. I shook my head. But the air draped around us, settling over my shoulders, so thick and heavy I couldn't shrug it off.

This is crazy. I have gone off the deep end. I've gone crazy.

The air churned, so dense I could almost see it. Swirling and twirling, it danced along with Calla's cartwheels.

I've gone crazy, and no one can blame me. I'll wake up back in the emergency room. It's the sedatives. More sedatives. I've lost it. I have lost so much that I've lost myself.

Nick cringed, either from the heaving air or from my expression. He took a moment to consider his words, then sighed. The air settled, seeming to gain composure along with him. He addressed Calla, who was still oblivious, swirling and twirling. "Please find Leo and go with him to the cove. Mommy and I will come for you after we talk, okay?"

"She's not going anywhere," I protested before Calla

could answer, putting a hand up toward Nick. Calla ran to my side as I knelt to her.

"This conversation is not for her ears." I recognized his tone. A soldier. He didn't speak, he commanded.

"No. She's not leaving me again." I held my ground, picking Calla up and hugging her close. She tucked herself into my hold, and I caught her familiar scent. So strong and stunning, I closed my eyes and inhaled deeper. *Lilies.*

She loved flowers as much as I did. Lilies were our favorite.

"Mama! Look!" Calla pulled away, and her tiny finger pointed to a blooming calla lily. Several more buds began to explode from the ground. Their little tips burst through the soil, erupting like a volcano, unfolding into flawless white petals.

Calla's namesake flower, the calla lily, grew wild in our park. She spent weeks impatiently waiting for them to bloom. Now, before us, a garden full of calla lilies sprouted, budded, and blossomed within seconds. Calla giggled.

We looked from the waving flowers to one another, a peace settling over the park. The garden seemed to suck up our tension, leaving behind a calming floral scent. I loosened my grip on Calla, and she wiggled free.

"I'm gonna find Leo and play at the cove!" She flitted away, like a butterfly dancing around a garden. She was so assured, so beautiful, I let her go. Her little body slowly disappeared in the field.

"Let's sit down," Nick suggested.

I turned, and there was *our* bench, in *our* park. I hesitated but followed him to the familiar white marble. We stood before it in silence.

"Gods?" I whispered.

Nick nodded.

"You and Calla are gods?" Again, he nodded in response.

He closed his eyes, and his lips moved like he was praying. He gestured for me to sit down on our bench, the wide, smooth stone that held our intimate secrets. It was big enough for us to sit together yet keep a safe distance. Cool and comforting. We sat engulfed in silence. I felt Nick's eyes on me, studying me.

"What about me?" I finally asked. "Why am I here?"

"I don't know."

"What do you mean, you don't know?" As I questioned, each word rose louder. "What is this place? *Where* are we?"

A breeze parted the air, scattering the scent of flowers.

"It's hard to explain." Nick hesitated. "A different realm. My home, Calla's home. Home for all gods of the Land. The Land where no mortal shall walk."

"Mortal? You mean, human?"

"We're all human, Mira." Nick looked to the sky. "Nature is two-fold. There's human and divine. Here we transcend those borders, born human with divine gifts. Gods." He looked to me, watching for a reaction. I needed more, but the air turned tense. Nick looked tense.

We had at least a foot between us, but as we continued to sit in apprehensive silence, the space diminished, and Nick's arms encircled me. His chin rested on my head, and he held me just as he had six years ago.

"What're we going to do?" he whispered. He lifted his head from mine and pulled me against him, his lips on mine. Kissing me again, a new first kiss.

It began sweet, as if drawing on a cherished memory. Quickly it changed, becoming rough and hungry. He held me closer, and the kiss deepened, his hand behind my head pulling me ever closer...

Years of heartache, and there was a lot of it, passed as our tongues collided. I felt them, saw them. Memories of the years passing quickly and quietly. And then happiness. Years of laughter, memories powerful and intense. So clear, like watching a movie. Our memories. Playing over and over. Tears, laughter, cries, whispers, and everything in between. And then they were gone. I pulled away, gasping.

"What was that?" The words barely came out. I held my fingers to my lips.

"That was us, remembering."

Birds chirped. Grass and leaves rustled. Nature sang in harmony with the wind, caressing my skin and soothing my senses.

So much time, so many events, life and death, had passed in six years. The memories left me breathless as they whispered words of affirmation. I remained motionless. Truth, understanding, memories... everything settled around like pieces of a puzzle, pieces of a puzzle where I did not know the picture, but I knew they fit.

The pieces, everything that flashed between us, pulled me together until I could no longer question words or logic. I didn't know how, yet I understood. I didn't know what, but I believed.

It felt right, it felt real, but I needed to hear it from him. I needed him to speak, the one person who held the picture for the pieces of this bizarre puzzle.

"Please, Nick, tell me more."

"There's too much. And even if I try, I'm not sure it'll make sense to you."

"I don't know what's going on." I looked around, again taking in the wonder of my surroundings. "But I believe. I believe you are gods. I do." I shook my head. "It's unbelievable, it doesn't make sense, but I feel it to be true. Here." I held my hand to my chest and pressed where my heart beat. "But I need to hear it, so please, just try to explain. Calla is a god, but why is she here? Why now? Did she die?"

There's nothing more we can do. I am so sorry. She is brain dead.

After a deliberate pause, Nick replied, "I brought her here. I took her." He looked down to his hands, which rested on his lap.

"You *took* her?" I whispered. "You brought her here?"

Nature stopped. The birds, the air, the swaying leaves.

Nick's eyes shifted, focusing on something in the distance.

"How could you? How could you take her from me?" My hands clenched into fists, but Nick caught my arms and brought them down to my side, pinning them against my body.

I watched as he breathed in and out, calming himself and calming me. He loosened his grip.

"I didn't take her from you. I brought her home. She is a god. This is where she belongs." He waved his arms toward the picture-perfect park, an artist's canvas of colors. Grass greener than emeralds, and crisp flowers vibrant with unearthly colors. The brilliant, blinding sun.

No, none of that mattered. Her home was with me.

"I gave birth to her, held her, fed her, watched her grow." My tone pitched. "I did it alone, too. You left us. She's my world. How could you?"

The screech of tires. Burning rubber. Gauze and tubes. Hair matted with blood.

"She was hit by a car. Did you do that?" I read his face and knew. Fury seethed within me, radiating from my core and pulsing through my body. The air quivered, and I knew it was my anger shaking the atmosphere. "Tell me! Did you do that?"

With sadness in his eyes, Nick nodded.

"Say it! Tell me!" The wind shuddered like angry ocean waves, roaring along with my rage.

Nick looked at me. "Yes. It was me."

FOUR

Six Years Ago

Clerks swiped the tables, glancing toward Nick and me, the only patrons left at Dark Beans.

"Are you hungry?" I asked, hoping to stretch our time. Afternoon had turned to early evening.

I learned so much about him in our three-hour coffee-shop conversation. A lifetime's worth. We covered our childhood, adolescence and adulthood-to-date with complete ease in conversation, chatting like old friends. He grew up in California, enlisted in the Army, and was a soldier stationed at the naval base in Illinois, located just over the Wisconsin border. On weekend liberty, he liked to explore new cities in the vicinity and live a little bit of a "normal, civilized life", as he put it.

Nick looked at his wrist, even though he wasn't wearing a watch. "Yes, sorry. I've got to check the time."

"Are you due back?"

"Liberty ends tomorrow night, but I took the Metro here—I don't have a car. Not sure when the last train leaves.

My plan when I checked the schedule this morning was to take the seven o'clock back."

I never wore a watch; it'd only get dirty at work. And I forgot my cell at home. It had to be nearing five, Dark Bean's closing time. I couldn't help with the train schedule either. I rarely left the city. My job working for the city parks system kept me within walking distance of my apartment, but I did have a car.

"I could drive you back." The words were out before I'd formed the thought. I reddened, hoping I didn't sound desperate. More so, I hoped for more time with Nick. Our story couldn't end here.

And it didn't. Nick agreed to my offer, and we left the coffee shop, again stopping at the corner of Ogden and Van Buren. This time, as we waited for the walk signal, we stood in companionable silence. The earlier awkwardness at that spot shifted to something else. An intimacy we couldn't deny.

As the light changed and we moved across the street, Nick's arm brushed against mine. I swear my skin tingled. And I swear he felt it too because he looked just as startled.

STEPPING over the threshold into my apartment, I spotted a folded sheet of paper that had been slipped under the door, Novalee's handwriting scrawled across the front.

Our girls' night! I'd completely forgotten. Novalee, whom I roomed with during and following college, now lived in the adjacent unit.

I picked up the sheet and scanned over her familiar lettering.

I heard your cell ringing through the walls when I called.

You left it at home again? Call me when you get this! Big plans for tonight!

Novalee, or Mama Bear, as I fondly called her, knew I not only forgot my cell phone often, but generally misplaced it.

"Everything okay?" Nick questioned, peering over my shoulder.

"Oh yeah, nothing urgent. It's from Novalee, my old roommate. I think I told you about her?" I knew I had. We were best friends for so long that most memories from the last decade included her. College roommates turned "real life" roommates. A few months earlier, we decided to venture on our own, moving into neighboring units. We needed the independence of our own space, but appreciated the comfort and security of having each other close.

"You want to call her?" he asked, waving me into the apartment. "I can wait, no worries."

"Okay, sure. Make yourself at home. In fact, if you'd like a drink, I have wine in the fridge. Please help yourself."

I found my cell upstairs on the carpet next to a blossoming African violet I had rotated earlier in the day. Flipping the phone open, the missing grocery list floated to the ground. Right, I'd tucked it in there for safekeeping. Unfolding it, I grinned. If I hadn't been aimlessly perusing the produce aisle, I possibly wouldn't have bumped into Nick.

Notifications for several missed calls and text messages blinked on the screen. I scrolled past Hank's name to Novalee's. She extended an invitation to an event that evening. My charismatic best friend was endlessly invited, and therefore inviting me, to socials ranging from rock concerts to cocktail hours.

My loft bedroom, which overlooked the compact living

room, didn't provide much privacy. I escaped to the bathroom to call Novalee.

"Mira." She answered before the first ring ended.

"Yes?" I giggled, then stopped. She usually started straight off with her requests, the A-type personality. "Everything okay? I got your text about the luau tonight at Strange Pete's."

"Yeah, everything's fine. I've just been trying to reach you forever! Where've you been, and without your phone!" Here was Mama Bear, worrying about me unnecessarily.

"Well, you'll never believe what happened." I lowered my voice, not wanting Nick to overhear my excitement as I laid out the day's events.

Slowly, as a mother would scold their child, she huffed out, "You took a strange guy home? He's there now? Some weirdo you met at the Metro Mart?"

I giggled again. "Weirdo, no. He's like a freaking Greek god. I mean, seriously, you should see him. I could bounce rocks off him." I snapped my mouth shut. But Nick was possibly the most attractive man I had ever met. *No, definitely.*

"Mira, being good looking does not make someone a good person." Her concerned tone turned serious. "This sounds really creepy. Who picks up women at a grocery store? Wait, did you say he's a soldier? Mira, he's trying to get laid. You know it, come on. Ditch him and meet me."

I knew it all right. She gave the reaction I expected. Until Novalee got to know my love interests personally, she was skeptical, even paranoid, of their intentions. Usually I appreciated her motherly protection.

"Um, I think you were the one telling me to 'get it on' with someone new. So really, I'm just taking your advice," I joked. Then again, maybe I wasn't. I never had one-night stands or sex on the first date, but Nick made me rethink my morals.

"You know I didn't mean that literally," Novalee groaned. "Fine, ask him if he wants to come to the luau tonight. I'm here for a Loft event, but it'll be fun—live music, tiki drinks." Loft and Associates was the prestigious law firm Novalee worked at, starting as an intern and rising in the ranks over the years.

"Okay, okay. I'll ask. But don't be mad if we're a no-show. If you saw him, trust me, you'd be skipping the tiki drinks and going for the leis."

"Just so you know, I'm rolling my eyes," she shot back, but I sensed a smile in Novalee's tone.

After ending our conversation with the usual "love you, sissy," I hastily maneuvered around the bathroom, stripping off the shorts and tank, splashing cold water over my face and applying a light layer of makeup.

Having thick, black lashes, I really didn't need mascara, but after two coats and a swipe of eyeliner, I blinked back at the results. Novalee was right. A little makeup transformed my unassuming eyes to a smoky, seductive brown.

Not wanting to keep Nick waiting, I hurried to undo my signature ponytail, combing it loose before twisting it back up into a ballerina-style bun. A hip-hugging sleeveless dress, conveniently hanging on the back of the bathroom door, and dangling earrings completed the look. Casual yet sexy.

Maybe I was overdressed, or maybe it was simply self-consciousness. I rarely wore anything besides jeans and cotton shirts, even on dates. Hank could attest to that.

Before dwelling further, I swung the door open and peered over the balcony to the lower level. Nick stood by the sliding glass door, gazing out to my cramped patio, glass of white wine in hand.

I inhaled, suddenly nervous I'd trip down the stairs even though I was barefoot. Nick's head jerked up in my direction.

"There you are." His voice was soft as his eyes swept over my face.

I carefully stepped down, my pulse quickening from the look on Nick's face. A look that made a woman feel appreciated, beautiful... wanted.

Wind picked up from the open patio, tousling Nick's hair. The effect only amplified the seductive air engulfing the room. My feet hit the landing and I exhaled. We stood motionless, staring at one another, waiting for the next step, but not quite sure what it was.

Nick broke the spell, setting his glass down on the coffee table while hastily moving toward me. I prepared myself, tilting my face up toward his, the need for him suddenly urgent.

Instead of a kiss, he placed his arms around my waist, and leaned into me until his chin rested on my forehead. We stood in a loose embrace, innocent but strikingly intimate.

Finally, Nick spoke, lifting his chin. "What are we going to do?"

Then slowly, sweetly, he brushed his lips across mine.

The kiss was gentle and innocent, yet it left me breathless. Nick pulled away, looking just as surprised.

"Tonight? What do you mean?" My voice was low and husky. He didn't answer, but his eyes locked again on mine, sparkling like emeralds.

We stood frozen.

Nick severed the connection, shifting his gaze away and

taking a step back. He stood taller, gaining control of his space. The magic in the room dispersed, thinning in the humidity. He picked up his abandoned wine glass. "Yes. What's our plan?"

"Well, we have options."

"Okay, what are they? I am pretty open to whatever the night holds, as long as it involves you." A flirty grin covered his face, and I resisted the urge to touch his dimples.

"For me?" I asked, spotting a glass of wine on the kitchen counter. Stepping past Nick, my elbow brushed against his arm. The simple touch set my skin on fire.

Nick nodded and held his glass toward mine. "To a memorable night, whatever and wherever it may take us." After a clink against my glass, he took a slow, deliberate drink, then motioned for me to join him on the sofa. "I know it'll be a memorable evening, a memory that'll mean a lot to me in the next couple of months. But that's the problem. I'm deploying soon."

Earlier over coffee, he told me about his work in the military. He was training with the Navy at the Great Lakes Naval Base before deploying with one of their units. He explained that although he was a soldier in the Army, he was taking part in a joint effort for this particular mission. I hadn't pieced together until now that tonight might be our only night.

My heart sank. I'd only known him for hours, but the thought of him being gone from my life just as quickly as he entered didn't seem fair.

"How soon?" I had to know.

"Nine weeks. After this workup, we leave."

Nine weeks. That gave us time. We could get to know each other in nine weeks.

"How long will you be gone?" *Please say nine weeks.* Nine weeks here, nine weeks gone, that seemed fair.

"Nine months." Regret thickened his voice.

I nearly spit out my wine. Nine months was a lifetime, literally the time it took for a new life to be created and enter the world.

"That's a long time." It was all I could manage.

NICK FINISHED his drink just as I finished mine. It was only one glass, but I felt light-headed, tingly from my finger-tips to my toes.

"Would you like another? I have crackers and cheese?" I offered, although I knew the crackers were stale. They were on the forgotten grocery list.

We couldn't leave yet. I didn't want to take him outside my apartment where we might be interrupted by others. Here we could go from carrying on an easy conversation, to enjoying each other in comfortable silence. No rush and no interruptions.

"I'd like another," I proclaimed. My voice came out high, almost shrill. I was wound up like a kid waiting for Santa on Christmas. Something good was going to happen, and I knew that something involved Nick.

My living room flowed into a thin galley kitchen. The compact space, June humidity and wine left my cheeks flushed and my neck damp. I pulled the refrigerator door open and welcomed the cold gust that escaped, closing my eyes for a second before searching for another bottle of wine.

A chardonnay on the lower shelf sat chilled. I couldn't help but hold it to my skin, cooling the tiny flecks of sweat that beaded my hairline. Nick watched, and I heard him exhale as I pulled the bottle away.

He was on his feet and to me in seconds, taking the bottle from my hands before brushing away the drops of condensation on my neck with his thumb. One hand traveled to the back of my head, stroking my hair, and the other landed on my cheek. He pulled me into him; our bodies pressed together while his lips skimmed mine, like a butterfly dancing over a petal.

"You smell like flowers." He breathed the words into my ear.

From there, it turned hungry. Our lips smashed together, eagerly exploring. One hand remained at the back of my head while the other moved firmly down my spine. With no space between us, I could feel the hardness of his chest.

Nick paused before his hand roamed further, stopping to cup my bottom and press me against an entirely different hardness.

Just when we made the connection, he took a step back.

I was breathless. He was breathless.

He studied me, and his eyes darkened to a deep green, like grass after a good rainfall. I inhaled long and slowly. Nick watched my chest as my lungs expanded. His eyes darted back to mine, and I recognized this look.

Hunger... and not for stale crackers.

FIVE

The Present
Nick kept his eyes down. Clouds rolled over the park.

I shook my head with disgust. "She's brain dead."

He sighed deeply, refusing to look at me.

"The doctors told me there's nothing they can do. Her head was so badly damaged, it was wrapped in gauze... tubes and wires... I couldn't even see her face." I tried to shake away the horrible vision.

"There's nothing more we can do. I am so sorry. She is brain dead." Dr. Lisle's voice echoed in my head.

"Nick, you killed her!" I jumped up from the bench, my hands clenched into fists.

"She was growing too strong!" He shot to his feet. Thunder clapped and lightning illuminated the sky. The blinding sun hid, leaving the park dark as night. Storm clouds huffed above us, angry and menacing.

I shivered, afraid of how quickly nature took cover.

Nick shook his head and the clouds scattered, instantly calming the sky. My chin dropped, my fists unclenched.

"I was watching her, but there's only so much I can do from afar. Little gods have energy and power that grows within them. If they don't know how to direct it or control it, it becomes dangerous. If not used properly, it can be disastrous." Nick grabbed my hand and pulled me back down onto the bench. The quarter-sized patch of skin where our knees touched sizzled. We jerked, both startled from the sudden jolt of electricity. "I need to sort through this. I don't understand what's happening."

He didn't understand?

"I saw her, Mira. I couldn't miss it. I was there." Nick hesitated, and then began more softly. "I am so proud of her. And I am so proud of you." He looked to the distance, speaking so quietly I had to lean closer, taking care not to touch him again. "I was there when she was born. You may not have seen me, but I was there, whispering to you, holding you. I heard her first cries just as you heard them."

Emotion caught in my throat as I remembered his voice whispering in my ear during labor. *"Be strong."* I thought it was my imagination.

"I saw her along with you, for the first time, just as you were seeing her. Besides you, she is the most beautiful thing I have ever seen."

The emotion in my throat traveled to my eyes, filling them with tears.

"I tried, Mira, I tried to nurture her from afar so she could stay with you." He looked down again, his eyes settling on his hands. "But she can't. She just can't."

My tears rolled, falling over my cheeks as light rain began to descend from the sky.

A realization fell over Nick, something so strong that the winds picked up, and the raindrops fell faster. They pinged against Calla's calla lilies, bouncing off the smooth petals and falling like hail to the grass. I could barely see Nick even though he sat inches away. He pulled me from the bench to my feet and gently swept away the tears and rain from my face. As he did, the sky cleared, again becoming bright and crisp.

Just as he'd shaken the storm clouds earlier, he swept away the rain. Yet, I recognized stress in the air, stifling like the humidity that follows a summer storm.

"No, it's not possible. It's just not." His voice turned low and urgent. "We're Land gods or gods of the earth. Calla is a nature goddess, flowers specifically."

Of course. Flowers always fascinated her. They dominated both of our lives. I realized the profound impact they had had on us.

"Look, mama! A lily!" She ran to pick a freshly budded flower, excitement bubbling from her. She crossed the street without thinking to check for traffic... before I could stop her... before the driver could hit the brakes.

My baby was killed in her mortal life by the very thing that made her immortal. Nick allowed me time to absorb the bitter irony.

"Land gods care for everything that is alive in the world of mortals. The Sky gods, or gods of the heavens, care for that of the afterlife." He pointed to the bright sky above. "Sky gods watch over what some people refer to as angels, mortals in the afterlife."

"The afterlife?"

"Yes, the afterlife, in heaven. Gods keep order. We help guide mortals, in life and death, and lead them in the right direction, but never force their hand. Where they go, what they do, is up to their moral compass. There is such a thing as heaven and hell. If your soul is deserving, but your mortal life was not, you're sent back to try again." Nick shrugged.

"It's much more complicated than that. We, of the Land, create life. From the Sky comes death." He noted my dark reaction and reached to comfort me, but pulled his hand back before making contact. "Death is nothing to fear. Heaven is a place of divine glory. I'll never be able to walk there, but it's just as beautiful here."

"You'll never see heaven?" I asked with surprise. Then again, he had just caused a horrific car accident involving my—*our*—daughter.

He shook his head. "Just as the dead cannot walk with the living, the Land gods cannot cross into the Sky's domain. To do so can be a mortal sin to a god." Nick raised his eyebrows. "A god can lose their station when they go unto another god's domain."

"You mean, if a Sky god tries to come here? That's a sin? A god can become mortal?"

"Yes. Even gods face punishment for their actions."

"So... why am I here? Am I a god?" What could explain my presence here?

"I would've known you were a god when we met among the mortals. I'd recognize you now. But... I just can't understand how you can be here, unless..." He stopped in thought, "But it's not possible. I'd feel if you were one of us." He held his hands to his chest. "Only gods of great strength can move between this realm and the mortal world. It's just... something's off."

He didn't feel it. *Something's off.* My heart deflated. I didn't belong in this beautiful world with Calla and him. The very thought of my presence baffled Nick.

"Can mortals come here?" I whispered with a wave to the park. "How can I..." The question lingered. I needed to know. Who was I? What was I?

I needed to know so I could stay with my child. I

hugged myself, feeling rejected and alone. And the breeze, which picked up in velocity, didn't help.

"There must be something in you. You may be half mortal and born of a god who hasn't walked in the Land for a very long time." He stroked his chin.

What brought me here? Was my pain in losing Calla so great that the gods had mercy on me?

"Are they letting me say goodbye... before Calla leaves me?" I asked reluctantly, unsure whether I wanted to hear the answer.

"Gods can't show mercy like that. When I first saw you here, I considered that Calla might have carried you. Her power is unusually strong, but it's not possible, unless—" Nick's hesitation was palpable. "Unless you're a walking god, but that's just not possible either." He noted my obvious confusion. "I'll start from the beginning, when the Almighty created his children, the mortals. Man and woman. Quickly he saw sin and disorder destroying his beloved creation. So, he created us, the gods, to protect humanity, allow the mortals to make mistakes, fail, but learn and grow. It's our divine duty to guide them, lead them through the cycle of life and death, but most importantly, protect them from evil."

Evil. The air chilled with that word.

"The Almighty created two domains, Land and Sky. We walk together among the mortals for the sake of humanity, but otherwise, we're separate for the strength necessary to protect his creation. *'Though one may be overpowered, two can defend themselves.'* A walking god is the forbidden union of Land and Sky. Simply put, it's a big no-no. A god born of both the Land and Sky walks among all domains, all gods. It's a very powerful force. Too powerful. So, they're stripped from their parents and taken at birth to be raised with the angels as our protectors. Angels in this sense are supreme beings, like saints, purely divine, not the silly stuff you see on TV. No wings or halos."

"The walking god is taken from their parents?" Like Calla was taken from me.

"Yes. And their parents—well, trust me, they're punished for their disobedience." He gave a definitive shake of his head. "You couldn't have lived among the mortals as a walking god and not known. I would have sensed it. Their energy is unique."

The Almighty. Angels. Protectors. Supreme beings. Walking gods. The severity of his words made me dizzy. A divine secret world I was now privy to.

"Besides, they're rarely sent to live with the mortals, unless it's a critical mission to help other gods. Sometimes, we're not enough, not strong enough, and we need their protection. They have immense energy and power. I've met only a handful of walking gods. One has become one of my closest friends, although he's now taken on a new station. He was sent as my protector, and helped me through a very sensitive assignment." Nick shivered from the memory. "I stared *evil* right in the eye, but he helped save my mission. I'd go as far as to say he saved me."

"Evil?" A cold breeze stung my cheeks.

"Yes, evil. Demonic creatures who have no humanity," Nick spat the words, leaving a bad taste in the air.

"Demons are real?"

"If the Almighty is real, how can you question the existence of demons?" Nick cocked his head.

"So, God, or I mean the Almighty, takes these walking gods? But where? And where are these demons, if the Land is here and the Sky is there?" I pointed to the clouds.

Nick looked up too. "Demons live in an eternal pit of

fire, raging and simmering. They build armies and come and go in the mortal world, trying to live among mortals, but we gods are way too powerful for them to ever stay long. They take up primary residence in what mortals consider the atmosphere... space. Think of them as burning stars. And they have a leader, who some in the mortal world refer to as Satan. Him and his followers are banished there, always livid, always bursting with fury and evil. They aren't allowed into our realms, yet they somehow find their way. Evil intends to take us over, but it'll never happen."

"How can you be so sure?" His certainty comforted me, but as I was learning, anything was possible.

"We care for our mortals. They may not know or believe in our existence, but nonetheless, their souls love us, and we love them. Even if a mortal commits sin, even the direst of sin during their living years, their soul can still be redeemed as long as they hold on to their humanity. True evil is rare, and while Satan has followers, his army will never be strong enough to overtake us. We control everything. He has nothing." Nick's voice vibrated with pride and energy.

My skin tingled as the sun glowed with his words, warming me inside and out. The rain had all but evaporated from my skin and clothes.

"Satan's army releases scraps of power every so often, but then they turn weak, burning out to the above. Besides, we always have warning."

"Warning? Like fire or lightning?"

"No. Lightning is a power of the gods. And fire, as you are aware of it, is also of the gods, not a demon's fire." Nick's voice rushed, now eager to tell me, as earlier apprehension from both sides slipped away. "It's one of many gifts."

Nick flipped up his palm where a cotton-ball-sized

cloud appeared. It puffed up, looking like cigarette smoke as tiny crystals fell over his hand, collecting into a puddle.

"Evil's warning is more chaotic. A diseased feeling among men. War, the feeling and possibility of demise and destruction. We know it's coming when men want to kill, when armies form and strengthen for the purpose of death." Nick flicked his fingers, scattering the miniature storm.

"You were a soldier!" I exclaimed. "Were you sent to us, six years ago... to fight the demons?"

"Not that simple, but yes. I am called Nicholas, but my given name is Niko, meaning 'Victory of the People'. I didn't lie when I told you then that I'm a soldier. When I met you, I was there for a very sensitive mission, a long-fought battle we needed to win. I was sent to ensure victory."

Nick looked invincible, unflappable, as he told me his god-given name and duty. He was a soldier, a victorious soldier, and his strength was undeniable. He stood tall with the clouds.

I recalled the first time I met him, how his physical presence seemed unnatural. He was strong, cut like granite. A god.

And I felt it down to my toes, he truly was a god.

If making me believe was his task, he was victorious.

SIX

Six Years Ago

Nick and I finally left the apartment, both reluctant as we untangled from the magic. We needed to eat, our heads light from wine on empty stomachs.

We crossed the busy intersection of Ogden and Van Buren for the third time that day, our hands tightly clasped. The journey of the day had taken us from strangers to friends to... something yet to be determined.

We made our way to the other side of the street, kitty-corner from Dark Beans. As we waited for the walk signal, the streetlight above us blinked on, illuminating a personal spotlight under the sun's descent.

Nick pulled me to him. "You are beautiful."

The glow danced over the hard contours of his face. He was beautiful. Being with him, next to him, I felt beautiful.

I smiled and studied his face unabashedly. An incoming beard shadowed his jawline, only exemplifying his tough edge. I felt safe with him. He was strong and commanding. A soldier, a protector.

Earlier in the afternoon, I'd questioned my sanity when leaving with a stranger. I'd wondered whether it was safe. Now I knew. The only thing in danger was my heart.

We didn't walk far, settling on an Irish pub a few blocks away. They often hosted live music on the weekends, and I was pleased to see a three-piece band setting up as we arrived.

Long lines formed around the bar, but as we twisted through the throng, patrons parted, and we found ourselves first in line at the hostess stand. I shook my head with a combination of confusion and amazement, speculating whether it could be Nick's charisma or intimidating presence that prompted our immediate seating. Wordlessly, I followed the perky hostess to a small table tucked away in the farthest part of the pub.

Her attention focused on Nick as she spoke, batting her eyes under obviously fake lashes. "Music will be starting soon. Enjoy your dinner."

Live music... Strange Pete's.

"Oh, I almost forgot! Novalee invited us to a luau." I glanced over to see his reaction. A luau could sound fun or tacky.

"Will I get laid?" Nick grinned.

My chin dropped, even though it was the same cheesy joke I'd used on Novalee. Nick burst out laughing.

"With leis, lei'd with leis... not... never mind, bad joke." Nick shook his head, his eyes gleaming.

An awkward chuckle slipped from my closed lips, and I wondered whether Nick could read my unspoken answer on my blushing face.

After ordering drinks, our table turned quiet as we studied the menu. I itched to touch him, to be closer, but even the wine buzz couldn't conquer my innate shyness. While I finished an extra cup of courage, I silently willed him to make the first move.

Either my body language was obvious, or we'd connected on some subconscious level, because Nick pushed to his feet and moved from across the table to the bench beside me.

"I want to be next to you," he whispered, his breath warm on my neck. The sides of our knees touched, shooting a shiver straight to my belly. He reached over to grab hold of my hand, and that shiver shot to my core.

An emotional, earthy Celtic group began to play on the makeshift stage. As the tip of Nick's index finger circled my wrist, I closed my eyes, overwhelmed by his sensual touches and the pub's soothing music.

My mind wandered, the folky Irish sounds evoking a vision behind my lids of a rolling, emerald green field. In the distance, a little girl danced. Swirling and twirling, she was too far away for me to see her face, but she seemed familiar. Maybe it was me as a kid, a snippet from my childhood.

When I was young, my parents and I took an extended summer vacation to Ireland, settling in a small coastal town while my dad completed a work project. I couldn't recall details of the trip. I was only three or four years old, too young for concrete memories. The music and ambiance of the Irish pub must have ignited a blast from the past, pieces stored somewhere deep in my mind.

Lost in my thoughts, the little girl continued to dance, now swirling and twirling to the band's music at the pub. Her shiny black hair and pink dress stood in stark contrast to the sparkling green field. She radiated under the sun's glow. A picture of innocence and purity.

"What are you thinking about?" Nick asked. The sound of his voice sent the little girl's image scattering.

I tilted my head up, studying Nick's green eyes. The same emerald hue as the field. His fingers, still circling my wrist, began to trail up my bare arm.

"This reminds me of a trip from when I was a kid," I replied, dispelling the shivers from his touch. "My parents and I went to Ireland for a summer vacation."

"Irish bars always bring back good memories."

"You've been too?" He nodded, and I further questioned, "Have you traveled a lot?"

Nick gave a half smile and took a sip from his pint glass. "I've spent more time away than here, in the States."

Of course. He probably was stationed away or deployed often. "Do you like it?"

"Traveling? Yes."

"Well, I guess I mean being away from home? Are you okay with that? I think I'd get a bit homesick."

My childhood home was a straight shot up the highway, about an hour's drive north of the city. Although now, my parents spent a majority of their time at their second home in Florida. My dad's job was mobile, and my mom hated the harsh Wisconsin winters. She seemed to hate Wisconsin in general. After I graduated from high school, they purchased the beachfront bungalow with the intention of being snowbirds.

"When I enlisted, I left home without looking back. I knew infantry would take me away, but it was an easy choice. Even as a kid, I knew I'd be a warrior." Nick stared at his pint, quietly reflecting.

I gathered from our earlier conversation he didn't have close ties to his family. Perhaps that's what motivated him to join the military, to find something he was missing, to be part of something bigger.

"I've been doing this so long, always moving, never in one place for too long. It's all I know now." His voice held an edge of sadness.

"How long have you been in?" I guessed his age to be around mine, maybe a few years older, early thirties at most.

"Long enough." Nick's tone indicated he wished to end the conversation. I didn't know many service members, yet I understood. Maybe talking about it summoned images or memories he wished to forget.

Our waitress arrived at that opportune moment with dinner. Nick ordered another Guinness, and I switched from wine to a gin and tonic. Whatever appetite I had was now replaced with a different craving. I wanted to leave. I needed to be alone with Nick. I tipped back my cocktail as he nursed his beer.

"I don't think I can drive tonight," I declared, setting down the empty glass.

"No, I don't think you can," Nick agreed. "Were you planning on it?"

"Well, to drive you back." Heat traveled up my neck and settled in my cheeks. "I don't think I can drive you back," I slurred for effect.

"Guess I'm trapped here. Oh, no." Chuckling, he put up his hands in mock surrender. He turned toward me and I quickly leaned in, catching his lips. I didn't care that my breath was heavy with gin. I didn't care that people around saw. I needed to touch him.

I needed to be alone with him.

Nick's eyes flashed as he read it on my face. "Let's get out of here." He pulled me up alongside him, leaving a couple bills on the table next to my untouched meal.

We stepped into the night, but didn't go far. Nick led me around the corner of the pub, and into the side alley. He pushed me against the rough brick wall, covering my mouth with his, and pinning my arms.

"Now I've trapped you," he whispered into my ear.

I moaned as his teeth nipped my lobe. My hair was still piled up in a bun, my neck exposed, as he took turns gently sucking and licking. I leaned into him, and he groaned.

"We should go." He pulled away, tugging my arm. His long strides outpaced mine, and I skipped to keep up.

We came to a fenced playground, a few blocks away from my apartment. Nick stopped to give me a hungry kiss, smashing into my body. With my back pinned against the metal fencing, his frame engulfed mine. Eager hands rubbed down my hips to the hem of my dress. He tugged at it, then abruptly stopped.

"Do you have any idea how much I want you?" Desire filled his face. He again pulled at my arm, guiding me down the sidewalk. The starless night was pitch black except for the scant glow from streetlights.

We stopped at the park in front of my building, the one my patio overlooked. Nick picked me up as we crossed under the wrought iron archway, carrying me to the white marble bench tucked away at the far end. He sat down, pulling me into his lap and shifting my legs so I straddled him. We kissed again, rough and desperate. His tongue roamed over my lower lip, then moved to my neck, nipping and sucking. With his hands, he pulled my hips against his hardness. Blooming bushes scarcely shielded us, but I didn't care.

Nick's hands loosened my hair from its bun. He pulled it free, allowing it to fall over my bare shoulders. I shook my head, sweeping the tendrils to one side to again expose a part of my neck, leaving it vulnerable to his touch. He continued to taste my skin. One hand stroked my hair, while the other lifted my chin to him.

"You look like a goddess," he whispered.

Moonlight swept over his face. He looked like a god.

SEVEN

The Present
"You nearly broke my mission," Nick said.

I kept my eyes on my hands, which rested in my lap.

"When we met, I was on an assignment."

Our relationship was intense, frantic and desperate from the moment we met until our final goodbye. Once we found one another, we clung on. But our time together quickly ran out. I cherished every second of our short story, holding it closely inside, protecting it.

I never told anyone the full details of Nicholas, the mystery man who fathered my child, who walked out of my life as quickly as he had walked in. Not even Novalee knew the depth of our brief courtship.

Nick and I spent nine glorious weeks together. Every minute together etched into my memory. Every sweet moment cherished.

"I was sent to prepare the most elite of armies, to calm them and guide them as they prepared for one of the most important missions of your time," Nick divulged as he leaned in. "I couldn't tell you then, but I was training with the Navy Seals. It was their mission to capture Saddam Hussein."

An involuntary gasp escaped from my lips.

"I could only guide those men to victory. It had to be their actions, their will. Thankfully, I was able to sort myself out, escape whatever spell you had on me, and clear my head for the mission." He closed his eyes. "I've never struggled like that, Mira. I've been among gods and mortals, in dire, deadly situations. I never lost myself like I did then. I wondered for so long how it happened. How did I lose my control to you? I loved you deeply, unlike any other love I have had, mortal or divine. A perfect love."

I felt it too. Startling true love, the kind that shakes you from inside out, changes you, and makes you better for all the right reasons. The kind you can never forget.

"For months, I couldn't speak of our relationship. My superiors knew the outcome; they knew you were with child. They promised to protect you—both of you—if I cleared my conscience, cleared my mind, and completed the mission." Nick stopped, taking hold of my hands. "I had to leave you. I had to concentrate on my duties and forget you."

His words stung, yet I understood. I also buried our memories. It was the only way I could go on. I seldom spoke to Calla about her daddy, and strangely, she rarely asked.

"I spent months with my men. After my conscience was clean, after I knew you'd be okay and taken care of, I felt victory. My mission would be over, and I could come home. I returned here, to the Land. Although I longed for us to be together, it wasn't possible. I'd committed a reprimandable act. Gods can have physical relations with mortals, but we

are not to become connected, attached. My punishment—"
Nick looked down to our connected hands, and his voice
lightened to a near whisper. "I was forbidden from seeing
you again. I could not return in my human form. While
some gods felt the punishment was just, I appealed the decision. I fought with all my might. Ultimately, the superiors
allowed me to keep watch for the sake of my child, but at a
distance. I was denied my greatest wish, my greatest desire
—to return to you. So, I did as best I could. From afar, I was
with Calla. She could feel me. I spoke to her and she spoke
to me, but they weren't with words you could hear or
understand."

Nick let go of my hands to brush away my tears. His
finger lingered on my chin. I couldn't speak, fearing I'd fall
apart if I tried.

Gentle drops of rain, like tears slipping from the sky,
began to fall again.

"I knew Calla would need to come to me, here, but I
thought I had more time. I thought I could teach her the
ways of the gods while she was with you. If I could help her
gain control of her power, at least until she was older, she
could have lived a normal life with you. I promise, Mira, I
tried to make it easy on you." He stroked my cheek. "I didn't
want to take her away from you. Seeing you together made
my heart full. We were a family, the three of us." He
stopped talking and clutched our hands together, pressing
them to my heart. "Even though we were not together, I was
always with you."

I shook my head, tears flowing freely as I sobbed. "I
know, oh, I know, because I felt you there too." Nick pulled
me into him. I settled my damp cheek over his chest. The
rain picked up, pummeling the bench. Nick looked to the
sky and loosened his hold.

"We need to go." His voice held a warning. Something was wrong.

"What is it? Calla? Is she okay?" Fear replaced my tears as a black cloud rumbled.

"Yes, yes," he assured while grabbing my arm and jerking me toward him. "It's raining."

We both looked to the sky, and as I rubbed away my tears, the rain stopped. Nick's eyes narrowed, his focus shifting between my confused face and the dry sky.

Without a word, he crushed against me. Kissing me. His tongue smashed mine, and the ground beneath us sizzled. Steam rose from the damp grass.

Nick broke away. The passion of the moment ceased. The mist evaporated.

"Mira." He appraised my face. "You made the rain. Our kiss caused the electricity. Something in you is growing strong, very quickly. We need to find Jake."

Before I was given a chance to question him, we were running, the ground slipping away like sand. Nick whisked me along so quickly my chest burned with panting breaths when we finally stopped. I turned around to look for the park, trying to collect my bearings, but all I saw was deep green grass shimmering in the sun.

Spinning around again, I eyed a cottage in the distance. As we neared, I appraised its cream stucco, steep sloping roof, and wide, rounded door. Flower boxes with red and yellow tulips lined the windows. All it needed was a tower, and it'd be a picture straight out of a fairytale.

I fully expected Snow White to step out, but as we approached the entrance, the door swooshed open, and a man stood within the foyer, seemingly waiting for us. He held the same authoritative presence and stunning good looks as Nick, making me wonder if all gods were created with an unearthly beauty.

"Father." Nick bowed his head to the man, who could not have been much older than us. I clenched my lips, realizing I'd been gaping.

"Niko," a deep voice answered. "I was expecting you." He looked over to me. "And you too. I'm Jake."

"You were?" Nick asked. "You knew?"

"I felt her," Jake answered as he ushered us in.

Nick took my elbow, guiding me into an open foyer. A large wooden table set with tea and fine china dominated the room. Serving platters brimmed with fruits, breads, and cheese. A warm fire blazed in the wide hearth behind the table. My pounding pulse settled at the inviting scene.

"Please sit. You must be hungry." Jake motioned to the chairs. He filled cups with steaming tea, handed them off and gestured toward the food. "Eat. Help yourself."

Nick reluctantly did as he was told, taking several pieces of fruit. He looked to me, signaling I should follow suit. Eyeing the platters, my stomach growled.

I gingerly picked from the mound of fruit and chunks of cheese. Jake watched, as if waiting for my reaction when I popped a red grape into my mouth.

A firework of flavor exploded as my teeth sunk into the plump flesh. Chewing, I experienced more than just a taste of natural sugar and gritty juice. I savored the life of the grape, from seed in soil, to fruit on the vine.

A fresh sprout, the bud of life. Little arms growing and reaching, tiny pebbles pulsing and plumping. Sun, rain, earth.

"It's delicious, isn't it? The fruit of the Land. I grow those in the back. Calla has been helping with all my plants," Jake interrupted.

"Calla?" My eyes flew open.

The fire crackled and sparked. Nick eyed Jake and he nodded.

"Calla's okay. She's playing at the cove with her friend," Jake answered.

I nodded back, and the fire settled.

Had I done that? Had I controlled the rain, steam, and fire? Jake noted the confusion in my eyes.

"You're a goddess." He answered my unspoken question.

"But how?" Nick asked, addressing Jake while keeping his eyes on me, studying me, as if I were the strange creature in this new world.

"I don't know." For not knowing, Jake looked surprisingly confident. He took a seat at the head of the table, positioning himself between Nick and me. "I'm Jake, Father to all in the Land, but I am just meeting you now, my child."

"A walking god?" Nick questioned with a tone that created an odd tension in my stomach.

"No." Jake's voice held absolute certainty.

I remembered Nick's words—a walking god, the forbidden love child.

Jake looked from me to the fire, making it roar and simmer. Then he looked from the door to the window, both swinging shut. "No, I don't believe you to be a walking god, but your energy is unusual... strong. Being here, it will only grow. You don't yet know how to control your emotion, your power, or its effects. Even we seasoned gods," he continued, motioning to Nick, "affect our surroundings with our emotions."

Yes. I recalled the clap of thunder, the storm clouds. Nick's emotions.

The gentle crackle of the fire hummed. Nick and Jake were both silent while I sat dumbly, waiting to hear more.

"Please tell me about yourself, Mira," Jake requested. He lifted a dainty teacup, which looked out of place in his large, calloused hands. With his flannel button down and distressed blue jeans, a beer stein seemed more fitting. "You like flowers, plants—all that grows from the ground. I know this. I see it in you, and I see it in your daughter."

Both sets of eyes were on me. Were they expecting me to explain my unbeknownst existence? I blinked back, blank for an answer. But Jake's eyes held such kindness and warmth, I couldn't help but relax. "Well, what would you like to know?"

Nick reached from across the table to cover my hand. I took it, and as our skin connected, our fingers glowed like embers of a fire. It didn't hurt, but the sensation and sight made me think of iron being slowly melded together.

Jake's eyebrows knitted with concern.

"What's wrong?" I asked. Nick's grip tightened, and our skin seared. I snatched my hand away.

"A divine message. Fate has reunited you, brought you together again, righting a wrong."

"Reuniting us?" Nick queried.

"Yes, Niko." Jake closed his eyes in deep thought. Several uncomfortable minutes passed before he continued with a deliberate, strong voice. "Niko, you have proven yourself an honorable and true god. Obeying me, as a son should his father. I watched you become a father. I felt your longing when you were forbidden from returning to your family. Now your greatest wish, your greatest desire, will be fulfilled. You sat beside me as my son. Now you will sit with me as my equal."

Jake looked at me. "Mira, before today, I did not know

you. Now, you are a child of the Land. This is your home, and we are your family. We welcome you with open arms." He shifted his attention back to Nick. Taking both our hands, we stood and connected into a jagged chain.

An energy radiated from within my body, glowing like the cinders in the hearth. It pulsated through my limbs, traveling from me to Jake, and then to Nick. In turn, their energy seemingly passed back to me, nearly jolting my legs from under me.

"Niko, you were born to be the God of Victory. You've always held true to your station. You have completed every mission with success. But you've been battling something within, your toughest conflict yet, as you long for your family. Today you will claim your victory."

Jake raised our hands as the chain turned blistering. "Hand-in-hand, you now walk together on a new path. Two gods, two souls, united. *'Though one may be overpowered, two can defend themselves.'* Hand-in-hand, you are bound to defend one another, to protect one another, to complete your divine duties." His voice boomed, vibrating against the walls.

He continued, and the embers in my veins grew to a fire. "What was once ripped apart, shall now be bound together."

Jake's declaration echoed throughout the room, shooting shockwaves with each seizing word. I shook with fear as red and yellow flames raged around us, engulfing the walls.

"Mira, be not fearful. *'There is no fear in love, but perfect love casts out fear.'* You and Niko are destined."

Jake freed himself from the chain and slapped his hands to the table, sending a final tremor through the air. It swept like a wave through my body, its force pushing me back into my chair, and knocking the wind from my chest.

White, choking smoke filled the room, making it difficult to see my hands waving before my face. I coughed, spitting out ash. My heart pounded like a hammer hitting nails, thumping against my ribs. Blood boiled through my body, burning my vision and veins. I cupped my ears, trying to drown out Jake's words which continued to vibrate and echo off the walls.

For the second time that day, a storm ravaged my very essence. And, just as the previous storm, this one—the pain, the noise, the smells—came to a sudden and complete end.

I opened my eyes and the smoke quickly evaporated. The walls surrounding us were destroyed, scorched by the same fire that had ravaged our bodies. I looked down to my blackened, singed clothes. *What* had happened?

What was once ripped apart, shall now be bound together. The words whispered, now soothing in my ears.

Jake's hands were still firmly in place on the table. As he lifted them, his seared imprints in the wood immediately began to fade, as did the soot and burnt destruction around us. "The days ahead may test you, your strength, and your beliefs. But faith, hope, and love will guide you. Even if you don't understand, they'll lead your heart on the right path."

I didn't look at Nick's face, but I knew his eyes were on me. And, although I didn't hear his voice, I felt his words, imploring me to look to him. My breath quickened, nervous and shy. I closed my eyes tightly, and a vision played behind my lids.

I saw myself. Dressed head to toe in white, sweet rosebuds made a crown for my hair and black curls flowed down my back. Calla lilies lined a path. Slowly, I made my way toward someone. *Nicholas.* He wasn't facing me, yet I knew it to be him. In slow motion, he turned around, sensing my approach. His face filled with emotion as his eyes fell over me.

His greatest wish.

Our eyes connected in my vision.

His greatest desire.

My eyes flew open. Our eyes connecting in the present.

What was once ripped apart, shall now be bound together.

I understood. We were married.

EIGHT

Six Years Ago

We had no regard for modesty as the moon provided a silver spotlight over the white marble bench. The air turned heavy with humidity and lust.

I straddled Nick, grinding my hips over his hardness. He groaned as his hands worked to remove my panties. I hastily unbuttoned his shorts, and he shifted so his boxers could be pulled away to free his erection. He guided me back down slowly, filling the part of me that ached the most.

A crack of thunder broke the sky as our bodies united. We began to rock, quickly finding our rhythm. Nick's hips turned forceful. Each thrust shot a wave of pleasure through my body.

Rain fell with the next rumble. Little droplets sizzled as they landed over my bare skin. Another roll of thunder echoed through the sky, shaking the ground. Faster, we continued to move in unison. Nick's eyes held mine. The storm reflected in his dilated pupils as his hands manipulated my hips, moving me along with him as we climbed...

farther and farther, ascending to the edge until we fell over together.

We climaxed just as blinding flashes of lightning lit the sky. Like a fourth of July fireworks display, they showered over us along with the rain. The elements raged and thunder groaned, only settling after I slumped against Nick.

We clung to one another with spent, limp bodies. Nick untangled an arm and stroked my back until our panting breaths evened. I lifted my face to the storm, letting the rain cool my flushed cheeks.

Modesty returned as the fervor in the air died. The rain lightened to a sprinkle, but Nick and I were already soaked. We peeled away sticky limbs, and then hurried across the street and into the lobby of my apartment complex.

Padding through the halls, our sandals squeaked. My neighbor, old Mrs. Cooper, gave a curious look as we passed. Amusement turned at the corner of her lips, and I blushed, certain our disheveled hair and clothes gave away what Nick and I had been up to.

We stumbled into my apartment in fits of laughter, shedding layers of clothes until we were both naked. I led Nick upstairs to my lofted bedroom. Giddy giggles gave way to quiet lust as we climbed into the shower, washing off sweat and rain. Our hands began to again explore one another, this time slow and deliberate in discovering each intimate curve.

Nick's fingers roamed over my shoulders and down my back, finally settling on my hips. He pulled me up to him, and again we connected. Cool water caressed our bodies, yet steam filled the shower, flowing over the curtain and into the room in a thick fog. It swirled like a sensual song, stroking my skin along with Nick's touch.

Feelings—more than primal lust—filled me as we climaxed again.

Our eyes remained locked long after the shudders of sweet release subsided. In the deepness of his stare, Nick's emotions spoke a wordless message.

Surprise, acceptance, fear, lust, love... and everything in between.

I reached out to brush away a curl that had fallen over his forehead. A droplet of water dripped from its tip, rolling down his cheek like a tear. My finger traced its path until Nick's large hand covered mine, cupping my fingers against his face. I looked up again into his eyes. No longer a stranger, my heart recognized him.

My heart had found its mate. I should have been surprised, but it felt too right to question.

THE NEXT MORNING, I woke in a tangle of limbs with Nick's heavy arms enveloping me, and my leg kicked over his. I wiggled within his hold, turning to study the features of his face. Dark shadows of a missed shave speckled the contours of his jaw. In sleep, Nick looked much less formidable, his sharp features softer. I rubbed a finger across his stubble and then brushed a curl, perhaps the same wayward curl as the previous night, off his forehead. His dark hair seemed longer than I thought allowed by military standards.

Unable to resist touching him, my finger swept across his chin, and I leaned in to lay a light kiss on his lips.

Nick's eyes fluttered open.

"Mirabel." He breathed out my name. "Good morning."

Blushing, I averted my eyes, but Nick gently grasped my jaw, tilting my chin upward.

"I could get used to that wake-up call. Much better than an alarm." He leaned in, kissing my forehead. "Breakfast in bed?"

"Unless we want condiments and wine, I might have to pick something up." I smiled. "Someone hijacked my grocery shopping yesterday. Not that I'm complaining."

I ran to a bakery down the street to get takeaway while Nick threw in a load of laundry, including his wet clothes from the night before. Having nothing for him to wear, he lounged in the living room with only a blanket to cover himself.

I returned with coffee and breakfast pastries. As the door latched behind me, Nick swiped the blanket from his body, setting it down on the living room floor for a picnic. His lips turned up in a devilish grin as he looked at me, extending his hand to pull me down next to him.

"I'm feeling a bit overdressed," I joked, glancing to his bare chest.

"That's because you are."

Nick tugged my shirt over my head, followed by the hasty removal of my shorts. Both naked, there was no prelude to sex.

The to-go coffees I purchased turned cold as the morning slipped away to rounds of lovemaking followed by stretches of rest.

Finally spent, we lay on our backs, looking up to the ceiling. Nick's hands moved from his side, brushing against my thigh to my stomach. He closed his eyes as he continued to feel my body, as if trying to commit every inch to memory.

His touch stopped over my right hip, at the place of my

one and only tattoo. The ink was embedded into my skin, yet, as if he felt it, his fingers lingered.

"It's a tattoo," I offered.

Nick propped on his elbow to get a better look. "Nice. What is it?"

"A big mistake, that's what it is." I rolled my eyes at the memory. "It's the decision of a slightly intoxicated teenager who was persuaded by her even more intoxicated best friend."

"A Celtic knot?" Nick leaned closer.

"Yep. A Sisters Knot." Novalee had begged me to get a tattoo with her, pleading that it would be a symbol of our eternal sisterhood, our best friend bond. Even at nineteen I knew it was a bad idea.

The dryer buzzed. I glanced at Nick, not wanting to move from the blanket, and definitely not wanting to get dressed.

"Clothes are dry," he stated the obvious.

I checked the clock on the wall. My heart fell. I desperately wished for more time, but it was nearing noon.

"There's a train that leaves at five, and I need to check in by seven—I have no intention of leaving here until the last possible minute," Nick said earnestly, his fingers lifting my chin toward him.

We reluctantly dressed. I decided to give Nick a tour of the conservatory, which was like a second home to me. Flowers were my passion, my life. Walking through the exhibits, he listened with genuine curiosity as I told him the names of the flowers, explained which were hardest to cultivate and listed my routine for managing them.

Nick plucked a white calla lily from a display, and I was about to scold him, but stopped as he reached over to tuck it behind my ear.

"White against black, like the moon at night." Nick's eyes were intent as he leaned in and kissed my forehead.

I swept a finger over a delicate petal. I'd never look at a calla lily the same.

After the gardens, we walked to the lakefront. An expanse of manicured lawn along the city's waterfront brimmed with people enjoying the perfect summer day. Nick and I kicked off our sandals and padded barefoot through the park to an open space. We lay with our backs cushioned by plush grass and silently watched puffy clouds float through the sky. Our connection was so strong, words weren't necessary.

Please don't let this end.

My silent pleas couldn't stop time. We wordlessly walked back to the apartment, hands clasped tightly together. Our pace slowed as we neared my complex. The reality of Nick's imminent departure loomed.

Inevitably, we found ourselves outside the park across from my building. Memories of the previous night warmed my body.

Nick glanced to the white marble bench in the far end of the park and grinned back at me. "You'll never look at that bench the same way again."

"Definitely not." I doubted I'd be able to look at anything in the same light after meeting Nick. He'd awoken something new in me that I hadn't felt or known before. My fingers touched the calla lily, still tucked behind my ear.

Flowers had always been my passion, bringing contentment, beauty, and peace to my life. But now, Nick brought something I hadn't known was missing... lust, desire, love. I felt filled, new, reborn.

Nick led me through the park and to our bench. The marble was much warmer in the summer sun than in the dark of night. *Our time is up. This is his goodbye.* My stomach sank as tears burned in my throat. I couldn't lose him, not after just finding him. I reached for his hand, but he pulled me into him, and we clung to one another.

A tear escaped from my eye, falling slowly down my cheek. He used a finger to wipe it away, then swept a kiss across my lips. "I need to go, but this isn't over." His words were strong.

They were a promise.

I STAYED by Nick's side until his train was called. He gave a final, gentle kiss, and then turned to join the crowd of departing passengers. As I watched him walk away, tears again flooded my eyes. Before I lost sight of him in the throng, he looked back, and his words echoed in the air... *"this isn't over."*

Nick kept his promise. When I arrived home from the train station that evening, a voicemail alert flashed on my cell. I hadn't realized I missed a call. Eagerly, I listened to the message.

"I just wanted to hear your voice. I miss you already." His voice filled a part of me that was already missing... him.

Later that evening I received a text message. Nick requested leave for the weekend ahead. I fell asleep easily that night, knowing I only had a few days without him.

The next nine weeks were filled with a lifetime of memories. Dancing until midnight, sleeping until noon. Laughing until the sun went down, making love until the sun came up. We did any and everything together, creating a magic that captivated our every moment. Nick's love filled me, every bit of me and my world, until he was a part of me and my world.

Everything around and within me changed with him. I was surrounded, filled, consumed by bits and pieces of him. How would I—how could I—go on when he was gone?

Nick tried to prepare me for what to expect during his deployment. He explained it was a very sensitive assignment, and he wasn't certain how much access he'd have to the Internet or a satellite phone. He would try to email or call once the communication lines were established and authorized for use, but he warned there were many unknowns and no timeline. He couldn't tell me much about the mission, but his tone implied danger.

I tucked the conversation away, not wanting it to spoil what time we did have together. Instead, I savored every second we were gifted. My heart burst with excitement as the long weekends neared, then fell heavy with dread as they quickly rolled by.

Tears stuck in my throat each Sunday as I returned Nick to the train station. Every time we said goodbye, I'd get a call within minutes of departing from the station.

"I just wanted to hear your voice. I miss you already."

OUR LAST DAY together was filled with highs and lows. As morning turned to afternoon, desperation consumed my apartment. Grey clouds dominated the previously clear sky, and the air was stifled with sadness. Everything around us seemed muffled by Nick's impending departure.

We made love one final time. Slowly and gently, our eyes remained locked as we connected. Mind, body, and soul. We watched each other's pleasure peak, never breaking contact. Unspoken words whispered his affirmation—he'd be gone, but he would still be with me.

Nick placed his hand just above my breast to my heart. "I need to go, but I will always be here." His fingers fluttered over my skin as he reiterated out loud the same thoughts that had murmured in my head. I could barely speak, fearing I'd fall apart, but Nick held me, stroking my body, and lulling me with soft words of comfort. He made promises, promises he would not keep. In the moment, they provided the assurance I needed to get through the day.

We said our final farewell at the train station. Tears streamed down my face. I didn't care as people watched, sensing some sad story playing out. We hugged, kissed. Minutes felt like seconds. Our precious time slipped away. An announcement played over the loudspeaker. It was time. Nick and I gripped one another.

"I'll be with you. I promise, no matter how far away I am, I'll always be with you." And then, I received one final kiss before he picked up his backpack and walked into the crowd.

Nick disappeared, but I could not move. The notice for the next train rang over the loudspeaker, yet my feet wouldn't budge. It wasn't denial. I accepted he was gone, but leaving would make it final, and I wasn't ready to let go. I'd never be ready to let go.

I remained planted in place, flooded by our memories, until the buzz of my phone interrupted the buzz in my head. Nick was calling. I didn't answer, letting it go to voicemail. I knew what he was going to say.

"I just wanted to hear your voice. I miss you already."

I kept the message on my cell until years later, when the old flip phone finally died.

Months later, when I learned of Nick's death, I didn't

cry. I could not cry. I felt numb. I felt loss. But I also felt life. I discovered I was pregnant just weeks after he left on the deployment. When the two lines formed on the pregnancy test, love and excitement overpowered my fears. Every emotion flushed my thoughts, including nervousness at telling Nick.

As fate had it, I didn't get to.

On an early October afternoon, I came home from work to find two soldiers waiting outside my apartment door. Stepping from the elevator, dark uniforms stood in glaring contrast to the crisp, white walls of the hallway. My heart raced with excitement at the initial thought that it was Nick, that he was back.

But the faces that came into focus were of two solemn strangers. I knew then. Before Nick left on the deployment, he had mentioned he'd be listing me as his Primary Next of Kin.

I ushered them into my apartment where they delivered the terrible news. *"Killed in action. An honorable death."* Strong arms embraced my body as I went through the obvious reaction, dropping to my knees and crumbling from shock.

But I knew, as if I'd always known, Nick was gone. I'd never see him again.

The soldier's words echoed in my ears long after they were spoken. The numbing loss could have engulfed me, but the new life Nick and I created together flickered and flittered within me, little butterfly flutters that let me know he was still with me. He would always be with me, even in death. His life carried on through this new life.

I was five months along before I told anyone, even Novalee. We'd seen little of each other since the summer. A hectic case at work had taken her away for weeks at a time.

On a snowy Friday evening in early December, I anxiously awaited Novalee's arrival. Her big project just wrapped up, and she wanted to celebrate. I left the door to my apartment unlocked as I contemplated how I'd fill her in on the pregnancy. My swollen belly bulged beyond its normal waistline. I couldn't hide it much longer.

With aching feet propped up on the coffee table, I relaxed against the sofa cushion and admired the freshly decorated, mini Christmas tree that sparkled in the corner of the living room. A double knock on the door startled me from the daze of twinkling lights.

"Nice tree, Mir," Novalee complimented as she breezed in. She stopped in front of me, wine bottle in hand, eyes narrowing as she took in my jogging pants and sweatshirt. "Um, what's going on? Thought we were going to Winetopia?"

I'd prepared a whole spiel, a wordy yet eloquent explanation. But as Novalee's eyes met mine, the words, "I'm pregnant," stumbled from my lips.

The wine bottle slipped from her hands, falling with a stunned thump onto the thick carpet. We watched it roll back and forth.

Novalee looked from the bottle to me, shaking her head in pure disbelief. "You can't be."

"I am."

"What? You had sex?"

"Umm... yes." The conversation turned very awkward, very quickly.

"What the hell? When?" she demanded, almost angry.

Completely taken aback, I answered in an equally irritated tone, "What do you mean, *when*? You want the date? Why are you acting like this?" I shook my head at her, tears sprouting in my eyes. I expected her to be surprised by the news. Surprised, but happy.

"I'm sorry, I'm just…" She picked up the wine bottle and awkwardly held it, her fingers clenching white around its neck. Then, as if resolving to herself that it was true, she set the bottle on the coffee table and sat beside me. "That was a horrible reaction."

We looked at each other and burst into laughter.

"In July," I told her after our giggles subsided.

"July?"

"Remember that guy, Nick?" My eyes welled again. I hadn't told her much about him, and she never got a chance to meet him. Following the luau at Strange Pete's, Novalee secured the project which had dominated her time the last few months.

"The Army guy? Wait. You're due in July?"

"Yes, him. But I'm due in April. July's the when." I wiggled my eyebrows as she looked at me, confused. "You asked when I had sex."

"So, you're—" Novalee stopped to count in her head, "You're five months along?" She looked from my belly to my face, her eyes lighting up. "You're going to have a baby!"

With a joy I'd been afraid to unleash, I cried into Novalee's arms, knowing with her by my side, it would all be okay.

THE MONTHS that followed passed in a whirl. Novalee hosted a floral-themed baby shower in my honor. A garden party for the little life blooming within me. I insisted on white calla lilies for the centerpieces as a tribute to Nick. My parents flew in from Florida for the celebration and to help prepare for their grandchild's arrival. They wanted to stay until they could meet her. A granddaughter. I'd known from the moment I felt life fluttering in my belly that my baby would be a girl, but my twenty-week ultrasound confirmed it.

As my belly got bigger, sleep became more and more uncomfortable. I'd wake frequently through the night from vivid dreams of Nick—dreams so real it'd take several seconds to return to reality.

Many nights the reality of his loss left me breathless. Somehow, when grief threatened to consume me, I would remember his promise. *"I need to go, but I will always be here."* I'd feel his fingers fluttering over my heart, his touch seared into memory.

The night of my due date, I woke in a sweat. *"Be strong, Mira, she's coming soon."* The voice I'd nearly forgotten whispered in my ears just as my eyes popped open from a deep sleep.

Instantly alert, I jerked to a sitting position. The sheets beneath my swollen body were damp. I couldn't tell whether my water had broken or if it was sweat from another intense dream. I remained frozen in place until a stabbing cramp shot through my back. *Oh God. This is it.* I hoisted heavy limbs and my balloon-shaped belly from the bed, then waddled to the bathroom sink. A near-crippling contraction brought my palms flat against the countertop. After several deep breaths and a splash of cold water to my face, I mustered the energy to call Novalee. She answered on the first ring.

"It's time." I didn't wait for her response, I clicked off the phone and bobbed carefully down the stairs.

Weeks before, my hospital bag had been packed and placed in the trunk of Novalee's car. We were prepared. We were ready. Every detail of my birth plan had been discussed and written together. All I needed now was to make it to the hospital.

"Be strong, Mira," Nick's voice again whispered.

Tears welled in my eyes, but another wave of pain took over before I could dwell on him. My face screwed up in agony as I swung open the apartment door, desperate for Novalee, who stood there waiting.

"Oh God!" I grabbed her arms, and my nails bit into her skin.

"Oh God!" Novalee repeated, flinching from the pain. She heaved and panted along with me. "Breathe, breathe, breathe!"

"Shut up!" A long contraction ripped through me.

After it passed, we moved quickly, making it down the elevator, to the parking garage, and into the car before another one hit. Novalee began timing. "Two minutes! They are *two minutes apart!*"

"Are we going to make it?" I asked desperately. "I can't have this baby in the car!"

Novalee glanced over nervously. The car sped up as she hit the pedal, now concentrating on the road instead of timing contractions.

"Why'd we choose Mequon, Nov?" I whispered in between contractions. "I could be hooked up with an epidural by now if we stayed local." The Mequon Center for Mother and Baby was at least a forty-minute drive, while Milwaukee General Hospital stood walking distance from our apartment building. However, Mequon was the only facility in the area that had birthing pools, and the idea of birthing in water called to me. It seemed right and natural. We'd gone over it a hundred times.

"Just hang in there, sissy. You're doing great," She gave a

hopeful smile, her hand momentarily leaving the steering wheel to squeeze my leg. "Love you, sissy."

I was certain we wouldn't make it to the hospital, but in the end, we did. The circular drive of the birthing center's grand entrance greeted my wet eyes, and I sighed with relief when I spotted my mom, Anya. Novalee had called her. It was part of our foolproof plan. I was to call Novalee, she was to call Anya, who was then to notify the center.

After being checked in triage, they informed us I was nearly six centimeters dilated. With the certainty of the baby's imminent arrival, the midwife led us to a private room.

Machines typical of a hospital lined the walls, while a large birthing pool dominated the center of the room. As I eyed the warm ripples on the water's surface, a wave of calm washed over me. The midwife, along with Anya, Novalee, and a nurse, quickly helped me in. I sunk into the soothing bath and breathed effortlessly.

"It's amazing, Mom. I'm so calm now."

"You're doing great, sweetheart," Anya reiterated Novalee's earlier sentiments, her eyes brimming with unshed tears.

From there, my baby girl quickly, quietly, *almost* painlessly made her way into our world. Novalee and Anya were positioned on each side of me when the time came to push. As the midwife walked me through the final stage, I heard Nick's voice again. *"Be strong."* With one long push, our daughter arrived.

Emotion and love choked the room as I looked to the tiny life Nick and I created. She was beautiful, even with a scrunched face and grime from birth. Dark hair spotted the top of her head, and her perfect lips formed an 'O' when she squeaked her first precious cry.

The sweet baby in my arms was a miracle. She was *our* miracle, Nick's and mine. Created from perfect love that lived on, even in death. Our testament, our love's legacy. I looked at her face, and all I could see was him. His presence so strong, so real, I wondered if he was truly with me, an angel watching over us.

~

AFTER BEING DISCHARGED from the hospital, I returned to my parents' home and back to my old bedroom. We decided ahead of time I would stay there to recuperate and avoid the stairs in my apartment until my body healed.

The security from my childhood home wrapped me up just like the security blanket I used to sleep with as a child.

But now, I wasn't a child. I was a mother, and the perfect baby girl sleeping sweetly in the bassinet was all mine.

If only she had a name.

Baby girl, as we called her, was nearly four days old and yet to be named. I'd thought of several options during my pregnancy, but now that I'd met her nothing seemed fitting.

Anya came through the bedroom door, quietly so as not to disturb us. She held the loveliest vase filled with white calla lilies.

"Who are those from?" I asked, surprised by the choice of flower.

"I'm not sure sweetheart, they were just delivered." Anya set the vase down on the dresser. "No note—maybe they're from your work mates?"

"Yes, probably."

Nick. They were from Nick. Although I knew it wasn't

possible, the thought made me smile. I looked down to my sweet, sleeping baby.

Calla. My lily. Calla, my lily. Calla, my life. Just like the lullaby Anya used to sing to me, *Mira, my miracle.* Now Calla would be my miracle. Our miracle.

As my mom moved to peer into the bassinet, I whispered, "Mom, meet your granddaughter, Calla."

NINE

The Present
    What was once ripped apart, shall now be bound together. Jake's words continued to hum in my head.

Nick watched, assessing my reaction as he read the obvious shock and panic on my face. His eyes darkened.

Moving to the hearth while keeping his back to us, Jake spoke with resolute authority, like a father advising his children. "Faith, hope, and love will guide you." Turning, he gave a long pause, allowing us time to absorb the hefty words that hung like smoke in the air. Then he addressed me, "You may be confused, dear Mira, but don't be afraid. It's a new, wondrous path you now walk upon." He gestured to Nick. "Now you, please, go together."

Jake's gentle words were an order, and Nick obeyed without reservation. I moved reluctantly, my legs burdened with heavy emotions. As I crossed the threshold and glanced back to Jake, he was gone, and I found myself alone with Nick. I couldn't face him. Not yet.

Married. When we were together in the mortal world, I was certain of his love. He was my destiny. When our nine weeks were up, and we had to say goodbye, I felt loss. But my heart filled with hope. Nick's love was so consuming, it filled any holes left from his physical departure. In the weeks that followed, I fantasized about our reunion. He'd return from the deployment with a ring and a proposal. It all shattered after I learned of his death. I resolved that a life with him would never be a reality. He was dead, gone forever.

Being reunited should have filled me with joy, something I'd once so desperately wished for—marrying the man of my desires and father of my child. Instead, betrayal and anger cursed the space between us. He had left us. He had taken my child. Perhaps his hand was forced, but still, my life had fallen beyond my control.

Because of him.

Jake proclaimed he would grant Nick his greatest desire, but what about me? I'd changed in the six years since we were together. He had changed. He was a foreigner to me now. I knew and loved Nick, the soldier. I did not know Niko, the god.

The god who took my child from me. The god who caused unimaginable grief.

I shivered, alone and frightened in this foreign land.

"Let's walk." Nick didn't take my arm or hand. Instead, he watched silently as I took great effort to move beside him, leaving a deliberate space between us. Thoughts and emotions clouded my head, pinging off me and onto him. He must have felt it, my reservation and reluctance, because he looked to me and winced.

We walked in silence, both staring ahead.

"Would you like to see the cove? Should we go to Calla?" he asked, trying to reconnect using our one commonality. I nodded, and he led me along a trail that cut through a field of tall, golden wheat. The waving stalks quickly faded away, and our path turned rocky as small pebbles and dried dirt replaced the rich soil. We made our way down to a ledge in the land. In the distance, water sparkled under the sun's rays. The gentle lull calmed my wrecked nerves.

As we continued, larger pools of water peaked through gaps in the shrubs. The trail quickly descended, and soon large, smooth rocks created a neat walkway. I spotted the cove. A stunning waterfall fell over a soaring wall of boulders. Dozens of children swam and splashed along the shore. Some bigger kids jumped from the tall ledges above the waterfall, arching into perfect dives, and sailing into the crystal water. The sweet music of children's laughter and chatter rang through the air.

I spotted Calla behind the waterfall, her hands clasped with a little boy's, who I assumed to be Leo. They swung each other around and then let go, sending one another flying into the water. As Calla's head bobbed up to the surface, she noticed me and squealed with pride.

"Mama!" she called out. "Look, everyone, it's my mama!"

Little faces turned with smiles and waves, welcoming me to their group.

"What is this place?" I whispered to Nick, wonder obvious in my voice.

"It's a little gods' playground." He grinned. "At least during the day. At night it becomes the adults' playground." I understood his seductive implication and flinched. I was not ready for him to talk to me with such intimacy yet.

I kicked off my sandals and noted with surprise that the pants and shirt I wore earlier were replaced with a modest swimsuit.

"How?" I motioned down my body.

"Your powers are getting stronger. A part of you must have thought of a swimsuit when you saw the kids in the water. Your thoughts can make things happen for you."

Yes, I had thought a swimsuit would be nice so I could join Calla in the water. Did I make it happen with a simple thought? Curious, I closed my eyes, envisioning my favorite yellow two-piece, the one I wore before the tolls of motherhood changed my body. Opening my eyes and peering down, the suit had changed. I laughed, running my fingers along my bare belly and my thighs.

"You're catching on!" The corner of Nick's lips twitched into the breath-stopping smile that used to make my stomach flutter. He no longer wore a shirt, and swim trunks had replaced his shorts. They hung low on his hips, hugging the strong muscles of his thighs. My eyes traveled up his body, awakening memories of the many lustful nights we'd shared. I remembered those nights quite well. Heat dotted my cheeks. Nick acknowledged the memories with a knowing smile, and I averted my eyes, focusing on Calla, who continued to splash in the water.

Surrounded by the energy and excitement of the children, I relaxed but remained pensive toward Nick. Everything I knew to be true was upended at the hands of this man, this god. I warily followed him into the water.

Nick dunked under, swimming around until he popped up just a few inches in front of me. Water dripped from the wet curls of his hair and eyelashes. He was gorgeous, still the Greek god I thought him to be many years before.

A playful smile softened his face. Our eyes locked as he held my gaze. I gave a gentle, defensive splash, but he grabbed hold of my arms and pulled me into him. His body exuded with desire, but I stiffened, torn from longing that radiated within me but still apprehensive and angry. He moved to kiss me, and I backed away, holding my arms up to him. We kept eye contact, and Nick understood. A line was drawn. His eyes darkened.

Calla called for us again. Nick, disregarding my obvious request for space, took my hand and led me through the water to our daughter. He scooped up Calla with his free arm. As the three of us connected physically for the first time, an energy flowed between our bodies, sending a small ripple along the water's surface. Calla giggled, and the current stalled. She wrapped her arms around our necks and squeezed until we were cheek-to-cheek.

"Mama, Daddy, we're all together now! A real family!" She again giggled, easing the tension between Nick and me.

We played in the water until the sun began its descent. As a rainbow of night colors bounced off the sea, the little gods began to scatter, heading home for the evening. Mothers and fathers—other gods—arrived to scoop up their children. The older gods looked to us curiously, nodding or bowing their head at Nick.

"Do you know them?" I asked.

He shook his head. "Most, but not all by name."

"Everyone knows Daddy," Calla chirped.

"Oh?" I asked.

"Yes, Daddy is very important. He's a high god!" Calla exclaimed proudly.

"We all have purpose and duty, but some have stations that make us more... powerful," Nick clarified.

"So, you're a high god?" I questioned.

"Yes, a very high god. You may have made some goddesses upset, having snagged me." He flashed a sexy, devilish grin.

"Snagged you?" Anger immediately flooded me, and I

snapped back bitterly. I knew he was being playful, but my fate had been sealed by him, without any regard to me. *His wants, his needs.* Neither Jake nor he had asked me what I wanted. My world, my life—everything—was uprooted by him. "Snagged you?" I asked again while taking steps away from him. The barrier returned. "More like the sacrificial lamb to satisfy *some* god, a god I didn't even know existed until this morning." My hands clenched in fists at my side.

The few remaining parents and children looked our way, my voice loud enough to catch their attention.

"Not just some god." Nick tilted his chin, lips flattening into a line. "Perhaps I need to show you just who I am." He lifted himself from the water and grabbed Calla's hand, effortlessly pulling her to the shore. "We will go home now."

It was a demand. He turned his back to me and began to walk away in long strides.

"You can't tell me what to do!" I yelled, remaining firmly rooted in the water. Calla was already running ahead to catch up with Nick. The temperature chilled by at least twenty degrees. A gust of cool air swirled the water's surface.

"I'm not going anywhere!" I repeated louder. Another wave of cold wind brushed against my skin. My swimsuit stiffened, crystallizing with ice. Nick kept walking. Furious, my hands clenched into fists. "I'm not going *anywhere* with you!"

Nick stopped in his tracks. He turned deliberately, as if collecting himself. His eyes narrowed, rolling over my wind-whipped face, down my shivering body, and settling at my toes, which remained defiantly in the water. I tingled from the cold. It emanated from his angry stare. He jerked his head, catapulting a thick wave of arctic air.

"Stop that!" Roiling with anger, I screamed again, "Stop

it!" The water crunched, rapidly turning to ice. "Stop doing that!" I jumped from the edge to the rough rocks on shore, and my toes burned as they collided with the hard, frozen ground.

Light snowflakes floated from the sky. Clad only in the bikini, my body shook. I pinched my eyes shut and attempted to conjure the image of dry clothes, a jacket, anything to cover myself. Nothing happened. Unlike earlier, my thoughts had no effect.

I felt stripped, naked, violated.

Nick's manipulation of the weather—and me—filled me with rage.

"I hate you!" I shouted with a voice I didn't recognize.

Icy blue and white ripples covered the path ahead. Clouds grumbled in the sky. The silver moon's reflection shuttered off the snow-glazed ground. My heart thudded as I stumbled along the path. "Nicholas!" I yelled. He was so far ahead, I'd lost sight of him. "Stop!" I cried out. "Stop!" The darkness and swirling snow made it hard for me to see, the trail now covered. Icy pebbles and rocks ripped into my bare feet as I staggered along, desperate to locate something familiar—the path to Jake's cottage, the park. Anything.

The moon hid from the storm, and blackness overtook the night. I could no longer see even a trace of the path. I fell to my knees. Desperate, scared, and alone.

Minutes passed, and I wept into my knees. Eventually the snow stopped. Lifting my chin, I whispered, "Please, come back. I'm sorry. I'm sorry." My breath came out in white, smoky puffs.

As I hung my head in defeat, a thick blanket covered my listless body, immediately warming my bones. Nick lifted me into his arms and carried me in silence. I went limp from relief.

Nick's body, which had held me so many times with tenderness, now stood hard and unyielding. The sky was black as midnight, but Nick navigated the path without seeing. We came to a clearing, and the warm, yellow glow from windows of a house offered a sliver of light. The front door swung open as we approached, and Nick carried me in.

I warily peeked around the great room. Similar to Jake's, a hearth with a crackling fire dominated the center. The kitchen and a staircase were to my left, while doors, which led to what I assumed were bedrooms or bathrooms, were situated to the right. Nick set me next to the fire, lowering me onto a thick carpet. As I adjusted the blanket, I noted modest flannel pajamas replaced the swimsuit.

Nick wordlessly moved to the kitchen. I kept my eyes down. I couldn't bear to see him or chance eye contact. If he'd meant to show me who he really was, it was not good.

Hearing his footsteps approach, I pulled the blanket tighter around me. Nick silently offered a steaming mug and plate of bread and cheese. When I didn't move to accept it, he laid it out on the carpet in front of me and then walked away.

Several silent minutes passed before I picked up the cup and drank from it. My stomach growled. I hadn't eaten anything all day, outside of a few grapes at Jake's.

All day. The events of the day washed over me like the icy waves at the cove. I pushed away the plate, suddenly too exhausted to eat.

～

I WOKE FROM A HEAVY, dreamless sleep. Sunshine peeked through cracks in the blinds. I squinted, and glanced around an unfamiliar room. *Nick's house.* I blinked, piecing together tidbits of the previous evening.

Calla's sweet voice interrupted my thoughts. I heard Nick directing her to wash her face and brush her teeth.

"Leo uses his mind to brush his teeth. He told me so himself!" Calla protested. "Why can't I?"

"That's lazy parenting. We will keep up mortal routines. Hurry up, sweetheart. I have pancakes ready for breakfast." His voice was soft, authoritative yet kind—a stark contrast to the ruthless cold he inflicted last night.

The anger and extremity of his actions paralyzed me for a moment. I rolled to my side and stared at the wall.

How could that voice—that person—which was so gentle toward Calla, act so cold toward me? Yes, I had made him mad, rejected him, challenged him. I even went as far as hurting him with stinging words... *I hate you!* I winced as the memory replayed in my head. But his reaction, his actions, were beyond explanation. What would I do? What *could* I do?

Taking the easy route, I opted to do nothing. I heard the door open and shut as goodbyes were exchanged, and Calla left for school. I knew Nick was still in the cottage. He made noises every so often—a chair pushing or a cabinet shutting. I lay on my back, staring at the ceiling while scenarios played out in my head. Should I go out there? What if he's still angry? What if he freezes me again? I flinched at that thought, shrugging it off. He wouldn't hurt me. He loves me. *His greatest wish. His greatest desire.*

But how could he do that last night. *How?*

The internal debate as to whether I should stay in the safety of the room or confront Nick continued, but after countless minutes, the decision was made for me. A gentle knock on the door set my heart thudding.

I tugged the blanket to my chest before softly calling, "Come in."

Nick opened the door, his formidable presence filling the frame. He sought to catch my eyes but made no effort to move forward into the bedroom. I held my breath.

"I am not proud of last night." Nick's chin dropped, his voice thick with regret and shame. "Please forgive me."

He didn't speak, yet I heard his plea. *Look at me. Please.* I unwillingly lifted my face to his, and our eyes locked.

Thoughts, words, and promises whispered in the space between us.

I need to go, but I will always be here.

Nick stood motionless across the room, yet the air swirled thick with his thoughts. I felt feathery fingers dancing over my skin, his familiar touch that had seared into my memory. Stroking my cheek, caressing my skin, moving down my chin to my neck, until finally resting over my heart, just as it had years ago.

Our memories came next. The endless nights we made love, the magic that held us captive, the part of my world that had burst with life because of him. I felt it roll over me again and again until I once again was consumed by bits and pieces of him.

I'll be with you. I promise, no matter how far away I am, I'll always be with you.

Then I felt pain. Nick's pain from being torn from his family, missing his child and wanting his true love. Years of suffering and longing.

Even though we were not together, I was always with you.

And then I felt the pain of last night, his heart breaking from rejection. He thought I'd be as happy as him by our reunion. It was his greatest wish, his greatest desire. He thought I'd felt the same.

I never left you. I never left.

The room echoed with his words, with every earnest promise, every simple sweet declaration of love.

"Please, forgive me," he quietly asked again.

I slowly nodded.

He nodded back.

We made an unspoken peace.

Nick continued to stand in the doorframe, waiting for me, for a signal either sending him away or calling him forward.

His greatest wish. His greatest desire.

I felt, just as I had the day we first met, we were destined. Fate brought us together. He loved me. *A perfect love.* I saw it in his eyes, his words, his touch. Memories of him washed over me again, eroding my resistance and reservation. I could not deny him.

His greatest wish is my greatest wish. Us, together.

It would always be him. Him and only him. My destiny.

I tugged back the blanket and gestured for him to come to me. Nick kept his eyes locked on mine as he moved from the door, taking deliberate steps to the bed. He sat next to me, and patiently waited for me to make the next move. Not breaking eye contact, I crawled into his lap and rested my head on his chest. Strong arms circled me, and I nuzzled closer into his hold.

"I'm sorry," he whispered into my hair.

I lifted my head to him, initiating a kiss. My mouth moved harder, probing his lips open with my tongue. Shifting from his lap, I straddled him. Hungry kisses traveled down his jaw line to his neck while eager fingers tugged at the edge of his shirt.

Nick stopped my hands, bringing them down to cup his face. *His greatest wish, his greatest desire.* I read it in his eyes as he spoke.

"If we do this, if we consummate the marriage, it is binding," Nick's voice deepened with lust. I nodded my head.

He is giving me a choice, and I choose him. I nodded my head again, smiling now, and he released my hands. I hurriedly lifted his shirt, then removed my own.

"Wait!" He took my arms again. "We can't. Not yet." Nick's eyebrows twisted with concern. "I can't."

I pulled back. "You can't?"

"Mira, I want this more than anything. Anything." Nick lifted my chin with a finger. "But consummating a marriage is not as simple as sex. I need to show you something."

Nick hoisted me from his lap, cradling me in his arms just as he did last night. But now our chests burned as hot flesh pressed together. He swooped out of the room, and up the staircase.

The door to a white, airy bedroom flew open as we approached the top of the second floor. Long, sheer curtains waved from an open window, and a lacey blanket with delicate pink rosebuds stitched along its edges adorned the wooden bed. Lush bouquets of white roses and calla lilies covered every open space.

"It's perfect," I whispered.

Nick carried me to the bed, setting me in the center.

"This is what I envisioned for us on our wedding night, Mira, not a scorched cottage or separate bedrooms." He shook his head. "I imagined you walking down a flower lined path, me waiting impatiently at the other end to get a glimpse of my raven-haired bride. I'd sense your approach, turning with bated breath."

Just like the image I had at Jake's cottage, when I saw myself dressed head to toe in white, the sweet rosebuds that crowned my hair, and the calla lilies lining the path.

"You see, one of the blessings of a marriage between gods is also its curse. I can feel your emotions, and you can feel mine. Last night, with everything heightened, I absorbed your doubt and fear. All your anger and resentment. It consumed me, and I lost control."

Nick picked up my hand, holding it tightly. "Downstairs, you saw my pain, my longing. Memories and moments of magic—the magic and wonder that I feel when I think about you. All that emotion, *my* emotion, consumed you."

He dropped my hand and moved to the edge of the bed. The short space between us now seeming as vast as the ocean. I already sensed him drifting away.

"This needs to be your decision. I want you to come to me on your own, without that influence." Nick's voice dropped to a whisper, "We can't do it. We can't bind the marriage."

TEN

Five Years Ago

My parents loved Calla at first sight, but Anya created a swift, fierce bond with her granddaughter. She rocked her through many sleepless nights, waking me for feedings, then whisking Calla away again. The respite allowed me to quickly heal from childbirth.

Well after my body and spirits revived, Anya continued her help with Calla's care, preparing bottles in the wee hours of the night, changing messy diapers, and soothing her during a colicky phase that seemed to go on forever.

At times, only my mom's touch or voice could calm Calla. She'd sing, *"Calla, my lily. Calla, my life. My life in the land."* Calla's glistening eyes would clear of tears, and her squawks hushed whenever Anya sang the special lullaby created for her granddaughter.

Calla filled a part of Anya's soul that seemed to be missing. I knew my parents wished for more children of their own, but fertility struggles plagued them. After I was born, they resolved to stop trying, and Anya cured her baby fever by working at a daycare until a mystery illness zapped all energy from her, and she was forced to quit. Now, Calla brought back a certain sparkle to my mom's eyes that had been missing for years.

My dad, Arthur, stayed particularly busy that spring following Calla's arrival. A research project kept him shut away in his study for hours at a time. He'd pop out every so often to gulp down a drink or snag a snack, always in a rush to return to his office. I wondered what this latest job involved.

In general, Arthur never discussed work. It usually involved boring topics, so I didn't bother to ask. But one afternoon, his flushed face and feverish efforts piqued my curiosity. As he breezed through the kitchen, I questioned him about it.

"So, what've you been doing in there?" I nodded toward his office. "Who's this project for?"

"The usual, Mira."

"Textbook or what?" Arthur didn't teach, but much of his writings included periodicals or textbooks for professors, subjects that didn't interest me.

"Yes, sorry sweetie, I have a tight deadline." Distracted, he twisted on the faucet and stuck a finger under the stream as he waited for the tap water to cool. Sunlight spilled in from the window above the sink. "Look at those roses, Mir. I'll have to prune them again. Third time this week. I've never seen them grow like this."

"I'll get it, Dad. I miss working."

SPRING TURNED to summer and my maternity leave would soon wrap up. I had to return to work, and my parents needed to fly back to Florida. Anya wanted to spend more time with Calla, but after months of supporting me, her energy waned. I wondered if the fatigue resulted from caring for a newborn or if there was more to it.

During my high school years, Anya's health had inexplicably deteriorated, leaving her endlessly exhausted and weak. After they bought the beachfront bungalow in Florida and began spending a majority of the year there, she appeared ages younger, more active, happier, and stronger. She claimed the cooler weather in the North wasn't healthy for her, and I believed it.

The night before my parents' departure, Anya snuggled a sleeping Calla.

"Please, please consider coming to Florida," she pleaded. For weeks, Anya asked, begged, for us to move.

"No, Mom, I can't leave." I always felt an attachment to my childhood home, but now a connection laid with the apartment, solidified by Nick. There, everywhere I looked I saw memories of him. *Our* park. *Our* bench. The bench that stood as a marble monument, immortalizing our love. I needed to get back there, where perhaps I could feel him again.

"Can you visit? Calla would love the ocean." Anya understood my deep fear of flying. The cross-Atlantic trip to Ireland when I was a little girl was the one and only time I remembered being on an airplane. The rocky flight left me traumatized. I'd never forget the panic and terror that consumed the plane after an unexpected storm raged above the sea.

"Someday, Mom," I promised. Somehow, I would make it happen. It'd been over a decade since they purchased their second home in Florida, but I had yet to visit. Anya was getting older, and trips to Wisconsin would be more difficult for her in the years to come.

Arthur shot Anya a stern look. "We'll be back soon enough. Mira has enough going on with heading back to work. Don't add to her worries."

Strange enough, the immense weight of being a single working parent didn't faze me. Nick's insurance policy and survivor's benefits provided sufficient money where I could cut my hours to part-time. Besides, the gardens and conservatory were a second home, and I was eager to get my hands dirty again.

CALLA'S sparse crop of hair grew in thick and dark, with soft curls like Nick's. I studied the features of her tiny face, seeing so much of him in her. Her eye color combined Nick's green and my brown, churning into a distinct hazel that resembled the deep waters of the sea. Calla would gaze at me with those big, stunning eyes as I recounted anecdotes about her daddy. I repeated the tales Nick had told me during our short time together, and then made up others to fill in the gaps.

There were moments when the gaps were too vast for words or stories. How would I ever explain his loss to Calla? How would I answer the many whys? Why would fate bring Nick and me together to only tear us apart? Why would I be given a baby, only to lose the father? Why was life so unfair? *Why?*

Calla would never meet the marvelous character from my stories. Never would she get a hug or kiss from her daddy. I'd mourn Nick over and over again, for her sake, that she'd never know him.

One afternoon as I watched Calla sleep, I dwelled for the millionth time on the cruel reality of our loss. "Nick... I wish you were here. I wish you could meet her," I whispered into the air. Calla woke minutes later. A gummy smile lit her face as her eyes fluttered open and settled on a spot in the distance.

"Dada." Her first word.

I imagined Nick sitting in that blank space Calla seemed fixated on. Maybe his spirit was there, watching over us.

"Nick?" His name slipped from my lips. Hearing it out loud hurled me back to reality, and I burst into tears. Calla's eyes shifted to me, now focusing wide-eyed on my face, and I cried harder. Her tiny lower lip trembled, and she wailed along with me, only spiraling me further, until I feared my grief would swallow me whole.

On that day, I swore to do better, to be stronger for Calla's sake. As painful as it was, I had to push thoughts of Nick aside, move past him, and concentrate on my daughter.

AS CALLA GREW INTO A TODDLER, her hair darkened to near black like mine. Her face transformed, drawing on more of my features. I sadly thought I was losing all sight of Nick in her. She became more like me than just in looks. She was my helper as I continued to care for the gardens in the city's park system.

Many days, Calla tagged along with me. She'd watch intently from her stroller as I plodded around colorful masses of plants and flowers, just as enthralled by nature as I was.

During the harsh Wisconsin winters, my work kept us indoors at the city's horticultural conservatory. I helped with the design and creation of their annual holiday exhibition, unveiling our efforts each year at the Holly-daze benefit. Poinsettia, holly, hypericum, amaryllis, ivy, stargazer lilies, and a myriad of other plant life filled the immense dome. Calla learned to identify the plants and recite their cumbersome names as she observed my team creating fanciful displays. After the holidays, we'd auction off or donate as many live arrangements as possible, but the dead ones often were tossed into giant garbage bins. The act caused tears and temper tantrums from Calla.

"No, Mama, no!" she'd exclaim, clutching the wilted petals and leaves. "Mine!"

I explained to her that plants grow and die, sometimes growing again the next season, sometimes needing to be replanted from seeds. Yet, each year when the time came to clean up the displays, Calla cried and mourned as if she were losing dear friends.

It prompted an idea. I unpacked the UV lights and flats that were stowed away in my storage closet. I taught Calla the cycle of life with plants. We started with seed packets and leftover soil from the conservatory's stock. Calla's daily responsibilities included watering the plants and shifting the flats. Small pots lined the windowsills and mottled the floor of our loft. Summer colors blossomed during the winter months as our tiny garden, and Calla, grew.

I often would find Calla babbling away to the plants. Living in an apartment in the city, she didn't meet many kids her age. So instead, she found companionship with the plants by talking to them, naming them, and telling stories to her little buds.

During the summer months, we spent our free time in the park outside the apartment. Calla didn't care that there wasn't a slide or swing set. She'd skip around the lawn barefoot and passionate with endless energy. Somehow, she always gravitated to the wild calla lilies that flourished in the far part of the park, behind the white marble bench that held her parents' intimate memories. She didn't know the secrets it kept, but perhaps, along with the lilies, she sensed something unusual about the space.

I never questioned the peculiar enchantment the calla lilies brought to the park. Being a tender perennial, the cold climate of Wisconsin should've hindered their growth, yet they grew hardy in our garden.

Calla's eyes would twinkle when she noted the first sign of a budding calla lily. "They're for me, Mama!" she'd proudly proclaim. "Right? Did they grow just for me? Are they mine?"

"Of course, they're just for you! After all, you are my Calla lily," I'd reply, my heart warming from our shared bond.

With my reassurance, she'd sing, "I am Calla. Calla the lily. Calla the life of the land."

YEARS PASSED and Calla blossomed into a charming little lady. Like her namesake flower, she carried a delicate and sweet disposition. Naturally shy and reserved, Calla came alive whenever her favorite friend, her Auntie Novee, came over to play.

Novalee, Calla's godmother, devoted as much time as her demanding career allotted. She'd beg to babysit, or "special fairy godmother time" as she referred to it, giving me breaks to spend time on myself.

While Novalee's job continued to take her away for weeks at a time, when she was home, the three of us were inseparable. Calla would cry and sulk when her auntie had to say goodbye before an extended work trip.

A few days after Novalee had taken off for a long project, Calla's disappointment wouldn't shake. Not only had it been raining for weeks, keeping us indoors, but poor Mrs. Cooper's kitty, Jasper, had just died.

We'd dropped off homemade muffins and hand drawn pictures to Mrs. Cooper, and Calla sulked in the kitchen while watching me clean up breakfast crumbs.

"Why don't you draw me a picture? Maybe tell me one of Novalee's stories?" I asked, trying to distract Calla. According to her, Novalee made up the best fairy tales.

"There once was a beautiful mermaid, with long red hair," she started. I pictured Ariel from *The Little Mermaid*. *Real original, Novalee.* From there, the story took a significant turn. "She had arms like us, but a tail like the fishies. She couldn't come on land because she had no legs. But she couldn't swim with the fishies because she had no fins. She was lonely. So, she was sent a friend who had wings for arms and legs instead of a tail. They had to hold on to each other forever, but together they could swim in the ocean, walk on land, and fly to the clouds."

I'd forgotten Novalee had a flair for the dramatic. Although she was a lawyer who now worked with logic and reason, I recalled the creative teenager that had enchanted an entire dorm with her whimsical stories. Even her English professor had encouraged her to pursue a career in creative writing versus law.

"Are mermaids real?" Calla asked, her eyes wide.

"I've never seen one, Cal, but I've only been to the ocean once."

"Auntie Novee said if you'll ever fly on an airplane, she'll take us to the beach! We can build sandcastles and try to find a real mermaid! Let's go, Mama! We can see Grandma and Grandpa! Please!"

"Someday, baby," I promised. "Someday I'll take you to the ocean."

"No, Mama! I want to go now. I want to see the fishies and the mermaids!" Her little hands clenched into fists, and she stomped her foot.

The best solution was to divert her attention. "I'll tell you what, Calla, if you help me with the dishes later, we can go to the park now."

The proposal did the trick. Calla pushed away the crayons and paper and ran to the sliding glass door. I joined her, peering through the glass to the blankets speckling the park below.

"Go potty, Cal," I said. "Hurry, the park's filling up. We need to get down there before there's no room left for us."

While Calla ran up the stairs, I stuffed a tote with snacks, sunscreen, books, and towels. She barreled back down, and I noticed she'd switched into her favorite pink sundress. Most days, pink was all she'd willingly wear.

"A little overdressed for the park?" I asked, knowing she'd get messy in the dirt.

"Mama, I look like a fairy!" Calla twirled, lifting her hands above her head as the flowy sundress swooshed around her legs.

She *did* look like a little fairy, all dressed up to visit her precious flower friends. "Okay, fine. Try not to get muddy. You don't want to stain your favorite dress, do you?" I warned, ushering her out of our apartment. While I locked the door, Calla hurried ahead to poke at the elevator button.

"Come on, Mama!" She waved me in. The door opened to the first floor, and Calla pushed past me into the lobby.

"Hang on, Cal!" I called out, struggling with our gear.

Blankets hung over one arm while the other held the bag. I had to use my hip to push open the heavy glass door of our building's entrance. Calla again swept by, skipping outside to the sidewalk.

"Look, Mama!" she exclaimed. "A lily!"

Before I could react—before I could call out to her, before I could make even the slightest movement—Calla charged across the street. Her excitement carrying her without thinking to check for traffic, before the driver of the car could hit his breaks.

All I can remember of the minutes, hours, and days that followed was the screech of tires, the smell of burning rubber, the blood matting her black hair... and those devastating words.

There's nothing more we can do. I am so sorry. She is brain dead.

ELEVEN

The Present

Awkward minutes passed before Nick spoke again. His voice firm, he repeated, "We can't do it."

"Okay, Nick. I heard you the first time." I folded my arms, acutely aware of my bare chest.

"Mira, please, I know this doesn't make sense, so let me explain," he pleaded. "I want you." His eyes rolled over my body before he jerked from the edge of the bed and moved to the window. "But I also want this to be your decision. The ceremony Jake performed was more than words. Your emotions are now linked with mine. You can absorb my emotions, physically and mentally, just as I can absorb yours. Until we consummate, it's not binding. I saw how you felt last night—your reservations, anger, and fear. I want you to go into this with open eyes. Without that divine intervention. Without my feelings influencing you. I want us both to know this is real."

Sunlight filtered through the gauzy white drapes. I lifted a hand to shield my face from its hazy rays and squinted back at Nick.

"Stay there," he commanded. "Just for a moment." His voice gentled into a request. I knew he wasn't used to asking. He took a step closer and whispered, "You look more from heaven than of the Land."

Nick stood a few feet away, yet I felt fingers stroking my hair. Maybe it was the wind, but I'm certain I felt the distinct caress of a finger brushing along the lower contour of my chin, and then stroking my cheek.

"I need you to get dressed," Nick said. The hand, or whatever it was touching my face, fell away. "Now."

I nodded, allowing Nick to lead me into a walk-in closet.

"If you don't find something you like here, I can get you whatever you need." He tapped a finger to his head. "Although, I do prefer to keep up mortal habits, especially in front of Calla."

I poked through the bulk of cotton sundresses, casual tank tops, and comfy shorts. The selection included items from my existing wardrobe and additional pieces I didn't recognize. Had Nick put them there?

"How'd you do it?" I lifted the hip-hugging, tie-dyed sundress Novalee had bought me for my birthday the previous summer, clearly more her free spirited-style than mine. "This is from my closet? How'd you get it here?"

"Mira, I promise I wasn't intentionally spying, but I saw you through the years. And trust me, you looked hot in that."

I blushed, lifting it from the hanger and pulling it over my head. "You remember me telling you about Novalee?"

"I never did get to meet her."

"Nope. She's going to freak out when she hears about this... Wait, I guess I can't really tell people. Not that they'd believe me."

"Nope. It's our secret. Besides, when we return—"

"Return?" I asked. Nick averted his gaze, and I got that sick feeling in the pit of my stomach that something was wrong. "What is it?"

He ran a hand through his hair. "We have a lot to talk about, Mira. I wish... I just wish we didn't have to face any of it yet, but we do."

"Face what?"

"Reality." Nick patted the spot next to him on the bed, and I took a seat. He looked out to the open window, staring blankly at the blowing curtains. "I haven't really gotten the chance to think this through, but we need to return soon. Both Calla and you remain *there*, at least in body." He nodded toward the window, adding to my confusion. "She's still in a coma. And you, you're in the emergency room in a deep sleep. The doctors have sedated you."

"What?" My jaw dropped.

"The doctors won't remove Calla's life support until they have your approval. You need to wake up and give them consent. Then, well, you'll need to leave your mortal life. You can do something gentle, like pills. It'll be quite feasible in the minds of the mortals, seeing how you went through such pain... the loss of your child."

"Leave my life? What are you talking about?" I blinked a few times. "What do you mean, give them consent and then leave my mortal life? We need to be dead there, before we can be here? But we're here now?" I waved my arms around and down my body, pointing out my obvious presence.

"No, not exactly. I mean, yes, you're here, but your mortal vessel remains *there*." Nick's arms gestured in the vague direction of the window. "Otherwise, you're in limbo.

Your body, that vessel, will remain there. The Sky can't take a Land god."

I shook my head. "No, no, that's crazy. I can't do that."

Nick took my arms, gently drawing me into him. "Mira, Calla and you can't grow as gods unless you're whole. Think of it like a body and soul being separated. You obviously have never been nurtured as a goddess. We don't even know your station yet. And Calla—it's not safe for her to remain in limbo while she's nurtured here."

"What do you mean, nurtured?"

"Gods and mortals can procreate. We aren't supposed to, and it doesn't happen often, but if we do, unless the new life is nurtured, our energy—the power of the new god—grows very weak and eventually dies within. Like a seed being planted, unless it's watered and cared for, it'll never grow. Calla flourished because I was there, teaching and guiding her from afar. But she grew too strong." He held up his hands. "I have a lot to tell you, a lot to explain. Maybe when I do, you'll understand why I needed to take Calla so quickly. And maybe once you understand, you can truly forgive me."

Too stunned to do anything more than nod, I let Nick lead me down the steep staircase to the living room below. As we walked past the hearth, embers flamed yellow and red, and a fire ignited. I looked to Nick, eyebrows raised. "So much for keeping up mortal habits."

"Sorry. Some of this is just routine." He smiled sheepishly.

We settled on the sofa, and he leaned into me. "Mira, I know this is very selfish of me, but I am so happy. Happy that I get to explain myself to you. Happy you're here." He took my hand, resting it on his lap. "And I know how selfish

I am for being so happy, because by me getting my family, you may lose some people you love in the process."

"What?"

Leaning back, he closed his eyes, took a big breath, and began his story.

"I watched Calla from far and near. When I'm here, in the Land, and I close my eyes, I can take myself anywhere mentally. If I want, I can be there physically, but that takes a lot of energy. Besides, it'd be too disrupting. Calla *knew* me, but if she saw me, even disguised, she'd recognize me as her father. It would be too confusing for her. So, I came in subtle ways. Visiting her in dreams. At times, I was just a whisper in the wind or a soft touch from a blanket. I craved to hold her, physically touch her, and you too. But I had to watch from far away. If I got too close, I could perpetuate Calla's strength or cause her too much confusion. Can you imagine if she came to you telling you she saw her daddy? She was too young to understand."

I recalled Calla's first word, when she'd looked up with a gummy smile and said, "Dada." Just as I'd thought then, he was there. He really was with us.

"There were times when I was close, and she could feel me. She'd giggle when she sensed my presence. I loved to hear her laugh, knowing it was *me* that made her happy, her dad. But her emotion could cause a flower to bloom or a plant to sprout. The flowerpots you had throughout the apartment made it really difficult. I'd have to swipe them before you saw those odd little flowers that bloomed by her laugh." His green eyes met mine. "If you saw that... that magic... I didn't know how you would react. It's not of the mortal world, being able to bring life like that. I had to be careful. Her energy was growing stronger, beyond her control. On days she was particularly happy, a whole garden could spring from the carpets, and I was on constant damage control, swiping away her creations. I'd scold her, telling her she can't do that, she can't create life on a whim. I had to teach her that in the mortal world, there is a cycle and flow to nature and life that we must follow."

"That's why I had the planters, to teach her," I said, soothed by Nick's gentle voice.

"She was too young to understand, and I was spending more and more time cleaning up her messes. I was concerned, but before I could determine a plan, I was pulled away having to deal with a situation here. In my short absence, something happened. She was troubled. The day I took her—" He shook his head in memory. "She must have been upset, disappointed, lonely. I wasn't sure if it was because she missed me or if there was something else."

The day I took her, she must have been upset. Yes, she was unusually upset. Upset Novalee was gone, upset I wouldn't take her to the ocean, upset Jasper had died, and upset that her daddy hadn't been visiting.

"When I saw her, I also saw *it*. A vine growing like a disease under your building. It had roots as thick as tree trunks, and was growing so fast, I could see it spreading like wildfire. I had to act fast before it erupted through the ground." He looked up, eyeing my face for a reaction. "Mira, she was so strong that her emotions, the innocent emotions of a child, were going to cause destruction and casualties of innocent mortals. Your building, the buildings around you, they would've crumbled. I saw you holding the door for her, and even though I knew the consequences, I made a decision. She looked to the park, and she could feel me, she knew I had returned. Her happiness created her favorite, a calla lily."

He closed his eyes, breathing in. "I called her to me, and

when she ran across the street, she didn't check for traffic. She didn't know that car was coming. I shielded her eyes and ears as the car hit. She was back here, with me, before she could see or feel anything. I promise, she doesn't know what happened."

A tangle of black hair matted with blood.

I wish he had shielded my eyes and ears too.

As if reading my mind, Nick solemnly whispered, "I wish I could have shielded you too. It all happened so fast, Mira. I had to act fast. That vine was a volcano about to erupt. After the accident, I contacted my friend—a god who lives among the mortals—to reach out to you, to help you, but he wasn't able to get to Milwaukee for a couple days. I tried, as best I could, to help ease your pain."

I couldn't speak of the accident, fearing I'd fall apart, so instead I asked another lingering question. My little girl was a goddess, and she belonged here. But I didn't know what exactly it meant to live here, in the Land.

"Nick, what will happen to Calla? Will she someday be a woman, marry, have a family here?"

"Yes." He nodded. "Some gods, such as myself, are sent to live among the mortals for a specific mission. Some gods remain here, cultivating their skill from afar. Calla may need to be among the mortals when she is older, for a specific reason or need. For instance, following a devastating act of god or man, such as a hurricane or forest fire, she or other gods who care for nature may be sent to assess the destruction, to help renew life. She's one of many nature gods, but she's strong, and as my child, she's destined to become a higher goddess."

"So, she'll grow up?" While I missed my baby being small, I'd hardly wish her to remain five years old forever.

"Yes," he assured. "She'll grow, eventually marry.

Maybe when she's, like, I don't know, say thirty?" He shrugged his shoulders, attempting to bring a little lightness to an otherwise serious conversation. "And her children will be gods, just like us."

"Just like us? How can I be a goddess?" I thought of my parents. Anya, always exhausted, and Arthur, always with his nose in a book. They'd never done anything extraordinary. "You've never met my parents, but I'd hardly put them in your category. They're old. They haven't led special lives. I mean, as far as I'm concerned, they're boring people. My mom's been sick throughout her life. And my dad..." I pictured him, with his wire-rimmed glasses always set down his nose like an old history professor. "Arthur's only interests are history and writing, boring stuff. I just can't see either of them being a god."

"A scribe!" Nick exclaimed, jolting up in his seat. "Your father—I can't believe I didn't piece it together before! Your dad is a writer, Arthur the author. I remember you joking when you told me about your parents. He's a scribe." His voice now certain, he nodded his head.

"A scribe? What?" I leaned into the sofa, unsure whether I could take any more surprises.

"A scribe is a demigod. They have no power, per se, but they hold a very important position among us. They're our writers, and they write about anything, everything, like authors in the mortal world. Scribes record our words. They write fiction for our entertainment, and nonfiction for us to learn. Most importantly, they record our history, so we always remember." Nick gave a firm jerk of his head, agreeing with himself. "Yes, yes, it makes so much sense now. A scribe is of the gods, but they don't have the same energy or power we do."

"My dad? I just don't believe it. Nick, he is—" I

frowned, picturing Arthur. "I just don't believe it." Constantly researching and writing, always learning, he loved history. I shook my head. He was too simple to be of the gods.

"Mira, my connection to you was so strong, but I couldn't feel you to be of the Land. As the daughter of a scribe, it makes sense for me to subconsciously see you as an equal. But also, as the daughter of a scribe, I didn't feel your energy in the mortal world." He motioned around, making the fire crackle.

"So, what you're saying is my dad is just a lowly guy here, in your hierarchy." I could hardly believe my dad could even be of the Land, but if so, was he the low guy on the totem pole? A demigod? "I'm sorry, I don't mean to sound petty or mad. It's just all so weird."

Nick chuckled. "Yes, I can see how it can seem weird. Really weird." He took my hand, rubbing the inside of my wrist with his fingertip. "Regardless, I'm thankful. Fate has smiled upon me, bringing you to me. And Mira, I hope this comes across the right way, because I know it sounds awful, but I am so glad fate had it that I took Calla that day. Had I not, you wouldn't be here with me right now. I might've never known you are a goddess. I'm sorry it was your despair that brought us together again, but I'm selfish. I craved my family, and now I have you. Both of you."

Yes. My devastation had brought me here. If Nick had been able to continue coaching Calla from afar, it was quite possible that the three of us would never have connected. I nodded my head to him in understanding, but a sad realization washed over me.

"Will I be able to see my parents again?" I asked quietly. "And Novalee?"

"In the mortal world, yes." He took a deep breath. "But

you need to make a decision, and soon. Your bodies are there, in limbo. We need to return and... deal with Calla... and then deal with you."

Deal with us? My stomach sank once again. "I see."

"I'm sorry. That probably sounds callous, but Calla needs to be whole, here. Even if we bring her back to the mortal world, she's too young, too immature, and too strong to control her powers. For those reasons, it's very rare for a child-god to be raised among mortals. I tried as best I could, but I obviously failed. She's safer in the Land."

"I understand." I really didn't. Too many thoughts swam in my head.

"When you're ready, we can do it."

"We can do it," I blankly repeated.

Nick lifted my chin with a finger, catching my eyes. His emanated with every emotion I couldn't voice. Sadness, worry, anger. Sadness and worry for me, anger towards himself.

"I'm so sorry I put you in this position, but it'll be okay. I promise. When you're ready, I'll be with you. We'll go there together, and I'll be with you all the way."

We sat silent and motionless for minutes until Nick spoke again, his voice resolute. "Calla's mortal life is done. It's modern medicine keeping her there. When you're ready to say goodbye, to allow the doctors to stop life support, I'll be there. I promise."

"You'll be with me... to watch Calla... pass on." He nodded in response. "What about me?"

"We never really die, even mortals. We move on to a better place. But this is your choice. You can remain there, or you can leave your mortal body and come here, with us."

"Leave my mortal body," I repeated softly. *Kill myself.*

Kill myself or live without Nick and Calla. I wouldn't win with either option. I sighed, a heaviness filling me.

My sweet parents. My mother, who even during her sickest moments, was my rock. My shining light. My champion. How could I leave Anya? How will she handle the loss of her only daughter and her only granddaughter? It would be too much. Tears smarted my eyes.

"I don't know how I can do it. I just don't know. My mother," I sobbed openly, and Nick embraced me, stroking my back. "It will destroy her if both Calla and I are gone. How will she make it through?"

"Your father can help her. As a scribe, he can write the words to soothe her. It'll be okay. I'll be with you. I promise." He repeated the sentiment, as if trying to convince himself.

Nick continued to rub my back, my pain and confusion diffusing with each stroke. I shrugged off his hands. I couldn't seem to think straight whenever he touched me.

"They don't even know." I thought back to the last couple days and Calla's accident. It happened so quickly. Life changed in an instant.

Immediately following the accident, I was too shocked to reach out to anybody. And the day after that, before I was given Calla's grim prognosis, I tried their cell numbers but was sent to voicemail. Arthur and Anya were on a trip overseas, my dad doing research, and Novalee was traveling somewhere for work. I couldn't leave a message of that magnitude.

Maybe Arthur could write the words to soothe my mom, but what about Novalee? She was more than a best friend. She was like a sister, and Calla was her goddaughter. With one of us, let alone both gone, I couldn't fathom her despair. Would Arthur write the words to soothe her too? How could I cause so much pain to those I love most?

"How could you?" I whispered, squeezing my eyes shut. "How could you do this to us, put me in this position?"

"I'm sorry." Nick patted my leg. "I'll make it up to you. I'll make things right, but for now, I can help you through this. I can help take away the pain, keep you strong. It's part of the link, our connection. Even though we haven't solidified the union, we're still bound."

Proving his point, Nick grabbed my hand and squeezed it. My anger, resentment, and fear seeped away. Like a vacuum sucking up dust, he drained all the negativity from my mind and muscles. Exhaling, Nick released my hand, and I slumped back against the cushion.

"I hope in time you will find forgiveness—true forgiveness. I want you to come to that on your own. We have eternity, Mira, and I will make it up to you. I want everything to be right going forward. For now, we need to concentrate on Calla."

Maybe it was the magic, whatever his touch did, but a large part of me had already forgiven him. It didn't make sense. How could it? How could I so easily forgive the man who'd taken my child? The man who'd turned my life—my very existence—upside down?

If I forgave him so easily, what would that say about me? What kind of mother would I be?

"I will spend eternity making it up to you," Nick repeated, reading my hesitation.

But I couldn't think of eternity, not when the days ahead seemed so heavy and bleak. I pinched the bridge of my nose, a trick I learned as a kid to ward off tears.

"How much time do we have?" I asked after several minutes of silence.

"We need to return soon. Calla will remain in the coma until you give consent to remove the life support. Once you come to peace with that, she'll be whole here. Then once you come to peace with your mortal death, we can all be together here."

"Why?" I breathed the words out. "Why?"

"Calla will be safe. Jake will watch over her. But there her mortal body is, for all practical purposes, dead. It's only being kept alive by machines," Nick said definitively. "You'll have time. I'll help you. You can talk to your parents. You can leave them with peace. You won't have to do it alone. I'll be right beside you."

"I don't understand, Nick!" I bellowed. His arms came around me, but I pushed them away. Whatever anger he'd sucked away returned with a vengeance. "How can you come and go, being here and there? Why can't Calla and I do it too?"

"I am a very powerful god." Nick looked me in the eye, his words vibrating off the walls, causing the fire to crackle. "Someday soon, Calla will be able to take herself 'here and there' as you put it, with ease. I am hopeful you will too. What brought you to this realm in the first place was profound grief, despair—*energy*. It can take years, centuries sometimes, for a god to have enough strength, enough energy to cross the domains with ease." His voice softened. "So, her vessel will remain. Can you imagine your bodies staying there, her in a coma? Even if I carried her back to her mortal vessel, can you imagine the questions and chaos that would cause? It'd be beyond a medical miracle for life to return after her prognosis."

Nick drew a deep breath and continued. "Calla is a young goddess, but she is already very strong. She needs to be here. We need to break the connection to her mortal body. She doesn't know yet how to do it, but she can quickly develop the energy and strength to return there, to that vessel. That is why, while it may break your heart, you must have them stop the machines."

Tears streamed down my face. This time, when Nick reached over to touch me, I didn't turn away. He swiped at my cheeks, his thumbs brushing tenderly against my skin. I couldn't understand how the simple gesture evoked such heat and desire, but what really baffled me was the sudden, urgent need to follow Nick's plan. To give the doctors permission to end Calla's life support. And, as insane as it sounded, to also follow through on the other part of the plan. The part where I ended my own life.

TWELVE

My hands were tied, but the when and where would be up to me. I could talk to my parents and Novalee, give them peace, and Nick would be with me when Calla passed. Somehow, the idea didn't sound as horrid, yet my stomach roiled every time I pictured Anya and Novalee.

If only Arthur had prepared me. Always levelheaded, Art concentrated on facts. Story time as a child included bits and pieces from textbooks, not fairytales that spoke of gods, demigods, and scribes.

The day's events were thick in the air when we left Nick's cottage. *Our* cottage. This magical land would eventually be my new home. As surreal as it seemed, the perfection surrounding us softened the blow of the day's discoveries.

A combination of resentment, anger, and fear mingled with love, passion, and excitement. To be with my husband, my soul mate, I'd be giving up the only life I knew. But every time I glanced at Nick, the very sight of him left me breathless.

He is my destiny.

The sun shone brightly above the gravel trail to Jake's home. As we walked, our paths crossed with other gods and goddesses. Some bowed as we passed. Some stopped, staring in surprise. Some gaped with obvious curiosity. One thing was for certain, all eyes were focused on me, assessing me.

I couldn't shake the stares and whispers as gods and goddesses continued to pass. Finally, I stopped in my tracks and tugged at Nick's arm. "Why are there so many people out tonight? Is this normal? And why are they all staring?"

Nick chuckled. "They are here to see you, to get a glimpse of you."

"What? Why? It's like they're... they're assessing me?"

"They are." He pulled me into him, then brushed a lock of hair off my shoulder. "I'm an old god, Mira. A confirmed bachelor. This is gossip to them. A high god getting married is news enough, and I don't think they expected I'd ever marry. They want to see you, who you are. They're curious, like in the mortal world when a prince marries a common-er." I flinched. "I don't mean it like that, but..." His voice trailed off.

I wondered if word had gotten out that I was the daughter of a scribe. The lovechild of the low guy in their hierarchy and a mere mortal, who'd *snagged* a high god. Was it just yesterday Nick made that comment?

"Okay, I get it. I get it." I held up my hands. "I guess you were right. I probably did make a few goddesses jealous when I snagged you."

Nick cocked his chin. "Well then, let's give them something to really be jealous about."

His mouth crushed mine, and I shivered from my lips

down to my toes, the ground beneath our feet trembling in response. Nick pulled back with satisfaction.

"Do you have any idea of the hold you have over me?" He breathed the words into my lips, still parted from his kiss. I shivered again, this time from the hunger in his voice.

WE FOUND Jake and Calla outside of his cottage, bent over a basket of vegetables. Dirt soiled Calla's pink T-shirt and speckled her knees. Spotting us, she waved a muddy hand.

"Mama! Daddy!" Calla squealed, dropping the garden spade from her hands and running to us.

"Look at this!" Jake motioned to the pile. "Your girl is amazing!"

"Mama, we planted these just this morning, and look!" She pointed to her bounty. Carrots, potatoes, beans, and onions heaped from the straw basket.

"She works tirelessly!" Jake beamed.

"Grandpa said I can't make them grow with my head anymore." Calla pouted, crossing her arms. "I need to be a patient of the bicycle of life."

"Yes, Calla, you need to be patient with the *cycle* of life." Jake's eyes twinkled, clearly amused by his student. "We did give them a little help. But just a little, right Cal?" He tapped his forehead with a pointed finger, and she nodded.

"It's amazing, sweetheart!" I crouched down to hug her.

"Grandpa's going to make stew, and I get to help him cut up everything!" Calla grabbed Jake's hand.

"Yes, that's right, let's get cooking. We have a lot to celebrate tonight. Come on." He waved us to the door.

I waited for Jake to cross through the door before turning to Nick. "Grandpa?"

"All the kids call Jake that. His station is Father of the Land, but he has no biological children of his own."

Entering Jake's home, a calm fire crackled in the hearth. I looked around the spotless great room, spying another woven basket atop the large wooden table, not catching any hint of the previous day's inferno. The kitchen was situated to my left, while a hall and doors were to my right.

"Are all of the homes here the same?" I gestured toward the hearth.

"No, but I helped Niko build his, and he helped with mine. Some gods build with their minds, but we prefer to build with our hands." Jake flipped up his palms to show me his callouses.

"It's amazing," I said, brushing my fingers over the smooth finish of the dining table.

"Are you happy?" Jake asked. "With your new home, that is? Is it the right size? It can be quickly changed to suit your needs." He nodded toward Nick. "He can build you a bigger wardrobe, an entire third floor, in the blink of an eye."

"No," I answered emphatically. "It's perfect." I closed my eyes with a light sigh. The bedroom with the dark bed frame, airy curtains, and rosebud blanket was seared into my memory. The calla lilies and white roses filling the room with their beauty and scent, perfection.

"Jake," Nick hesitated, looking to Calla. "We have some answers. Some decisions. We'll need to speak once the little one goes to bed."

"I see." Jake poured a large glass of a red wine. The intense color reminded me of the extraordinary grapes from the day before. "Here." He passed the goblet to me, then poured another for Nick, and juice for Calla. "A toast. To the newlyweds."

"What's a newlywed?" Calla asked.

"When a man and woman get married, they are just wed, newly wed." Jake patted her head. "Ready to toast, Cal? To your parents!"

"Toast!" she exclaimed joyfully, clinking her glass against Jake's.

I glanced at Nick. Married, but not. Could life get any weirder?

~

CALLA TOOK a final bite of dinner, tossed her fork across the plate, and then gave a dramatic yawn. She didn't fuss when Nick wrapped her in a flannel blanket and set her on the sofa.

Jake opened yet another bottle of wine. I refilled my glass for the fourth time, unable to resist the stunning taste of mulled grapes. Nick laid out the day's revelations. Jake nodded in agreement with Nick's assessment that Arthur was a scribe. He also concurred that I needed to return to the mortal land.

As Nick talked it through with Jake, I sifted through my conflicted emotions. Somehow, our odd predicament seemed slightly less bizarre. The copious amounts of wine probably helped with that, but I also realized there was no use in dwelling. What was done, was done. The path had already been paved, starting with Calla's accident. Now there was no going back.

I swallowed the lump in my throat.

The severity of our actions would probably catch up with me at some point in the future, but if I wanted to make it through the days to come, I had to accept it.

For now, I needed Nick more than anything else, even if it was him that set this crazy plan in motion. I needed him.

More importantly, I wanted him.

Nick and Jake's voices floated above me as they discussed the plan, which Nick had already gone over with me. After I fell asleep that night, he'd help me "travel" back to my body. There was no plausible way for me to do it on my own. I had neither the knowledge nor the power, so he'd use his energy to carry me back.

"Mira?" Nick called.

My eyes popped open. "Yes? Sorry."

"Remember what I told you? Carrying a fellow god can be taxing, so it might take me some time to recover before I can make it back to you."

I nodded, and then returned my attention to Calla who looked like a glowing angel, complete with a halo, sleeping by the fire. This would be the image that carried me through the days to come. My innocent daughter.

GLOOM AND ANXIETY hovered over the gravel path on our walk home. I kept pace with Nick, who effortlessly carried a sleeping Calla. Her head rested against his shoulder, oblivious to the discussion regarding her life—and death—that had just played out.

At the cottage, Nick settled Calla in her bed. I peeked from the doorway into her room. Mint green paint covered three walls while a detailed garden mural occupied the fourth. Beneath a large picture window lay a toy bin, overflowing with stuffed animals, dolls, and games. Centered in the room was a hand-carved bed, similar to the one upstairs, either Nick or Jake's handiwork. Resting on the pillow next to Calla lay her favorite stuffy, Leon, the plush little lion Novalee had given her as a baby.

Nick remembered. Calla never went to bed without Leon.

He left me to spend time alone with Calla. I cradled her small frame, taking in her floral scent and committing her peaceful face to memory. I rubbed my fingers over her delicate skin, resting them over her cheeks.

Finally, before leaving my daughter for the night and days to come, I apologized for what I had to do. I had no idea where I'd gather the strength to carry out the plan. A tear slipped from my eye, falling onto Calla. I brushed it away, leaving a shimmery glaze on her cheek.

She'd looked like an angel by the fire. Now, in this flowery bedroom with my tears glistening on her cheeks, she looked like a fairy.

In reality, Calla is neither. She's a goddess, and this is her destiny.

Nick stood in the doorway with remorseful eyes, watching as I clutched Calla's tiny hands, the little hands that used to stroke my chin every morning as I woke. I longed for the simplicity of those mornings, when my only worry was a few extra minutes of sleep.

I gave her a final kiss then joined Nick in the hallway. I didn't look back when I crossed through the door.

Tense silence filled the house. Nick led me up the stairs to his bedroom. The calla lilies and roses glowed under the moon's shine, twinkling through the sheer curtains.

"You're sure this'll work?" I asked wearily.

"Yes. Just as I brought Calla here, I can bring you back." His confidence, the confidence that can only come from the

God of Victory, was assuring. "Remember, carrying another god takes a lot of energy. I may not be there when you wake, but I promise it won't be long."

"I'm scared." My voice trembled. He nodded knowingly.

"Be not fearful. There is no fear in love, but perfect love casts out fear." Nick placed his hands over mine. "I am with you. I am yours. When you are weak, I will strengthen you. When you fall, I will carry you. When you weep, I will hold you. *Though one may be overpowered, two can defend themselves."*

Nick's words floated in the breeze, and I felt my fears drift away with it. No longer able to keep my eyes open, his voice lulled me to sleep, still garbed in the tie-dyed dress and strappy sandals.

PART TWO

Though one may be overpowered,
two can defend themselves.
A cord of three strands
is not quickly broken.
(Ecclesiastes 4:12)

THIRTEEN

The screech of tires. The smell of burning rubber.

My eyes popped open, my head twisted side to side, searching for Nick. Instead, a bright, blinding overhead light came into focus.

Was it a dream? Was it all just a dream?

I waited for the wave of nausea to pass before digging my elbows into the stiff mattress. Attempting to push up, my heavy limbs groaned in response. I slumped back against a starchy pillowcase.

"You're awake." A nurse hovered under the door frame before coming to me and silencing the beeping machines.

"Nick?" my raspy voice escaped in a low plea. "Is he here?"

"You..." The nurse considered her words, taking a long, deliberate breath. When she exhaled, her calm eyes met mine. "You collapsed. You had a nasty fall."

The IV. The blinding overhead light. The stinging scent of antiseptic.

My heart pounded. I looked around, acutely aware I was back in the emergency room, in the same cold room with the same sad-eyed nurse who was speaking the same compassioned words.

"Let me get Dr. Shanahan. He may want you to rest longer." And like déjà vu, she placed her hand on my shoulder, giving a gentle squeeze of comfort.

No, no, no. The words screamed in my head. I closed my eyes tightly, willing myself to remain silent. My attempt futile, small whispers escaped my lips. "No, no, no."

The nurse patted my arm, concern swimming in her eyes. "Mira, please breathe." She grasped my hand, squeezing it. "It's okay. It's okay."

Nothing is okay.

"Is he here?" I asked again through sobs. Confused, the nurse shook her head side to side.

Nick, where are you?

I sunk my pounding head into the pillow. "What day is it?"

The nurse continued to hold my hand, murmuring, "Please breathe, Mira. You... You hit your head. Just try to relax."

"What day is it?" I screamed, snatching my hand away. She took a step back.

"Tuesday." I had startled her, yet her eyes remained kind. "You've been asleep for a few hours."

I wept on and off for the remainder of the morning. The doctor on rounds stopped in and explained I'd suffered an anxiety attack, collapsed and hit my head against the ventilator in Calla's room. But I already knew that.

"Do you remember what happened?" he asked.

I squeezed my eyes shut before answering. "Yes, I can't see her again. Not yet."

"Just rest, Mira. When it feels right, you can see her." I

looked to him, and he nodded the same pitying nod I'd grown accustomed to.

My head bobbed in agreement before I rolled away and buried my face into the stiff hospital pillow. Tears continued to drip, saturating the pillowcase while my eyes focused blankly on the colorful ebbs and flows of the vitals monitor.

Remember, please. The leftover haze of drugs and throbbing pain clouded my thoughts and made for a fuzzy picture, but there was Calla, when I first saw her in the Land—all of her, from infant to present. *Remember.* Her excitement over cartwheels, her skipping along in a field of flowers, the calla lilies blooming, the intense taste of the grape, splashing in the cove, getting ready for school with daddy, a basket full of vegetables...

Once they started flowing, the memories became a flood, and I relived every moment, ending with the final kiss when I had watched Calla sleeping peacefully.

It was real. It had to be real.

THAT EVENING, Dr. Shanahan released me from the emergency room. I signed papers as a nurse went over instructions at discharge. She then guided me to the fourth floor of the hospital, to the trauma center where Calla remained in critical condition.

The elevator door opened, and the nursing station stood before me. I averted my eyes, focusing on the placard for the respite room. The quiet space was reserved for family members of the hospital's most delicate patients, available for our use day or night.

I wasn't yet ready to see Calla. I needed to keep the

sweet images I'd just retrieved at the forefront of my memories. But being near her, on the same floor as her, comforted my spirits.

The blood-stained clothes I wore in the ambulance to the hospital on the day of the accident had been discarded by a staff member. They'd generously donated a clean jogging outfit bearing the hospital's logo. I realized I'd eventually have to return to the apartment for a shower and change of clothes, but I wasn't ready for that either. How could I see Calla's toys, her clothes, her stuff? How could I leave her alone here, even if it was just her body, and go home? I'd wait for Nick. He'd help me sort through all of this. He promised.

After turning my cell phone back on, it immediately buzzed with dozens of notifications. Friends, neighbors, and colleagues who'd heard about the accident offering words of sympathy. Yet the three people most important to me remained in the dark. I clicked to call my parents, but it went directly to their voicemail. I tried Novalee next and also got a recording. I couldn't remember where she was headed for this trip. London rang a bell, but she traveled so much I hardly kept track. My parents were in Ireland, my dad doing historical research for a periodical.

My dad, the scribe. It sounded bizarre, unrealistic. Gods, angels, demigods, scribes. A sick feeling in the pit of my stomach grew as I considered reality. It had to have been a dream, a dream created by the cocktail of drugs, but it was all I had. The only thing I could hold on to, my only hope.

Instead of focusing on the absurdness, I needed to recollect every minute of the Land.

Nick didn't appear any older since I'd seen him last in the mortal world, about six years ago. I wondered if he thought I changed in the time since we met. I was lucky to have lost my pregnancy weight quickly, but my body seemed different after childbirth. Could he tell? Did he notice that my breasts weren't as firm, my muscles not as defined? Being a single mom, I didn't have as much time to devote to myself.

But he's seen me through the years, he's been with us this whole time.

I shook off the doubt. I had to believe. It was my last sliver of hope. *No,* I shook my head, remembering Jake's words. *The days ahead may test you, your strength, your beliefs. But faith, hope, and love will guide you. Even if you don't understand, they'll lead your heart on the right path.*

I felt the love. I had to maintain faith and hope. Nick would come.

THE RESPITE LOUNGE held minimal furniture, a few sofas and end tables with reading lamps, and a television in the corner. Old magazines sat on a coffee table. The room was empty, and I was glad for the solitude. I stretched across one of the sofas. My body ached from stress and shock, and my head still throbbed from the fall, but somehow, I was able to slip into sleep, waking several times to turn and stretch.

When the sun started to rise in the morning, I sat up and rubbed my eyes, doubting I'd be able to drift off again. I checked my cell to confirm the time. A notification for new emails popped on the screen.

At the very top was my dad's name. Blowing out a distressed sigh, I clicked his message. A lengthy detail of their activities from the last week filled the screen. Arthur apologized for the delay in communicating, saying phone and internet access was sporadic as they traveled through Ireland. Bad weather had squashed some plans, and Mom wasn't too happy leaving before she got dry time by the cliff. They planned to extend their trip for several weeks.

The cliff, as Anya referred to it, was an area very dear to her. She was abandoned as a newborn and lived with a family near the cliff for a short time before being sent to an orphanage. Her childhood wasn't pleasant, but she always felt drawn to the cliff, the only place where she'd been a part of a real family. After high school, she returned. It was there she met Arthur, an American studying history abroad. They fell in love, married, and returned to the States. When Arthur again had a research opportunity in Ireland, our family returned for a month. Anya was reunited with her beloved seaside town.

The return flight from that trip was the one in which our plane had lost control over the sea, leaving me with a lasting fear of flying.

I clicked "reply" and began an email to my dad. I didn't know where to start so I let muddled thoughts flow into rambling words. Each paragraph brought the Land back to life, but also the oddity of the events.

Who would believe this? Rereading my message, it was doubtful even to my own eyes. I deleted the email and started tapping at my phone again.

Dad, why didn't you tell me about the Land? I backspaced until the screen went blank.

Strumming my fingers against the screen, I eyed the window. I needed a break, to think this through before I sent anything final off into cyberland. I had to clear my mind, figure out whether I truly believed the last few days were real or a desperate act of my imagination.

THE STUFFY HOSPITAL CAFETERIA, located five floors down in the basement, bustled from the morning rush. A throng of people waited for the hot breakfast foods, twisting in a line along the length of the diner, and out the wide double doors. Not eager to wait, I opted for coffee and a fruit cup from the take-and-go cooler.

With few seats open, I found a space between two strangers at a communal, high-top table. I sipped coffee and reread my dad's message, doubt swirling in my head. Was the Land real, or a desperate figment of my imagination to cope with Calla's loss? I had no concrete evidence, only flashes of memories from my brief visit to the enchanting wonderland. If only I could reach my parents or Novalee. If only I had someone to talk through this with.

Nick, where are you?

He warned it'd take time to come to me. I had to remember that. Yet, being here at the hospital without him, the calmness I'd felt from his words, his nearness, fell away, leaving me uncertain and afraid. What if it *was* just a dream? A story created by my mind, a desperate way to cope?

Doubt again clouded my resolve, and I mindlessly popped a waxy, red grape into my mouth.

The grapes! The fruit of the Land. The firework of flavor that exploded in my mouth. The taste and feel of the grape that evoked surreal images. The life of the grape, from seed in soil, to plump, juicy fruit on the vine.

I closed my eyes, and for the shortest of seconds, I relived the moment in Jake's cottage, sitting at the table, when I first tasted the fruit of the Land.

A fresh sprout, the bud of life. Little arms growing and

reaching, tiny pebbles pulsing and plumping. Sun, rain, earth.

In the fleck of time my eyes were closed, I felt something so real, so intense—the heat of the sun, the earthy scent of soil, the sweet taste of the fruit—it could not have been my imagination. *It is real.*

Opening my eyes, I giggled then, a loud, high-pitched laugh that escaped my lips as my hands fluttered to cover my mouth. The man sitting next to me jerked from the squeal, and a few Cheerios toppled off his spoon. Sheepishly, I apologized and looked down to the cup of pastel-colored melons and dull grapes.

It was real. It is real. I repeated the words with absolute conviction, and then hit reply.

Dad,

I'm sorry this is short, but I don't have much time, and I need to get this out before I lose my courage. There is so much I need to ask and tell you, but I can't put it in an email. So please call me. It's urgent. I'm at the hospital with Calla. It's going to be okay. I think you'll understand, but regardless of what happens, she'll be okay.

I've tasted the fruit of the Land. I've seen beautiful gardens grow. My eyes have been opened to a new world. I will be okay too.

If we're gone before I can talk to you, please explain to Mom. She might not understand, but you will. Please help her, explain to her in your words, that we need to leave.

Love,

Mirabel

FOURTEEN

After reliving a taste of the Land, I couldn't fathom choking down the rest of the fruit cup. I chucked the container into the trash. Besides, an urgent desire to be near Calla churned anxiously in my stomach. I wasn't ready to see her, but I needed to be close.

A group of visitors and medical personnel clustered in the congested hall near the elevator. As I approached, they seemed to clear a path for me, and the door slid open. I was the first to enter, settling with my back against the wall as the space filled.

"Fourth floor, please," I said in a shaky voice, keeping my eyes down. The man nearest the buttons poked upon my request.

The door creaked shut, cutting off my view of the cafeteria. Confined within the small space, it seemed to buzz with a slight electricity, a nervous excitement. Buttons for the second and third floor illuminated, yet the elevator bypassed those levels, opening first at my stop on the fourth floor.

Keeping my head down, I hurried past the nurses'

station and into the respite room. Someone had switched on the television, and a morning talk show hummed in the background. I took a seat and picked up a magazine from the pile.

The rest of the morning dragged on as I waited. And waited. Morning talk shows turned to afternoon soap operas. The television's noise floated through the room while I kept checking the time.

Nick, where are you? I pleaded for a sign, for anything. The hours crawled on and by late afternoon, I'd flipped through every single magazine. I needed to get out of the room.

I reached for the doorknob just as someone pushed in from the other side.

"Oh, sorry!' a pleasant voice called. Not in the mood to chat, I excused myself, brushing past a young woman. She laid a hand on my arm. "You must be Mira?" I turned back toward her, mumbling a yes in response. "I'm Samantha, Calla's caseworker. I don't mean to interrupt, but if you have a minute can we chat in my office?"

A caseworker? I sucked in air, then nodded my head, silently pleading for Nick.

Where are you? I need you.

I wasn't sure whether I welcomed this new sensation of needing Nick again. When it came to Calla's care, to my mental strength and well-being, I'd always been on my own, in control. As a single parent, I had to be.

Samantha led me to an office on the fifth floor. I settled into a brown leather chair while she offered clarification on her role at the hospital. She was to educate family members in sensitive situations, such as Calla's, of options we had for our loved one. Eventually I'd need to make decisions. I fidgeted, picking mindlessly at the corner of the business card she'd handed me, as she again offered condolences, and then explained the practice of organ donation.

Samantha's face softened when she detailed the process and emphasized the gift—the blessing—it would be to other children and families. My face froze as I digested the idea.

"Stop!" I cried, pushing to my feet. "I can't! I can't even think about this right now!"

Nearly tipping my chair over, I fled from the room, tears streaming down my cheeks. Frantically, I jabbed at the elevator buttons with a desperate need to get out of the hospital.

But what I really needed was Nick.

My hands clenched into fists. He promised he'd be here. Where was he? I charged out of the lobby on foot, running down the sidewalk.

Before I realized it, I was blocks from home. My pace slowed as I neared the park, *our* park, averting my eyes when I came to the spot on the street where the accident occurred.

Water drizzled from the fountain in the park's center. I fixated on it, holding my breath and following the criss-crossing path toward my building. Summer's hot sun cast a warm glow over the budding bushes and fresh grass, yet the park appeared dull... lifeless.

Calla, goddess of nature, was gone.

MY APARTMENT WAS JUST as we'd left it days ago, on the morning we set out for a picnic. Dishes from breakfast sat in the sink, and Calla's toys scattered the living room floor. My eyes darted to the patio. The jungle of plants covering the terrace had wilted and slumped from lack of water. Or perhaps they were mourning Calla.

I sniffed away tears as I slipped upstairs to the loft bedroom. The shirt Calla had discarded after changing into her favorite sundress sat in a puddle next to my bed. I dropped to my knees, rubbing the fabric against my cheek and to my nose. Her light flowery scent lingered.

I wouldn't wait any longer for Nick. I needed to see Calla.

Leon, Calla's stuffed lion, lay abandoned on her pink pillow. My fingers ran over his squishy body, and I wondered how he'd made the long trip to and from the Land. How could he be here and not Nick?

Because it's not real, it's your imagination.

My resolve again faltered, struggling between reality and fantasy. I'd always worked with a level head. Post-its and lists, order and routine. All of that had been thrown by the way-side when I met Nick. Maybe that was what drew me to him. He was so unexpected, our love so sudden, sweeping me off my feet and turning my orderly life upside down.

Life again was slipping beyond my control.

Remember, please remember. The scent of Calla, the wintery air, the taste of the fruit. Dreams do not evoke those sensations.

I stroked Leon's matted fur, stiff and soiled from the hundreds of kisses and messy adventures he'd shared with Calla. She never slept without him, even in the Land.

I wanted to wait for Nick to be with me when I saw Calla, but perhaps like the Cowardly Lion, her little stuffed friend could give me the necessary courage instead.

~

A STABBING HEADACHE shivered at my temples. I brushed my damp hair into a ponytail. The hot, steamy shower didn't help in relieving any of my aches or pains. Scouring the medicine cabinet for an Advil, I came up empty handed. I'd have to stop at the Metro Mart on the walk back to the hospital. I sighed, stuffed Leon the Lion in my bag, and scurried out of the apartment without caring to lock the door behind me.

Bounding down the streets of my neighborhood, I passed the corner of Ogden and Van Buren, barely glancing at Dark Beans. I stopped going there after Nick died.

Pain pounded full force, pulsating from the bridge of my nose to each temple. I pushed away thoughts of Nick and entered Metro Mart through the automatic doors, which opened to the produce department. The drug aisle was situated on the opposite side of the market, near the other entrance. I didn't pay notice to my surroundings, walking through the maze of fruits and vegetables.

Something stopped me. A feeling. An unnatural force. I stood frozen, inhaling shallow breaths of the crisp, air-conditioned air.

Slowly I twisted around, as if in a dream, afraid to startle myself awake.

There he was, standing by a crate of tomatoes. He picked one up, a playful smile spreading across his face.

"Nick," I whispered.

He lifted the tomato in an offering—just as he'd done years before with the mango. My lower lip trembled. Nick's deep dimples and sparkling green eyes created an instant flutter in my stomach. The simple sight of him left me nearly breathless.

But his presence, solidifying the truth of the Land, snapped me to reality. I hurried the few steps to him and threw myself into his chest. His solid body barely budged against my weight.

In Nick's arms, my pulse pounded so hard I was certain everyone could hear it. He stroked my back, and it slowly settled. As his hold loosened, the crushed tomato dropped from between our bodies, splattering at our feet. Wide-eyed, I looked from it to the bright red stain that stretched across Nick's white tee shirt.

"Your shirt," I whispered.

"Yours too," Nick grinned, eyeing the matching splatter on my tank top. Before I could reply, he brushed a finger under my chin, his lips sweeping across mine. "Sorry it took so long, but I'm here now, and I won't leave your side again."

All lingering fear and anxiety melted away. The headache was gone. I felt whole, complete, in control again.

"Let's see Calla. I haven't had the courage, but I'm ready now." I grabbed Nick's hand, leading him out of the produce department where our story had begun all those years ago.

WE HEARD the beeping machines before we saw her. Nick exhaled a long breath.

"I don't know how you can find forgiveness for what I've done." He spoke without looking at me. "Not in taking our daughter, but for leaving you alone in your grief. I can't bear seeing her like this, even knowing she walks immortal."

I clasped Nick's hand, unable to resist the urge to comfort him. *"Though one may be overpowered, two can defend themselves. A cord of three strands is not quickly broken."* The voice was mine, but the words were not. I jerked my hand away, our chain broken, and looked to Nick in confusion. "I don't know where that came from." I gaped, open-mouthed, holding my hand to my lips.

He watched me, carefully studying my face. "It's a prayer of unity. Ecclesiastes, from our ceremony?"

"I hardly remember the details of the ceremony."

Nick shrugged. "It's getting late. We're both tired."

"I don't think being tired made me recite that," I stated dubiously.

"It's the link, Mira," Nick said, handing me my bag. Leon's mane poked from the top. "Let's get dinner. We can talk about it later. I need to eat, and you should too." Exhaustion darkened Nick's face.

I stroked Calla's arm, then leaned in for a kiss on her cheek. The tubes running from her nose and mouth no longer fazed me. Before leaving, I pulled the stuffed lion from my bag and set it next to her.

"For courage," I whispered. Hers and mine.

FIFTEEN

The cafeteria was on the verge of closing. Only a minimal selection of prepackaged dinners were available. I picked at the wilted lettuce of an overpriced salad and wondered if anything in the mortal world would ever taste as fine as the fruit of the Land.

Concerns for the days to come faded as I thought about my new home. I found myself desperately wishing we could act soon. I wanted to be back there. Back with my daughter. Back where every sensation tingled with life. I looked around, thinking of the park this morning, my cramped apartment, and the dead plants on the patio. Everything here was lackluster, dull, dead.

"We should do it soon, Nick."

His eyes narrowed, curiously. "Your parents? Have you reached them?"

"No, but I sent my dad an email." Nick's brow raised. "Nothing too detailed. I asked him to call me as soon as he's able. They're somewhere in Ireland. He said access to the internet is sporadic."

"Do you think you should wait to talk to them?"

"I don't know. Now that I'm here, I want it to be done. I want to go back. I feel like I'm missing something. Not just Calla, but my senses seem off. I'm sure it's the stress and anxiety. I just need to get it done."

Nick rubbed his chin, then leaned forward. "I understand." He took my hand from across the table. "I was insensitive... thoughtless. When I talked so cavalierly about ending Calla's and your mortal lives. Now that I've seen Calla, I understand how difficult this is for you. While I'm happy you feel more confident about our path, I think you need to be here for your parents. We need to help your dad. He can write the words, soothing words, to help your mom." He shook his head. "I'm a father, a father who has seen the face of death in his child. I cannot let Calla and you leave your mom this way. We'll use our strength. Arthur, you, me —our strength and energy can ease your mother's pain."

I'd gotten ahead of myself, so eager to ease my anxiety that I lost sight of my mother.

And what about Novalee? I needed to speak with her too. My shoulders sagged. Uneasiness filled me. Nick read it on my face. It stifled the air.

We were interrupted by a couple arguing at the table behind us. My eyebrows rose to Nick. I couldn't see them, but from his position, he watched intently. Then I heard cries from a child across the room. At the table beside us, an older man yelled into his phone. The young woman on the other side of us appeared sick with nerves as she took bites of her dinner.

Looking around, the room and everyone within erupted with agitation.

Nick shifted his eyes to me. He gave me the same curious look he had before. Then, placing his hands over mine, he let out a long calming breath. The room turned silent and still for the shortest of seconds, then picked up in an amicable murmur of conversation.

"What was that?" I whispered.

"You're getting stronger." He smiled, looking pleased.

"I did that?" Realization sunk in, and I looked around the room. My eyes brushed over the couple behind me, then returned to Nick. "I made everyone angry?"

His head nodded slowly. "Sorta."

"I don't understand. You look happy." Again, he nodded his head. "Why would that make you happy? I don't want anyone, especially people in a hospital, to take on my feelings." Paranoia made my eyes dart over the room.

"Now you are aware." He pointedly looked around as well. "And now that you're conscious of it, you can control it. You're growing stronger, and you'll need to maintain that control in the weeks to come."

"Weeks? I don't want to be away from Calla for weeks."

"We can leave your mother with enough love to fill any holes left by Calla and your mortal deaths. We can leave her with peace." Nick traced a finger from my wrist to the tip of my thumb.

A gentle breeze. Waving green grass. A blossoming lily. Death, white and bright. A new beginning, not the end.

"We can leave her with that," Nick whispered, his hand cupping mine.

WE ENTERED A FULL ELEVATOR. People squished together to make room for us. The small space buzzed with excitement. Nick leaned close to whisper to me. "Control, Mira. Remember, you have to control your feelings." And with that, he squeezed my hand and the elevator abruptly quieted.

We stopped at the trauma center's front desk, and I requested to speak with a doctor and the caseworker. I told Emilie, the nurse assigned to Calla, that I needed to discuss a plan going forward. Taking note of my calm demeanor, she visibly relaxed, nodding and gently smiling. Emilie pulled up Samantha's calendar and scheduled me a time for the following morning.

Nick and I went to Calla, although visiting hours would be over soon. She slept with Leon tucked beneath her arm, just as I'd left them.

"Do you think it's okay if we go to my apartment tonight? I need to sleep in a real bed." As selfish as I felt leaving Calla alone, my body desperately needed the rest. "Maybe you can stay here, and I'll go back now, then we can switch?" The words were out, and I regretted them immediately. I needed Nick.

But he made the decision for me. "No, we'll go together. Calla is surrounded by love in the Land. She'll sleep well, whether we're here or not."

I left a list of instructions with Emilie. She made notes of my requests, as futile as they may be, nodding her head when I asked her to call if there were any changes.

"I'll watch her like she's my own," she promised, placing a hand on my arm before snapping it away. "What's that scent? It reminds me of my mom. I always loved her perfume but can't remember the name of what she wore. We lost her a few years ago, but you know how sometimes a certain scent can just take you back?"

I didn't know how to answer. I never wore perfume. I lifted my wrist to my nose, smelling nothing, not even the antiseptic scent of the hospital's soap.

∾

A STARLESS NIGHT darkened the sidewalk on our walk back to my apartment. I realized it was the first full week of June. Summer would soon fill the days ahead, the best part of the year in Milwaukee. Festivals, farmers markets, concerts in the park—things I looked forward to throughout the long winter months. I turned to Nick, to ask him more about life in the Land.

"So, what do people—gods—do in the Land for fun? Do you have parties? Barbecues? Game night with friends?"

Being the first in our group to have a baby, my circle of friends quickly dwindled. Some stopped inviting me to events, maybe because they assumed I couldn't make it, while many friends made the effort, lifting me through a dark period with open arms. My stomach sunk, realizing I'd be leaving them as well.

"The Land is like here except better. Much better. We can ski down a mountain and swim in the tropics, all within a day's time." Reservations of abandoning my life in Milwaukee diminished as Nick's velvety voice soothed. "You want sunny skies, a light rainfall, or even a snowstorm? It can be done with a nod." *Indeed.* I cringed, thinking back to a few nights ago, when he flipped the summer air into a blizzard. "But I don't like to live like that in the Land. We must appreciate our surroundings and not take advantage of our power. Yes, it's a benefit, and the Land is our play-ground, but our existence is meant to be the example for mortals. I wish to do things the proper way, walk where I need to go, build with my hands. Accept help and give help. At times I do use my god-given power when perhaps I shouldn't. But to be a true god, we must walk with the mortals, understand their ways, feel their struggles."

"Is that why Jake is teaching Calla to plant from seed and soil?"

"Yes, and I hope you're in agreement." He stopped walking and looked at me. "As we parent together, it's my wish to teach her the mortal way, the hard way, to achieve success. She must make her bed herself, dress herself, use the restroom, and use pen and paper for homework. Too many little gods are becoming idle as their parents fail to teach them. Jake is struggling right now, a single parent per say, to keep his children on the chosen path."

"A single parent?"

Nick chuckled. "Oh, he has no biological children, never married. With his station as Father to the Land, he is meant to guide us, lead us on the right path, help us determine right from wrong." Nick nodded to the sky. "His counterpart left decades ago. Hunters have searched and searched, but Mother disappeared without a trace. It's believed she was sent on a critical mission. Otherwise they certainly would have found her by now."

"Hunters?"

"They're kind of like bounty hunters or the police. You don't want to mess with them. They find gods who've defied their fate, refuted orders, or abused their powers." Nick grinned. "It's a curious new world you're now a part of, Mira. Someday, we'll sit down and I'll teach you the intricacies."

A curious new world indeed. One which included hunters, demigods, scribes, high gods. I pictured Jake, the carpenter who built exquisite work using his hands when he could accomplish the arduous task with a mere thought.

A curious new world where my mind could create tangible things, and my emotions affected the weather.

But what about *my* world? The one where Calla and I

deliver Mrs. Cooper's mail every evening. The one with the bakery on Brady Street that makes our favorite cinnamon rolls. The one with my conservatory and the annual Hollydaze display.

This world, right here.

Nick watched, his eyes narrowing as anxiety stiffened my posture. I exhaled before continuing to walk. He followed silently until we came to the opening of the park, *our* park, and stopped under the wrought-iron archway.

Reaching out, Nick clasped my hand.

The silver shimmer of the moon. Panting bodies. The shudder of thunder. Fireworks and pleasure. A flash of lighting. Rumbling and moaning. Desire and lust. Running, reaching, falling over.

I gasped and Nick grasped my elbows, steadying my footing. The images and sensations passed in an instant, yet they spun me up and spit me out like a tornado. My body tingled, and my legs trembled. I tugged an arm free and brushed back my hair, even though it was still secured neatly in a high ponytail.

"What was that?" My voice trembled, my fingers settling at my temple.

Nick looked ahead to the white marble bench. "Our first night."

"Did you do that?" I whispered.

"Not intentionally," Nick replied softly. "It's the link that Jake created."

"What?"

"Can we talk inside?" He nodded toward a couple stumbling into the park, clearly drunk.

I looked blankly at Nick, suddenly overwhelmed. Overwhelmed by the emotion and energy that seemed to thicken in my blood with every passing minute. It was too much, too consuming.

Without a word, Nick placed his hand under my elbow and led me across the street and into the lobby of my building. He dropped his hand to press the elevator button, and I scooted away, desperate for breathing room.

While we waited for the elevator, I fished out my keys, and unlocked two postal boxes.

"See this?" I rasped, pulling out a thick stack of envelopes. "Who's going to give Mrs. Cooper her mail when we're gone? She's almost ninety, Nick. Who's going to help her?" I slumped against the wall, sliding down until my butt rested on my heels. Tears leaked from my eyes. "What's happening to me? One minute I want to get this done and over with, be back in the Land, and the next I can only think about Mrs. Cooper, and my life here. I'm going crazy."

WITH THE DOOR LEFT AJAR, Nick's commanding voice boomed from the hallway as he delivered Mrs. Cooper's mail.

"That's very kind, Mrs. Cooper," I heard him say. "I'll be sure to relay it to Mira. But, please be assured, Calla feels no pain." He continued chatting with her, and his soothing words drifted around me, light and peaceful, rolling over my shoulders like an airy blanket, making my eyes so heavy I could barely keep them open.

"Mrs. Cooper will be okay," Nick said, the door clicking shut behind him. "Sorry, did I wake you?"

With my head slung over the armrest, I groggily sat up, blinking a few times, recollecting the thoughts that had wafted away. "I must've dozed off."

Nick took a seat at the upholstered chair opposite me, the one Calla had picked out because she thought the silver bevels looked like gems.

I stared at him for what seemed like hours before snapping my fingers as it clicked in my head. "You told Mrs. Cooper some story so she could go on without us? Is that what you meant by saying she'll be okay?"

"Yes." Nick tilted back the glass of wine I had poured for him. When we'd come upstairs, I figured we both could use something to loosen the mood.

"I could hear you through the door." I nodded toward the entryway, which in the small space was only a few feet away. "I heard you, and it felt like I was floating. Like I was on a cloud."

He set the glass down and waited for me to continue.

"I need to know more about the link." I shifted in my seat, leaning toward Nick. "If you want me to go into this with open eyes, then I need to know everything. So, spill it."

Nick stood, picking up his wine glass and moving to the patio door. He stared through the darkened pane. "Think of it as natural instinct, or a mother's instinct, but with souls. With the link from Jake's ceremony, our souls are now connected, seeking each other. They'll do whatever it takes to protect the union. So, when you are sad or have pain, it's now instinct for me, my spirit, my voice, my touch, to comfort and soothe you."

Maybe I wasn't going crazy after all. Each instance when my emotions threatened to take me over the edge, Nick's voice or touch had somehow talked me down.

But what about the panting bodies and silvery moonlight? That was so intense, I felt it in my core. A tingle so real, I'd nearly orgasmed.

"What about the memory of the park?" I asked, my cheeks warming.

Nick caught my eyes, his narrowing to a dark, seductive green.

"Our souls will also do whatever it takes to *bind* the union. It'll keep pulling us together, mind and body, until we consummate."

SIXTEEN

Two steaming cups of take-away coffee from Dark Beans sat on the kitchen countertop. Nick perched on a stool with a newspaper in hand. His hair had dried after an early-morning shower into loose curls, one of which fell over a brow. I instinctively reached to brush it away, but snatched my hand back before making contact.

"Good morning. Sleep well?" His warm breath brushed against my ear.

We'd gone to bed, Nick on the couch, me in my bed, with lingering questions and unresolved issues.

"Honestly, I fell asleep as soon as my head hit the pillow." Having him so near, the hairs on my arm stood on end, and I shivered. "Is that the link?"

"No," he said definitively. "That is because you like me."

"Nick?" I hesitated. "What if I keep second-guessing everything I do and questioning everything you do? How can I be sure it's our true feelings and not just our souls working in cahoots?"

"Because it doesn't really work like that, it doesn't

change who you are or what you want," he said, chuckling. "But I understand, and I want you to know this is real, even if it means severing the link. That day, after Jake performed the ceremony, I felt all your anger, resentment, and hesitation. I want—I need—to earn your trust again. As soon as this is over, we'll sever the link, and I'll court you properly. I'm going to right all the wrongs. I promise, Mira."

Nick gave me several options the night before, including one which I knew pained him to say. I knew because the hurt emanating from him hit me in distressed waves. I could send him away, back to the Land, to break the link.

The other option, the more plausible one, would be the conscious effort on both our parts to control the urges. No lingering touches. No emotions by osmosis. No sweeping, sultry memories. Nick would be able to use the link to calm me when I needed it, but would not manipulate my feelings.

Most importantly, Nick promised that until the tremulous events of the upcoming weeks were a distant memory, we would not consummate the marriage. He said he'd wait an eternity for me to come to him on my own, without divine influence. He wanted me to know it was real.

"Even if you beg. Even if you buy tiny, sexy lingerie. Even if you get me stumbling drunk and beg while wearing said tiny, sexy lingerie. I will resist until the link is broken and you come to me of your own free will, and as the God of Victory, I will not fail you."

Through his humor, I saw the truth on his face. Now, he saw the answer on my face.

"I'm staying? Guess this means I should buy a toothbrush." Nick grinned, sliding down from the stool and embracing me.

"You knew I wouldn't send you away." My voice came

out airy as I looked down and wiggled out of his gentle hold. His innocent embrace had my blood pumping. "Seems we're already breaking the rules," I whispered under my breath, smiling.

My smile quickly faded as reality set in. Knowing I couldn't have him, only made me want him more.

∼

WITH AN EMPTY REFRIGERATOR and an aversion to the hospital's cafeteria, I suggested we stop at a restaurant on our walk to the hospital. After giving Nick a few options, he chose Constance Café, an old-timey diner a few blocks from my apartment.

The hostess looked a bit taken aback when we walked in. Nick had that effect. Not only his jaw-dropping good looks, but his dominating aura. He held an enchantment over mortals, especially the women.

Instead of the hostess's eyes appraising Nick, she turned to me with a shy smile. "This may sound weird, but you remind me so much of my mom." I nodded curiously, and she continued. "Just something about you. So weird. I haven't seen her in months." Her words trailed off. She looked at least a decade older than me, making it all the stranger that *I'd* remind her of her mother.

She shrugged, then led us to a table where a waitress delivered menus and ice water. Before I had the chance to ask Nick about the odd encounter, I saw his face darken and followed his stare to the door, where, of all people, Hank sauntered in.

Hank and I had mutual friends, so I'd run into him every so often. Rumor had it he preferred younger women these days, which was confirmed by his date, a petite girl at least ten years our junior. I willed the hostess to place them across the restaurant, but like a bee making its line to honey, they were seated next to us in seconds.

Hank's eyes lit in recollection, then settled over Nick. He leaned over, whispering something to his date before leaving her to visit our table.

"Hey, I heard about your little girl. I'm so sorry." Hank placed a hand on my shoulder. Nick cocked his head, his tension palpable. Hank looked to him, extending his hand. "Hi, I'm Hank."

Before thinking, I replied, "This is Nick, Calla's father."

It took a moment for Hank to make the connection. "I thought her dad was killed... I'm sorry." He reddened, stumbling over his words. "I'm so sorry, that just came out, I didn't—" He quit speaking as Nick's eyes narrowed.

I recalled the gossip that swirled around so-called friends who thought Calla was the result of a one-night stand. Even years later, it stung.

Flustered, I stared wide-eyed as the napkin in my hand slipped away. Silently it hit the floor, but as if a glass instead had fallen and shattered, all eyes in the restaurant turned on me. There was a pregnant pause until Nick held up a hand and people went back to their conversations and meals.

Nick looked to Hank, his eyes squinting. "Yes, I am Calla's father. You will go back to your table. Have a lovely conversation with your date, and forget you saw either of us."

Like a puppy, Hank turned and did as he was told.

"What did you do?" I looked in awe to Nick.

"Seems I'm breaking the rules quite a bit lately." He shook his head in mock disapproval.

"Wow. Impressive."

The link with me was one thing. Calming Mrs. Cooper

with his words last night was another. But making Hank forget an entire encounter took mind manipulation to an entirely new level.

After we finished breakfast, I glanced back at Hank, who was engrossed in conversation with his young date. I grinned, knowing it was Nick's commanding words that kept him captive, because I also knew Hank rarely liked hearing anything other than the sound of his own voice.

∽

WE CONTINUED on our walk to the hospital. The city streets and sidewalks buzzed with summer tourists and hurried businessmen. Less than a block away, a young man approached us reluctantly, eyes darting to Nick and his formidable size, then back to me.

The young man looked down, clearly embarrassed. When our eyes connected again, raw emotion consumed his face.

"I thought you were... my mom died last year and..." He trailed off, and I instinctively put my arms around him, embracing him. Negative energy lifted from him, physically and emotionally, like a battery being sucked dry. He pulled away, standing taller and stronger. "Thank you." He rubbed at his eyes. "Thank you."

Nick and I stood speechless. The man walked away, glancing back at me a few times with a small smile in place.

"Mira." Nick looked intently at my face, then pulled me into his arms. He pressed his nose into my hair. Holding my shoulders steady, he leaned back to again study my stunned face. After what seemed like minutes, his eyes traveled down my body, resting on my belly. "If I didn't know better, I'd think—"

I took a step back.

"Something about you has changed."

"What?" I asked, my voice barely audible.

Now that he said it, I felt it. *Different*. A maternal feeling, so strong, I resisted the urge to put my hand across my belly like I used to do when I was pregnant. Curiosity ripped through me.

Curiosity or nerves because I suddenly felt sick.

"What's going on? What now?" My eyes stung with tears.

"You're radiating. I see it now." He glanced at my stomach, shaking his head. "And the mortals can feel it."

The nurse's comment, the hostess, the young man. Mortals who could feel some strange supernatural instinct. A mother's instinct?

My stomach roiled with a sudden wave of nausea, so intense I started to stumble. Nick's arm flew under my elbow, steadying my footing. "Let's sit down." He guided me to a bench a few steps away.

A gentle rain began to fall along with the tears slipping down my cheeks. "Breathe, Mira, it's okay," Nick coaxed.

I tried to slowly inhale in through my nose and exhale from my mouth. Frantic thoughts made it impossible to slow my racing heart. *It's too much.* The rain fell faster, pinging off our heads and to the concrete.

"I won't stop it unless you want me to," Nick whispered.

"I'm okay." I squeezed my eyes shut. When I opened them, a final drop of rain fell from the sky, pointedly falling onto Nick's cheek.

"We really need to work on your control."

I burst into giggles, going from crying to laughing in seconds. I watched from under wet eyelashes as Nick grinned along with me.

This beautiful god was my husband.

Linked or not, I was falling again.

~

THE SUDDEN STORM left my sundress sopping wet. We sloshed through the hospital's lobby. I glanced at the clock above the elevator, realizing we wouldn't have time to return to the apartment and change before our appointment.

Minutes later we were standing in Samantha's office on the fifth floor. I apologized profusely for being late, one of my pet peeves, and one of the many reasons I lived by lists and schedules.

Samantha seemed a bit aloof, perhaps dazed by Nick's sex appeal. I couldn't blame her. He was a god after all, and he looked the part.

She quickly snapped out of it, offering us a seat and asking Nick what his relationship was to Calla. I'd only given the hospital my parents' and Novalee's information for emergency contacts, indicating on the admittance and insurance forms that Calla's father was deceased. I held my tongue and let Nick offer an explanation.

Nick told her he was Calla's uncle, and my heart ached that he couldn't claim her as his own. He'd missed so much of her upbringing. Although he may have been "there" spiritually, he didn't have hands-on involvement. No hugs, no kisses. No early morning wakeup calls. No dirty diapers, or tantrums. Even the unpleasant moments made parenthood a beautiful, extraordinary experience.

The meeting continued, but I only half listened. I hardly noticed Nick's voice pitch with anger.

"Well, how do you feel, Mira?" Samantha asked of me.

"I'm sorry, what was that?" I looked from my hands, where my attention currently resided, to their faces. Nick's palms were flat on the desktop.

"As we were discussing yesterday, organ donation. I know this is a very, very difficult time—"

"Absolutely not. Calla will be cremated. I'm taking her ashes to the cliff to be scattered into the sea." The words rushed out just as my hands flew to cover my mouth. Nick cocked his head.

"Okay," Samantha replied, eyes widening.

I tucked my hands away, and Nick continued to stare at me with obvious confusion.

"Samantha, I hate to cut this short, really, I appreciate the meeting, but," I stammered, pushing my chair back, "we have a lot to discuss, and—" I needed to get out of the confines of the small room, which seemed to be closing in on me by the second. I jumped up. "I think I'm going to be sick."

Fleeing from the room, I escaped to the bathroom down the hall just in time to clutch the toilet bowl. Swiping at my mouth, I wished for an ounce of Nick's powers. If he could create an entire third floor addition to the cottage with the simple nod of his head, I figured a brush, towel, toothbrush, and maybe a change of clothes shouldn't be asking for much.

Taking a deep breath, I splashed cold water over my cheeks and rinsed my mouth before leaving the bathroom.

Outside the door, Nick leaned against the wall waiting for my exit. He looked up, concern wrinkling his brow. "What was that?"

"Food poisoning? Nerves? I don't know."

"No, with Calla. Cremated? What's the cliff? Where

did that come from?" He placed a hand under my elbow. The simple gesture quieted my reeling belly.

"I don't know. It just came out. But it makes sense. My parents are there now—at the cliff. I'm not sure exactly where it is, somewhere along the southern coast of Ireland. It's my mom's birthplace. We need to bring Calla there." I held my hands to my heart.

"Okay." Nick nodded. "Have you heard back from your dad?"

"No, I'll email him again and tell them to stay put until we come to them. This plan is right."

A sense of urgency took over. The first step was already in place. A meeting with Calla's team of doctors had been scheduled for the following morning. In the meantime, I shot my dad a quick message telling them to stay put and also asking for the specific location of the cliff.

We returned to my apartment so I could shower and change. Nick used my laptop to research flight options.

"Where exactly are we going? Should we fly into Dublin?" he called from outside the bathroom door.

"It's on the coast. I don't know the name. I was only there once when I was three or four." A toothbrush dangled from the side of my mouth, but a pressing idea came to me. "Nick, let's drive to my parents' house. I don't want to snoop through their stuff, but I'm sure my mom's birth certificate is somewhere in my dad's office."

We loaded into my Subaru and made a quick stop at the hospital to see Calla before getting on the road.

Calla's face softened from sleep, and Leon the Lion was still tucked securely under her arm. I smiled at Nick, feeling more normal than I had in days, as if I'd purged my belly of all fear, anxiety, and dread.

"My sweet girl, we'll be bringing you home soon," I whispered as we left.

I spotted Emilie at the nurse's station and waved. "We need to run home, but I have my cell on me. Please call me if anything changes."

She nodded and smiled, but I read the sad reply on her face. There'd be no change.

SEVENTEEN

As we pulled into my parent's long, winding driveway, we were greeted by overgrown grass and half-dead bushes. I grimaced, realizing my dad's prized rose garden in the back probably met the same fate. During the long stretches between visits, my parents kept a landscaper on retainer to care for the grounds, but it appeared the workers hadn't been there in months.

Using my spare key to access the front door, I pushed it open, fully expecting a room of spider webs and gothic dust. Flipping the switch, I waited for the foyer light. Nothing happened. Nick shrugged, and then moved inside to open the blinds. Sunlight splattered the walls.

We maneuvered through the living room, down the hall and into the first bedroom, the smallest one which had been converted into my dad's office. Nick worked on cracking the desk drawer's lock while I looked through the books on Arthur's numerous shelves. All were history or educational.

Oh Dad. I wish I had asked more about your work, what you do. I wish we'd made that connection. With remorse, I let my fingers run down the binding of a thick, leather book.

A loud crash interrupted my thoughts. Nick had pried the drawer open, but the force caused it to pull from the tracks. Papers, pencils, staples, and other random junk scattered the floor.

Adding an extra layer of surprise, my phone buzzed.

"Who is it? Your dad? Maybe he senses we're here?" Nick asked, looking up from his crouched position over the drawer.

I flashed him the screen, showing an unidentified number, then lifted it to my cheek. "Hello?"

"Don't worry, but I need you to come to the hospital. Immediately." It was Emilie.

"What's wrong?" I demanded. My hand trembled along with my voice. "Is Calla okay?" Nick hovered over me, trying to hear as well.

Emilie's voice dropped. "I don't want to get your hopes up, but there's been a change. Just come."

"We'll be there in an hour." I tapped to end the call, then directed over my shoulder to Nick, "Grab everything. The whole drawer. We'll go through it later."

Being in such a rush, I didn't think to close the blinds, let alone lock the front door. As I made my way to the car, Nick dropped the drawer, its contents spilling out a second time. My head swiveled toward the commotion.

"Mira—" I followed Nick's wide-eyed gaze to the bushes lining the perimeter of the house.

Previously half dead, they now perked in full bloom.

NICK'S HANDS clenched white-knuckled at the steering wheel. The desk drawer lay at my feet, its contents daring me. With unsteady fingers, I picked up the first few files and skimmed through my parents' financial records and real estate information. I set them to the side and grabbed the next folder, sliding out two spiral bound notebooks.

Thick, black words printed in Arthur's neat hand-writing spread across the cover. *To Anya—So We May Remember*.

A journal dedicated to my mother? I had no idea that my father wrote anything besides facts. I looked to the second notebook. My fingers traced the title. *To Mira—Our Miracle of the Sea*. A journal dedicated to me.

"My dad has a couple personal journals in here." I patted the folder. "One is addressed to my mom, and the other is to me. Is that kind of weird? I can't picture Art writing in a journal?"

"Well, Mira, he's a scribe. He probably has a more comprehensive library than you think."

"Can I read them?"

"Scribes have intricate methods of writing. If he doesn't want you to see it, there are ways he can protect his work." Nick glanced at the drawer and files. "Did you find anything about your mom? Her birth record?"

I pulled the contents from the last folder. Envelopes with my dad's block script offered a brief description of the contents. I lifted the lip of the one identified as *Birth Certificates* and pulled out three slips of thick paper, unfolding the first. It was Arthur's. Scanning the information, I confirmed the date. Born January 1, 1950, in Staten Island, New York. Anya's was next. Her birth date listed January 1, 1950, location County Cork, Ireland. I always thought it was kismet they had the same exact birth day and year.

"This is it!" I waved the copy excitedly and, in the process, dropped the last certificate to the floor. I crouched to pick it up, nearly hitting my head on the dash, when a word caught my eye.

County Cork, Ireland.

Still leaning over my knees, I scanned my legal name and birth date, my stomach sinking.

"What's wrong? Is your mom's record there?"

"My birth certificate. My parents always told me I was born here. Well, not Wisconsin, but in Baltimore. This says County Cork, Ireland, the same birth place as my mom."

A sick, overwhelming flood of nerves clenched my stomach. I shoved everything into the envelope. Tears stung in my eyes as yet another truth in my life clouded in mystery. Why would they lie? I shoved everything back into the file folder.

Nick maneuvered through the hospital parking ramp, cutting the engine after pulling into a tight spot. Slamming the door, I took a deep breath. I couldn't chance losing my calm, especially not knowing what exactly we were walking into.

We silently navigated the now familiar halls of the hospital. The elevator door opened to the fourth floor, and I spotted Emilie behind the nurses' station. She held up a finger before picking up the phone and gesturing us forward. Setting the receiver back down, she whispered, "I just paged Dr. Lisle. He's on his way."

"What's going on?" Nick towered tensely over Emilie. I laid my hand on his shoulder, unable to resist the urge to comfort him. He took a breath and began again. "I'm sorry. Can you tell us anything, or must we wait for Dr. Lisle?"

"He's on his way now. He'll be here any minute." She bubbled with anticipation, her words bouncing off me.

"*What* is it?" I cried, and now it was Nick's turn to calm me.

Thankfully for poor Emilie, she didn't have to respond. Dr. Lisle bounded around the corner, eyes lighting with an odd combination of stress and excitement.

"Her brain." He waved his arms emphatically. "There seems to be some repair. When they were changing her gauze, her finger moved. We set up scans." He was almost out of breath. "And there was activity."

"Oh, dear God," I cried and hugged Dr. Lisle, then pulled back. "What does this mean?"

"I don't know, honestly. I don't know. If anything, it means *hope*." His head shook like a bobble doll.

"Thank you, Dr. Lisle," Nick said, his tone curiously flat.

"Don't thank me. This is the work of God," Dr. Lisle proclaimed. Nick and I stiffened awkwardly. *It certainly is.* "It's a miracle, really. In all my years, I have never seen anything like this happen. I've only heard of one case—in the entire recorded history of medicine—where someone regained brain activity following a firm diagnosis. Calla was medically brain dead." He stressed the word dead. "I guess in medicine, sometimes there are no answers, only miracles." He removed his wire framed glasses, wiping tears away. "Someone must have been praying for you. Or someone up there pulled some strings."

Yes, indeed.

"A miracle," he repeated, still shaking his head in disbelief. "She is a miracle. Mira, she's *your* miracle."

"My miracle," I repeated softly.

My miracle. Mira, my miracle. My miracle of the sea. The words sang between my ears so loudly, they vibrated behind my eyes. I took a wobbly step backwards before bolting to the bathroom for a second time that day.

EIGHTEEN

"I'm so sorry, Mira." Dr. Lisle said. He and Nick were waiting outside the bathroom door. "I'm sorry for the shock. Really, I don't want to give you false hope, but it's something for us to go on."

I looked to Nick, whose face was devoid of emotion. Another wave of uneasiness rolled through my body, but I swallowed it down.

"Would you like to see Calla?" Dr. Lisle asked. He led us through the double doors and down the hall to Calla's private room.

The tubes remained in place, but the gauze had been removed. Dr. Lisle explained they'd do another scan in a few hours. In the meantime, they were closely monitoring her. Calla's team of doctors would assess the results and determine the next step for her care. He stressed there was no set protocol in her case. When a patient was considered brain dead, it meant life was not possible without the machines. She remained in critical condition, but now there was hope.

The doctor left us to spend time alone with Calla. I

studied her face, suddenly seeing so much life in my little girl. Besides the tubes and a few bruises, she looked healed. What could this mean? What about our plan? Questions pinged in my head, and the room smelled heavy and dense, like a summer storm.

"I would go to see her in the Land, but I can't leave you alone. Not now," Nick quietly said from the corner of the room. "It'd take me too long. I don't know what this means, Mira."

"Do you think something's wrong?" I asked, concerned by his deflated tone.

"I don't know. Honestly, I have no idea what's going on. Jake wouldn't let her slip back unless there was a reason. He's very strong, very aware. There has to be a reason."

The exhilaration from Dr. Lisle's news wore thin. My baby showed signs of improvement, but Nick's stifling concern, which covered me like an iron blanket, smothered out the elation. A headache twanged behind my eyes, and my belly growled. We hadn't eaten since breakfast, and I had gotten sick twice since then.

"Let's eat," I suggested. "Maybe a full stomach will help us sort through this."

On the way down to the cafeteria, I remembered the journal.

To Mira—Our Miracle of the Sea

"The book! The one dedicated to me, *Our Miracle of the Sea*. I don't know how I could forget, but the book!" I grabbed Nick's arm.

"Okay?"

"Dr. Lisle called Calla a miracle. My miracle." Nick looked confused. "When I was a kid, my mom used to sing a lullaby she made up for me. *My miracle. Mira, my miracle.*

My miracle of the sea." I sang it softly just as my mom used to sing. "My dad's book—there's got to be a connection."

Nick rubbed his eyes before pushing back the crazy curl that always seemed to flop over his brow. "Maybe."

"What's wrong? I don't think this is just coincidence."

"Yeah, I know." Three thick lines wrinkled his forehead, and I resisted the urge to smooth them out. Nick's reaction confused me, but I figured we both needed a few minutes to digest this newest twist.

We stood motionless for a several seconds before the hand dangling at my side lifted to rest on Nick's bicep. His anxiety lifted under my touch, swelling into my fingers, filling each digit like a balloon. I pulled my hand away, wiggling my fingers in front of my eyes, watching in amazement.

"Thanks, Mira." He smiled.

I stared at my hands. Just as Nick had sucked up my angst and fear so many times over the course of the last few days, I finally returned the favor.

Brushing off curious stares from other cafeteria patrons, Nick and I went through the buffet style line, then picked a table in the farthest corner of the dining hall. I concentrated on chewing my dinner, but thoughts of the day's events swirled so thick around us, I was certain they'd puffed like a rain cloud above our heads. Breathing through each revelation, the air thinned until Nick and I again were two unassuming people, simply eating the special of the day.

But questions remained.

Why would my parents lie about my birthplace? And why was Calla, my miracle, showing improvement? There must be a connection to Arthur's book. It had to hold answers. I set down my fork, barely having eaten any of the bland chicken and rice casserole. Nick warily sighed as I insisted once again that we get the book.

"Look, I'm as confused as you, Mira. I don't like this feeling. It's strange to me." He fidgeted with his fork, and I realized why Nick appeared so uneasy. The God of Victory was now in battle for his own family. A first for him, going up against something unknown.

Rubbing a hand over his arm, I whispered, "It's okay. We'll get through this, the three of us. *Though one may be overpowered, two can defend themselves. A cord of three strands is not quickly broken."*

Nick's fear evaporated under my roaming fingers. I was so amazed at my newfound ability to help ease his anxieties that I didn't think to question the strange words, the foreign phrase, that rolled so easily off my tongue.

FOLLOWING DINNER, Nick and I returned to the apartment to deposit my car and pack an overnight bag. Although the trauma center's respite lounge had sinfully small sofas, we needed to be close in case there were further changes with Calla's condition.

"Nick?" I asked as I placed my toiletry bag into the duffle. "Can you create things here, with your mind? Like you did in the Land?"

"Yeah, but it's different here. In the Land, it can be done with ease. Here, let's just say it takes a bit more dust and a lot more concentration. After all this," he waved his arm around, signifying our time in the mortal world, "I'll teach you. Although, I think you're already halfway there. You're getting stronger."

I held up my hand, wiggling my fingers in front of my face. "I still don't understand where that came from."

"It's instinct now, the need to comfort. I'm not sure if it's just the link or if something's growing in you. Maybe it's your station, revealing itself slowly?" Nick took my hands within his and rubbed a finger along the fat part of my palm, his touch innocent, yet strangely seductive. I plucked them away, trying to stay focused on the conversation.

Calla, a nature goddess, and Niko, the God of Victory. They had defined duties. Who—or what—was I?

Giving a final glance to my newly charmed hands, I put them to practical use by zipping up the duffel. "I think I have everything for tonight and a change of clothes for tomorrow." I patted the bag. "But if I forgot anything, I'm sure we can find some dust and a quiet place for you to work your magic."

"There's a different kind of magic I'd like to show you." Nick's eyes darkened to a lusty shade of green that sent my heart thumping. He cocked his head to the side. "Do you trust me?"

"Yes?" I replied, although it sounded more like a question than an answer.

"Let's go." Nick lifted the bulging duffel bag, and bounded down the stairs, out of my building and across the street. I wordlessly followed him to the park, where he paused under the wrought iron gate at the entrance.

"Do you trust me?" Nick asked again, his voice so quiet I stepped closer to hear. Hungry eyes swept over my body, nearly knocking the breath from my chest. All I could do was nod for a response. Leaning down, he brushed a feathery kiss on my cheek. "I've made a promise to you, one I vow to keep, but when you look at me like that..." Pausing, he scanned my face with such intensity and desire that my legs trembled. He didn't finish the threat. Instead, he scooped me up and carried me through the park to the marble bench.

Our bench.

It welcomed us just as it had six years ago, shielded only by the blooming bushes and a near-black sky. Nick laid me across the white stone, like an offering to the moon. Looking up, he jerked his head and sent the clouds scattering. Silver light illuminated the grounds, glistening over the flowers and rippling along the trees.

Like actors under the moon's spotlight, nature watched with bated breath.

Nick brought his attention back to me, sweeping his eyes over my body. The little hairs along my bare arms stood on end, electric from the desire radiating between us. He towered above me, our bodies not physically touching, yet I could feel his thoughts roll over me like the caress of a hand and mouth. They nipped at my neck, cupped my breasts, then traveled down my body to the part of me that ached most. He settled there, and my legs readily parted.

The moon trembled along with me, awaiting Nick's next move. His mind ignited a flame. His thoughts filled me with fire. My blood simmered.

As I lay, willing him to touch me, he stood strong, solid, like a marble statue. Eyes closed, his lids twitched with thought, and I swore I felt the feathery stroke of his fingers and tongue probing me, bringing me to the peak. I clutched white-knuckled to the bench and moaned for him. His eyes fluttered open, and he came to me.

"As much as I want to touch you, I am keeping my word. And as the God of Victory, I will not—I *cannot* fail," Nick whispered as he sat next to me, keeping a deliberate distance. "I will be patient, and I will wait, Mira. I know one day, after this is over and the link is broken, you will come to me, and our vows will be complete. And I can wait, because when you do come, we will know it heeds from the heart, from the soul."

∼

DRUNK FROM THE moon and dizzy from Nick's words, I stumbled alongside him as we silently made our way back to the hospital. My shallow breaths finally evened when we stepped out of the elevator at the fourth floor.

A nurse we hadn't met before stopped us. Her soft eyes appraised Nick before settling on mine.

"I heard about your miracle." She glanced at the duffel slung over Nick's shoulder. "Where're you headed? You're not going to sleep in that little room, are you? Listen, I'll grab some pillows and blankets for you."

I hadn't thought to bring pillows or blankets. My life usually was kept neat and orderly with sticky notes and lists. Always ready, always prepared. But that was the old me, my old life, the one I'd soon be leaving. Maybe it was Nick's fault, his presence stole my attention. I couldn't seem to keep my head straight around him.

After the display in the park, I was certain it wouldn't get any better.

The nurse quickly returned with an armful of blankets and pillows. "Here, if you need anything else, just ask. We have lots of supplies back there that might make your time here a little more comfortable." She waved in the direction of the nurses' station. "Okay? My name's Sandy, and I'm here for the night."

She stepped through the door, leaving Nick and me alone.

Staying overnight at the hospital made sense in more than one way. Not only would we be near Calla, but in the open, public lounge, there'd be more distractions and less temptation to touch Nick.

~

I WOKE the next morning to find Nick's solemn face staring blankly at his hands as he sat stiff on the sofa opposite of me. The black-and-white-checkered duffle bag rested on the floor between his feet. Mumbling a good morning, I stretched within the confines of my own small couch.

"Mira." Nick lifted his head as he breathed out my name.

My heart skipped. The seductive sound of his voice, the hungry way in which he looked at me, maybe it was the link, but being near him, simply being in the *same* room as him, was making it harder and harder to resist. I itched to curl up in his lap, touch his face, kiss his lips.

"Did you shower already?" My voice came out low and husky. His freshly-shaven face and change of clothes confirmed my answer, but I needed an icebreaker, something to halt the intimate tension. "Were you at my apartment?"

"Yes. I needed your passport. Sorry, I dug through your stuff."

"My passport? What?"

"We need to go to County Cork, the cliff." Urgency replaced intimacy as Nick pushed to his feet and walked to the door. He peered out the sliver-sized window.

"What? What about Calla?" I asked, rubbing my eyes.

"We'll take her with us."

"What is going on? Did something happen during the night?" I perched rigidly in my seat.

"Sort of. We're on the verge of something. Something big, and we need to be prepared." Nick turned from the door and stepped back to his sofa.

"What do you mean? Stop being so cryptic, and spit it out already." A thought hit me. I pinkened with panic, perspiration beaded my neck. The mere idea of flying made me dizzy. "I don't have a passport."

"I realized that." He removed three small blue books from the bag.

"Where'd you—"

"I created them." He slyly tapped his head. "Dust and concentration."

"But I don't understand. What *exactly* is going on?" Hot and confused, my stomach twisted. I wasn't used to or prepared for this constant feeling of losing control.

"Okay." He inhaled deeply and released his breath slowly. It hit my face like a cool, calming breeze. "In the middle of the night, I popped awake and couldn't get back to sleep, so I went to see Calla. When I got to her room, something seemed off." Nick shook his head. "Then I saw *it*. Thick, green moss, creeping along the walls. She's returning to us. She's coming back."

"She's getting stronger!" I exclaimed, popping up from the sofa. "She's coming back?"

The look on his face sucked the excitement from my belly.

Nick continued to shake his head. "Something's wrong. Jake wouldn't let her slip away like this. There's got to be a damned good reason. We need to get her out of here, and soon, before it gets out of control—before we *learn* that reason. I cleared away the moss, but as she returns, it's going to be more difficult. What'll the doctors and nurses think? What will they do if they see that?"

"So, what're we going to do? Check her out of the hospital? Don't you think they'll find that even crazier? I don't even know if they'd allow us to."

"We'll just have to take her."

I appreciated his confidence, but just *take* her?

"Mira, about your apartment... it's overgrown with life. Sprouting in the carpets, growing along the walls. We need to get out of here. *Today*."

"Today?" My lower jaw dropped.

"I'll talk to the nurses and keep them distracted while you bring Calla to the car. I can divert their attention."

"What?" I turned my back on Nick and walked to the picture window. "Okay, so I'm just going to grab our comatose child? What about the tubes, the IV?"

"I'll take them out before we do anything."

"What if she stops breathing? We'll kill her just as she's coming back," I whispered, keeping my back to him, staring at the street below.

"We need to get her out of here before she fully returns. Not only will it raise too many questions, but her power and energy are obviously growing. We need to find your parents, find County Cork, wherever this cliff may be, and say our goodbyes. Then we have to return to the Land."

"You think that's the plan? She's coming back just for us to leave again?" I turned around and faced him.

"No."

"So, what is it?" I asked, fear hefty in my tone. Nick used his hands to wave my emotion away, like pushing a curtain back.

"I don't know, but in the short term, we need to take her and get on the next flight to Dublin. Maybe your dad will have answers for us. Who knows?" He patted the duffle bag. "The scripts are in here. They're blank."

"Blank?" Our one hope for answers. How could they be blank? The two bound notebooks were titled with a clear dedication for Anya and me. Why would Arthur have gone through the effort of locking the book in his office, but leave them blank?

"Nothing. No title, no dedication. For me, it's just a plain notebook. I think they were written to be read by the intended only. Your dad wrote them for you and your mom. As a scribe, he's probably protecting his story and made it for your eyes only."

"Should I read it first then? Before we do anything *crazy*?" I emphasized the last word. The whole thing was crazy but removing the life support from my little girl just as she was showing signs of improvement seemed beyond comprehension.

"There's no time. I'll explain later, but for now, please trust me." His voice firmed.

I nodded, still trying to understand how quickly—again—everything had changed. I sat down. "Okay."

"Okay. Thank you, Mira." Nick looked tenderly at me, his shoulders relaxing. He rubbed his hands over his thighs. "This is what we'll do. We'll go to her. I'll remove everything. I'll stop the monitors and take the IV out. You can shower, change. You don't even need to be in the room when it happens. If something goes wrong, you won't be there to see it—if that's what you prefer."

"I can't leave, Nick. If she... passes... I want to be near, be with her."

"There's a shower in the bathroom connected to her room. If anything goes awry, you'll be close. You can take a shower, try to relax. I'll take care of the hard parts," Nick assured.

"Okay, but I think the hardest part might be getting her out of here. Don't you think they'll notice us carrying her out? Even if we manage to sneak past them, they'll freak out when they notice she's gone."

Nick picked at a long strand of my hair, twisting it around his finger. "Already thought of that." He dropped it, then calmly tapped his head again. "Gods shouldn't use powers to manipulate mortals, but we have these gifts for a reason, and this is definitely a moment to bend the rules. We need to leave. There's no other way."

Just like with Hank, he'd wipe us from their memory. The memory of the little family with the brain-dead girl.

I rubbed my eyes as Nick laid out in exact detail what we would do. He'd detach Calla from the machines and change her out of the hospital gown into clothes he had brought from home. Once we were fully prepared to make the exit, he'd talk to the nurses. I'd wait one full minute before carrying Calla directly to the elevator and down to the parking garage where he'd parked my car in the same spot as the previous day. If something went amiss in our plan, I was to continue without stopping, and Nick would do the damage control. He told me to think only of the path, from here to the car, and not let any other thought or feeling enter my mind. If I kept that visual, I'd be safe from inter-ference.

With the duffel bag in hand, Nick and I went to Calla's room. He worked his part of the plan while I took a shower in the attached bathroom.

As Nick predicted, the stream relaxed my frazzled nerves and tight muscles. The heavy feeling in my belly slipped down the drain along with the water. My worries lifted in the steam, rising above me, and dissipating into the air.

I towel dried and changed into fresh clothes, a floral sundress I'd gotten on clearance a few years back. Splashes of vibrant flowers filled the soft cotton, fitting to welcome our little fairy back.

No, our little goddess.

My chest tightened. Calla will be in my arms in just minutes.

Breathe, I reminded myself. *Breathe, and remember the plan.*

Nervously, I peeked from the bathroom door, and the weight on my chest lifted as I observed Calla's rising and falling.

Nick hastily changed her out of the hospital gown and into her favorite bubblegum-pink pajamas. With an even voice, he reiterated the next part of our plan, breathing deeply to keep the serene atmosphere of the room.

"We're almost there, Mir," he coaxed. "Wait one full minute before exiting. Keep your focus. Here to the garage. Just visualize each step as you make your way down. The elevator, the first floor, the car. You can do it."

I nodded my head, mesmerized by his voice. After he left to complete the next phase, I eagerly rushed to Calla's side. Even with the commotion, she remained asleep on the bed. I scooped her into my arms. Her head rested against my shoulder, just as it had a million times in the past.

I deliberately breathed in and out, while counting down.

Ten . . . nine . . . eight . . . seven . . . six . . . five . . . four . . . three . . . two . . . one . . .

Just as I opened the door, I gave a final look over her

room and spotted Leon laying abandoned on Calla's pillow. I grabbed him and began our escape.

To the elevator... to the elevator. I repeated in my head, visualizing the button for the first floor. The door opened, and I crossed into the empty elevator. *To the first floor... to the first floor*. The words filled my thoughts like sentences in a book. The elevator door slid closed and descended without a touch of the button. It reopened to the lobby. *To the car... to the car*. I was on third base, almost to home plate. *To the car... to the car*.

No more than two minutes could have passed in the time it took me to carry Calla from her room to the car. Homerun. It was over. I exhaled with immense relief, another weight lifting from my chest, and settled Calla into her booster in the backseat. I buckled myself in the front before feeling all tension exit my body in waves.

As relaxation engulfed my body, my fingers unclenched, and Leon fell to the floor. "Thank you," I whispered, picking him up and holding him close.

Nick was to us minutes later. He looked calm and assured, as if he just aced an exam. He climbed into the driver's seat and passed the duffle bag to me. Pride reflected in his eyes. "We did it. *You* did it. You're amazing."

Blooming trees greeted us as we exited the city and continued onto the state highway. Nick navigated south toward Illinois. We didn't know where we were going, but we were on our way.

NINETEEN

I decompressed in silence, glancing nervously to Calla several times for assurance. Fast asleep, she didn't stir, but her chest and shallow breaths confirmed life. Freed from the tubes and out of the hospital gown, she looked normal. Like her normal, sweet self. Healed and whole.

Soon, we crossed the Illinois border. I asked Nick to stop at a gas station for a bathroom break and to grab breakfast. He stayed with Calla while I ran in. When I returned, I made a paranoid sweep of the lot. If Nick's charm didn't work, police would be looking for us by now.

Nick had moved to the backseat. Calla's head rested in his lap. He gently stroked her silky black hair. I set down our food, opened the door, and climbed in next to him.

Together, our family reunited, I grasped Calla's listless hand and settled it over Nick's, cupping our hands together.

Hand in hand, we were bound. Three pieces in a puzzle.

Sizzling, fusing, binding.

We were one. And in a flash, we saw it. Life and death and the memories made in between.

A spark of white, the burst of lightning. A streak of red, the flicker of a heartbeat. A first breath, the squeak of a newborn's cry.

Rapid thoughts radiated from our connected flesh, and Nick and I were swept along with Calla as her life returned. Booming like a firework, blinding like the sun. Memories so quick and fleeting we could barely make sense of the images that flashed in perfect, clear pictures.

I saw her, still sticky from birth, a crop of black hair matted to her head. Then, cooing and babbling, her first words, first steps. Giggling and growing, she was a flower blooming. Laughter and song, she was nature singing. Flowers lifting in a sun-soaked garden, she was swirling and twirling, her hair and dress fanning out in dance. Colors so bright, images so crisp, my eyes burned.

The memories were sparklers bursting around us, fusing us, skin melding like iron.

Flesh, blood, love.

As suddenly as it began, it stopped. We remained motionless, but our hands now moved on their own, traveling down Calla's small frame. Her complexion flushed with life, blazing like a sunburn, as she revived under our touch.

Speechless, Nick and I watched as our daughter returned.

Calla sat up, looking around with hazy eyes. She yawned with little hands stretched into fists over her head, and then settled back into the space between us. Her head swiveled from Nick to me, then to my feet where Leon lay, again abandoned.

"Leo!" she squealed. "You said you'd be here!"

Leo? The little boy from the cove. Could it be?

We remained in the backseat, quietly watching Calla

recover from the journey that led her back to us. Our family reunited.

A cord of three.

Calla yawned again, clutching Leo. "Mama, I'm starving!"

"The food!" I shrieked. The bag of breakfast sandwiches and coffee sat untouched outside of the car.

"We need to get back on the road." Nick's voice was calm, but I eyed him.

"Okay?" I asked.

"We have to keep moving. I have us booked on a direct flight from O'Hare to Dublin. It leaves in three hours. That should give us just enough time."

"You booked a flight? When?" He glanced at me and raised his eyebrows. He must have done it while I was in the oasis. "Nicholas, are you going to get in trouble for all this rule bending?"

"I've had centuries of good behavior. I'm due a little fun."

Centuries? I hadn't thought of it before. Exactly how old was he? I wanted to ask but the question felt irrelevant. He had a world's worth of experience, lifetimes of adventures. How could he find me interesting? Appealing? He must've had hundreds of relationships. Lovers. He never married. An old bachelor, he said so himself. So why me? Why after all this time would he settle down with the daughter of a demigod?

I tried not to let my insecurities ruin the mood of the car. Excitement bubbled in the air as Nick wove through heavy traffic to Chicago O'Hare International Airport, our next destination on this ever-changing path.

The idea of flying, let alone over a vast ocean, brought tension back to my shoulders and stomach. I tried to push the thoughts aside and concentrate on the present, yet a lump traveled from my stomach to my throat, and I couldn't swallow it down.

Nick found the exit for the international terminal and parked in the hourly lot. My eyebrows rose as he cut the engine.

"Umm, do you know how much this is going to cost?" I nodded toward the rates, which were plastered at the pay station.

"This is it. We're leaving, and we won't be coming back. At least not to this life."

This is it. We're going to abandon my car along with my mortal life.

THE TRIP through ticketing and security went surprisingly smooth. There were no issues with the passports Nick had created using his mind and a little dust. Calla slept through the entire ordeal, only groggily waking for the minute it took to lead her through security, then she was whisked again into Nick's arms.

After settling near our gate, I relaxed enough to swallow the lump, drowning it down with a chug from a water bottle. Nick leaned back in his chair, calmly holding onto Calla. Her little body showed slight movements from the light breaths and heave of her chest.

I whispered to Nick, not wanting to disturb her, "Is it normal for her to be this tired?"

Nick shrugged. "It's not often that little gods travel to the mortal world, but yes, it takes a lot out of us." He shifted her, so she was curled in his lap like a kitten. "We need to keep her calm until we're safe over the ocean." His voice soothed. He nodded to the window where trees waved unassumingly in the breeze.

We had over an hour's wait until we could board, which meant I had over an hour's wait to work myself up over the flight. I set off in search of a distraction at one of the gift shops, thumbing through their selection of novels and magazines.

The journal!

The one thing that may hold answers or clues. I scurried back to Nick, lifting the duffle bag that rested between his legs, but he placed his hand over mine. "Wait until we are there," he warned. "We need to be clear of any thoughts that might affect our flight. We can't take any chances now. Everything is in place."

I had no idea of *anything* being in place. We had our flight, but what then? Nick noted my shoulders, which slumped as I dropped the duffel. I sunk into the seat next to him, running a hand through my hair.

The days ahead may test you, your strength, your beliefs. But faith, hope, and love will guide you. Even if you don't understand, they'll lead your heart on the right path. Little whispers in my ears sang like a soft lullaby. My eyes felt heavy. My muscles relaxed.

I shuffled onto the plane with cumbersome limbs. Fuzzy announcements followed the purr of the engine as our plane lifted into air. During the seven-hour flight, both Calla and I slept. I'd wake, look to Nick and then Calla, but the calming haze, the whispered mantra, would lull me back to sleep.

An overhead announcement catapulted me back to reality. Our plane was off the coast of Ireland, descending into Dublin. My eyes jerked open, and fear flooded my veins. I clenched my seat cushion, looking wild-eyed to Nick. His face softened from serene sleep.

"Oh, my God," I whispered. The plane started to shake. "Oh God, Nick." I urgently poked his arm, trying to jostle him awake without disturbing Calla, who was nestled between us.

Hitting turbulence, the plane rocked. Images of my mother, father, and me flashed with each jolt, bringing to life my long-buried memory of our cross-Atlantic flight from Ireland to the United States, the trip that left me with a lasting fear of flying.

Anya's eyes pinched shut, and her worry consumed the cabin. She grasped my hand as the overhead speaker crackled with a desperate announcement. "We seem to have hit an unexpected storm, folks. Please return to your seats and fasten your safety belts." The captain's voice tried to exude confidence, but his distress wafted through the air. My mother snatched her hand away. Her blue eyes paled. She squeezed them shut again while her lips twitched with silent sounds. I reached for her, but she brushed me off, and I looked to my father, who was feverishly writing in a journal. "Mama!" I cried, again grabbing her arm. The plane plunged, whipping my head back and forth. Tears stung my eyes. Arthur seized my arms. His pen fell to the floor, and the pages of his journal flapped as the plane took hit after hit. "Shh, shh," he whispered, his eyes shifting from Anya back to me. The distress on his face matched the choking air of the cabin.

"Nick!" The plane jerked with my voice.

His eyes fluttered open, and he grasped my arm, exerting a controlled calm through our connected flesh. It seeped from his skin to mine like a drug, and I sighed from the immediate relief.

"Buckle up, folks, might get a little bumpy as we make our final descent into Dublin," the captain announced.

Nick slumped back in his chair, but his hand remained tightly clasped around my arm. He'd used his power to calm us, to keep Calla and me comfortable so we could sleep. Having expended his energy, he must have drifted off to sleep, and without him, I woke in a panic.

Control, Mira. Now that you know, you can control it. I hung my head, realizing the immense power and responsibility I now carried. I'd spent much of the last few days feeling so very out of control that I needed to focus on what I could control.

Calla slept between us, oblivious to the commotion. The plane smoothly descended into Dublin.

People shuffled past our seats until the rows emptied and only Nick, Calla, and I remained. The stewards asked if we needed assistance in exiting. We were three worn passengers who, unknown to them, had taken a much longer journey in getting to this final destination.

We lumbered through customs, floating along with the current of people. Nick carried Calla, while I clutched the duffle bag. Neither of us had the energy to think of our next step, so when we saw an advertisement for lodging off the airport's second terminal, we figured it was a sign.

I hardly remembered check-in, let alone crawling into the crisp sheets of the king-sized bed.

"MAMA! Daddy! My belly is so hungry!" Nick and I woke to an energized Calla, who was bouncing between us. With no idea or care as to where she was or how she got there, she clasped her hands together. "Can I have cereal? Or a cupcake? Or cookies? Grandpa lets me eat cinnamon rolls and sweetie pies all day!"

"Grandpa?" I asked in confusion. "Arthur?"

"Grandpa Jake." She looked back earnestly, and held her hand to her heart. "He does, I swear. Can I have one, please?"

Jake! I forgot Calla was his charge while we were away.

"Well, we're going to have to talk to *Grandpa* about this. I don't think sweetie pies all day sounds very nutritious." At the thought of pie, my stomach growled.

Nick stretched sleepily, still waking. "What time is it?" he asked, rolling to his side and hauling Calla along with him.

Looking to the alarm clock on the nightstand, I plucked the room service menu before noting the time, which neared noon. I handed the menu off to Nick, and then dug through the duffle for my cell phone. It'd been off since we boarded the plane in Chicago. I assumed I wouldn't have cell service but could hopefully still access the hotel's Wi-Fi. I needed to check my email to see if Arthur had replied to any of my frantic messages.

The cell's screen illuminated, and gasped when the date blinked back. We'd been asleep for over twenty-four hours. No wonder my stomach churned.

Little hands patted my arm. "Mama, don't be scared, okay? Grandpa Jake says it's all in the plan." She turned her attention back to the cartoon Nick had flipped on.

"What? What did you say?" I choked out.

The menu dropped from Nick's hands. He looked dumbly from Calla to me before putting his arm around her, forcing her to look at him. "Did Jake say anything else? Did Grandpa say why you needed to come back here?"

"Yes, Daddy." Calla rolled her eyes, a move I didn't expect until the teenage years. "It's our destiny."

Her eyes darted back to the television, and Nick peered over her head to me. "We may not understand, but we'll be okay. We'll figure things out."

"I guess..." I hesitated, about to elaborate, but stopped. Calla was with us, and for now, that was good enough for me.

"You're doing amazing, Mira." His eyes connected with mine, holding them. A little twinge of passion flickered before he passed the menu. "Let's order, then hit the road."

"Okay, but where are we going? I don't know where the cliff is. Should I read the notebook?" Nick shook his head. "But why not?"

"You can in time. We need to get where we are going, then it'll be right."

"Get where we're going? We don't *know* where we're going!" My voice pitched. The pictures hanging on the walls rattled. "Then *what* will be right? I'm so tired of this." I stopped as Nick's eyebrows rose, and his chin nodded toward the vibrating artwork. *Control, Mira.* "Okay, okay. I get it." I flipped my hands up in surrender, then tossed the menu onto the bed. "Order me pancakes. I'm taking a shower."

I hurried to the bathroom. Too many questions swirled in my mind. *Control,* I reminded myself. Before anxiety and fear overwhelmed me, I turned the shower to hot and let the fog in my mind mingle with the humidity in the air.

After drying off with a scratchy towel, I realized that, once again, I'd forgotten to pack the simplest of tools—a hairbrush. Long gone was meticulously mindful Mira. I squeezed my eyes shut, thinking how lovely it would be to brush my hair, to do something as *simple*, as *normal*, as brushing my hair.

Releasing a big sigh, I opened my eyes... and a hairbrush sat on the previously empty vanity. I looked at it suspiciously then poked a finger at it. Yes, it was there, I wasn't imagining it. I laughed, picked it up and studied it.

"Nick, look what I got!" I called, waving the brush as I stepped through the bathroom door.

"Nice, Mir, but some clothes would've probably been better." Nick's gaze wandered over my naked body. "Seriously though, well done." He came from the bed and pulled a fresh towel from the rack, sneaking a quick look before wrapping it snugly around my shoulders. "It's a good thing Calla's here," he whispered, "because you are awfully tempting." I shivered, Nick's eyes again rolling down my body. "Room service should be here soon. I'm suddenly... ravenous."

I tugged the towel tighter, clutching it like a security blanket. A few nights ago, Nick showed me what his mind could do. Even more tempting was the reality of what his body could do. I shivered under his intense gaze.

"Check the closet before they show up," Nick whispered. He brushed his thumb over my lower lip, and then silently slipped into the bathroom.

With the sound of the shower, I shook off vulgar thoughts and peeked in the closet. A large black suitcase sat inside. Lugging it to the bed, Calla and I inspected its contents. My measly hairbrush was nothing compared to the piles of clothes that had been folded nicely and placed neatly within. Nick must've worked his own magic while I showered.

As complicated as the life of a god could be, it sure seemed easy at that moment.

WHILE CALLA and I ate breakfast in the room, Nick returned to the airport to reserve a rental car. He was back within the hour, and we were on the road driving south by the early afternoon. When we exited onto M11, Nick nodded out the window to the sparkling grass and rolling, green hills.

"Beautiful, isn't it?" he asked.

"Yes." I twisted in my seat to get a better view. "Where are we headed?" Nick didn't have a map, but maybe he had asked for directions when he reserved the car. My cell no longer had data. Until we stopped somewhere with Wi-Fi, I couldn't pull up GPS.

"Mama!" Calla's finger smashed against the window. "Can we stop, please?" Excitement wafted through the car, a pungent, floral scent so strong I couldn't help but agree.

"Let's stretch our legs. Calla hasn't run around or played for days." I thought of her journey from the Land to Milwaukee to Dublin. She'd been through so much in the last week and hadn't complained or whined.

Nick took the next exit off the highway. I had no concept of direction, but he appeared confident. Countryside continued to pass peacefully until we found ourselves entering a small town.

Eyeing a sign for The Everly Inn, Nick turned from the main thoroughfare onto a country road which wound around a hillside until finally ending in front of a quaint inn.

Several small cottages were spaced evenly behind a large main building. Matching planters adorned the windowsills of each stone cottage, giving it a fairytale feel. A blue awning had stenciled, white letters reading, "Restaurant, Lounge, Bar".

We climbed out of the car, and Calla bolted into the grassy field. I called after her, telling her to stay close by. When she turned around, pure pleasure covered her face. Among nature, she was home. I gave an approving nod and she kicked off her sandals, padding further into the lawn.

Calla always loved running around our park barefoot. Now her feet glittered as she skipped and twirled in dewy grass. I stayed near the car, planted in the pebbled lot of the inn while Nick went to see about a room.

Several minutes later, his low voice came from behind. "Welcome home."

"What?" I mumbled, acutely aware his body was inches from mine.

"I got us the little cottage over there." Nick's arm brushed against mine as he pointed to the building farthest from the main inn. "We can stay as long as we need."

"How long do you think that'll be?" I spun around, colliding with the solid wall of his chest. I took a shaky step back, and tilted my face upward just as he brought his down. His nose grazed my cheek.

Nick's husky words vibrated against my skin as he pulled away and quietly spoke. "They have a business office for you to check messages. Maybe Arthur's emailed you back. And look at that field. The innkeeper said there's miles and miles of trails. Calla has space to expend her energy. This can give us some down time, allow Calla to recover from her journey until we hear from Arthur. Gives us time as a family. And maybe after the little one falls asleep, some time alone. How's that sound?"

I didn't need to reply. My body was loud and clear as I leaned into him.

TWENTY

The next several days passed uneventfully as each of us recovered from the rollercoaster week in our own way. Calla slept off and on, either from jet lag or the taxing journey, and spent her waking minutes playing in the vast field behind our cottage. Nick got acquainted with the small village, taking several trips into town to buy supplies and speak with the locals.

As for me, I poured myself into cooking and baking, although I wasn't any good at either. Beating eggs, whisking batter, and scrubbing pots seemed to get my mind off the bizarre journey we'd begun, and it kept my mind from wandering to Nick, whose presence was an electric current.

We kept the atmosphere light, not discussing Calla's return to the mortal world, Arthur's journal, or what it all could mean.

On the third day, I found myself dreading the journal. Our journey stopped dead in its tracks, but I liked where we landed. The quaint cottage and its idyllic countryside, Nick and me parenting seamlessly, as if we'd always been a family of three, and Calla flourishing along with early summer's bloom. Whatever answers the notebook held, it could possibly take us away from here. I wasn't ready to let go of *here* just yet.

That night, after Calla had fallen asleep, I washed dishes while Nick sat at the two-person, pub-style table. The one room cottage had a layout similar to a hotel room, with all three living spaces on top of one another.

"Nick?" I called over my shoulder. "Are you busy?"

He looked up from the map he'd been studying.

"I think it's time for Arthur's book." I watched as his face softened. "You think so too?"

"Only you can say, baby. It's been a good couple of days." Nick stood up and moved beside me at the sink.

Baby. The term of endearment, along with a hint of his woodsy scent, turned my belly to mush. I turned my back on him.

"I wish you'd just tell me instead of being ambiguous." My voice loudened, and I stopped, glancing toward Calla. "For all we know, it could be filled with blank pages. I feel like I've been holding my breath, waiting until the next twist in *this plan* derails us. Maybe it's time we use the resources available to us." I grinned, proud that I'd spoken without my annoyance or anxiety jumbling the mood.

Nick chuckled and threw up his arms. "Okay, it's time."

"You were waiting on me? Because I can't control my emotions?" I gave a soft, playful punch to his arm. Water from my sudsy hands dripped down his bicep. I watched it trail around his muscle. Heat rippled through me, and I murmured, "No faith in your wife?"

"That's the first time I've heard you refer to yourself as my wife. I like the way it sounds." He caught my eyes, looking more like a sexy devil than a god.

"Don't try to flirt your way out of this." The wife bit had just slipped out.

"Honestly, you might not like what you read. We have no idea what stories those books hold." Nick's eyes softened. "You need to be prepared to learn things about your parents and yourself that you may not like or agree with. Good or bad."

"Can you take Calla on a walk tomorrow, give me some space to read? Maybe it's better if I'm alone."

"Yes, of course." Nick placed a hand on each of my shoulders. His lip dropped, as if he were going to say more, but instead it turned up into a limp smile. "Whatever you need, Mira. Time or space. I'll give you whatever you need."

I knew he wasn't solely referring to the journal.

"WHAT ABOUT ANTS?" Calla asked, shoving a chocolate donut into her mouth. Nick had brought coffee and pastries from the inn's bakery, delivering them to us while we watched cartoons in bed.

"Eat up all the crumbs, and there won't be anything left for them," he directed as he picked up a fritter.

Calla polished off her treat, licked her fingers, and then held them to Nick for approval. He scooped her from the bed, tickling her until tears rolled down her cheeks. The scene made me flush with love, and I didn't hold back as my emotion blanketed the room. Nick glanced my way with a knowing grin.

He set Calla down, swiped away her tears and turned to me. "We'll go as soon as I get Calla changed out of her jammies." His eyes traveled down my body, then back up to meet mine. Although I wore a plain, modest nightgown, my hands flew to cover my neck. Nick's grin widened. "Come on, Cal." His eyes remained locked on mine. "Let's give Mama some time to herself."

The journal provided a sobering distraction to Nick and his suggestive tone. Whether or not it was intentional, every simple gesture, touch and look felt provocative and intimate, causing my heart to pound and my body to tingle. I couldn't seem to think straight or focus with him around. Now, alone in the cottage, my head cleared.

I swept a finger over the dedication on the cover of Arthur's journal. *To Mira—Our Miracle of the Sea.* My story told in the words of my father, the scribe. I sighed, preparing to reenter the magical world of gods, goddesses, scribes and demigods.

Oh Dad. Why couldn't you tell me all of this?

I gingerly flipped through the notebook. Black block letters filled the front pages, but a good portion of the end was blank. My story was yet to be finished, but I was about to learn of its beginning.

My dearest Mirabel,

Should you be reading this, it means two things have occurred—you've learned we are part of something beyond ourselves, our own wants and needs, and we are on our way to complete a most important plan. You may not yet know what it is, but along this journey, you will find your way. Like a map with unmarked roads, it'll be long with bumps and twists along the way. There may be storms and sunny skies that delay or propel you. The route you take will most certainly change, and change again. Have faith. Maintain hope.

Your story begins with your mother and me. Our history and love dates back to a lifetime ago. Unfortunately, it is our sin that paved the path you now travel.

It began with me, Arthur, a scribe born to write stories for my people. I was a good pupil but lacked discipline and spirit. I was lazy and uninspired. It's no excuse, but I simply was young and immature.

When I met your mother, I knew her to be my muse. A goddess who inspired words spoken from the soul, she ignited my senses. When I looked to her, I could taste her strawberry-gold hair. When I watched her, I swam in the ocean of her blue eyes. When I touched her, I felt heaven on earth. Every sensation lit on fire.

Finally, words filled me. They erupted like a volcano, and I wrote feverishly in her presence. I became the scribe I was fated to be—because of your mother, my muse.

The one soul who set mine on fire was my fate. With her, I fulfilled my destiny. Yet our love was not meant to be. We should have let go, but we couldn't. Ultimately, we committed a sin that led to our separation. I lost my love, and I lost my life.

I was reborn a scribe who could not spell, let alone write. For years I traveled, wandering the earth alone, moving from continent to continent. As fate would have it, I began studying history and literature, which led me back to my divine path.

A research project brought me to the southern coast of Ireland. My spirits revived as I absorbed the elements around me. I would sit above the ocean, peering down to the waves crashing along the shore, inspired by its force and energy. Stories and poetry filled pages upon pages. I threw them to the sea, not knowing what to do with the fiction that flowed through me and out of my pen.

One morning on my way back from the cliff's edge, I saw a beautiful woman with hair red like fire. I felt a sensation, hot and burning like the sun. She was familiar to me, yet I did not recognize her. I knew her, but I had never met her. When I ran to find her, she vanished. Like a mermaid that had slipped away into the sea, she left behind no trace. I returned day after day; my studies faltered, but I could only think of the woman by the sea.

It was a particularly rough day when we finally met again. The sea raged. Its waves crushed the cliff, roaring like a child's tantrum. I returned to the safety of the trail above the shore when I spotted your mother. Our eyes connected, and I recognized her as the mermaid in my imagination, but she was a stranger.

The next day I sought her out at the shore again. And again. Every day we met at the cliff's edge, and slowly she opened to me—I learned of her past. The reborn Anya lacked the energy and power of a goddess. Shy and reserved, jaded from a hard and lonely life, she was an orphan and had returned to the place of her birth to find answers. Instead, she found me.

Our love grew again, quickly and feverishly. When it was time for me to return to the States, we could not part, not when we had just found each other again. She agreed to come with me, and we were married days later.

The first decade of our life together was filled with music, flowers, love, poetry and passion. Your mother inspired me daily. With her, I completed my degree in history and literature, I went on for a master's degree, and began a professional career. I embraced a life with mortals and was full. I was complete.

Anya, however, grew desperate for a baby. It was all she wanted, to be a mother. We tried for years, but this was before the advances in fertility. We had few choices other than to keep trying the natural way. Anya prayed, pleaded and *begged, but every month her prayers went unanswered. Months, then years, of unanswered prayers passed. She became angry and stopped praying. She lost faith. She lost hope. She pushed me away. Blamed herself, and blamed me.*

Years of longing for a child, feeling unfulfilled, left our marriage damaged. I was no longer inspired by my muse. She had become bitter. The woman who enchanted me for so many years was gone. She no longer smiled or laughed. She stopped speaking to me. Most days she did not leave the confines of her room.

Our marriage continued to suffer. I pleaded with her to seek help, but your mother made no effort to work with me in repairing our marriage. At my breaking point, I announced I was leaving. I bought two plane tickets, one for each of us, and gave her a choice. She could come with me or stay behind. If she came, we would leave our troubles in the past, promise to start new and work to rebuild our life. If she chose to stay, I would not come back. I left, setting her ticket on the table and leaving the fate of our marriage in her hands.

As I waited on the plane, I grew nervous. She was not coming, and the sense of loss nearly suffocated me. The woman I married had been gone for a while, but this was final—I meant it when I said I would not come back. If she did not join me on that day, I would put life with her behind me. I would start again on my own.

The captain made an announcement, and I began to mourn the loss of my wife and our marriage. The empty seat beside me was Anya's answer. She was not coming. With tears in my eyes, I looked out of the window of the plane.

Saying goodbye, those tears slipped down my cheeks. It was the first time I could remember crying. Caught up in so much emotion, I did not pay attention to the announcements that followed. I rested my head against the window and watched as the plane backed away from the gate. My eyes remained closed as the engines revved, preparing for takeoff. "Goodbye," I whispered.

The plane began its ascent. I kept my head down and my eyes closed. But I felt the slightest touch at my leg, a gentle squeeze. Looking to my side, your mother was seated next to me. She had come.

For the first time in months, we held hands. Words were not exchanged, but it was a start. We landed several hours later in Dublin.

We took our time making the way to our new home. Ultimately, the path took us back to the small seaside town where we had first met. We rented a little, one-bedroom cottage high up on the cliff that overlooked the sea.

The woman I married began to return. Several weeks passed and her spirit swiftly healed. She used to hide in the darkness of our bedroom; now she spent nearly every waking moment outside. Daily, she'd make the steep trek down to the shoreline to walk along the sea and watch the crashing waves. She began to meditate, sitting for hours on the rocky beach, breathing in the energy of the ocean.

Your mother was whole again. The emptiness in her was filled with something new. The sea had restored her.

It was then that our miracle occurred. Your mother was pregnant.

After discovering life growing within her, she radiated. I would find her by the sea, the sun shining around her in a halo, setting her red hair ablaze. Her skin glowed iridescent, like pearls in an oyster's shell. She was breathtaking, looking like the mermaid I thought her to be years ago. Her mere image again ignited my senses—touch, taste, and smell. My muse had returned to me.

But I began to worry about the daily trip she took from the cottage high on the cliff to the sea below. She persisted. I began to walk her down every morning, keeping her steady as her belly grew. I checked on her throughout the day and helped her back up the winding path when the sun began to set.

Your mother was well into her third trimester when my concern came to a head. Anya explained that the sea had brought her out of the darkness. The sea brought her back to life. It brought her new life. The baby, growing in her, was its gift. Now they were connected—the baby, her, and the sea. She feared if she stopped visiting, it might anger the sea. She insisted that until the baby was born, she needed to pay her daily homage.

I didn't understand, but I no longer objected. I continued to help her, every day walking her to and from the ocean's edge.

The sea was unusually rough the day you were born. I had just left your mother, settling her on a big blanket and leaving her with a basket of food. She felt the pang of a deep contraction as soon as I'd gone. She called for me, but I was too far away to hear.

Pain ripped through her as the contractions continued, quickly intensifying to active labor. She moved around clumsily, encumbered by her large belly, finding no comfort in the coarse sand. Finally, on all fours, she rocked back and forth, screaming through the pain of a tearing contraction. She crawled into the cool waves, desperate for anything that might offer relief.

It was then that the rain started. I was alerted by the storm clouds and quickly made my way back down the path to the edge of the sea. I found your mother in the ocean. "The baby is coming," she cried, her voice roaring above the wind *and waves. I rushed into the water, stunned by the cold. Just up to my shins, I did not understand how she could be immersed in the icy waves. She clung to my legs, screaming and pushing, until you were delivered into the world, into the sea.*

TWENTY-ONE

My mother had been a goddess too. I reread the sentence. Yes, explicitly written, she was a goddess, reborn, and stripped of her station. Tears welled in my eyes as I absorbed the truth of my parents' relationship. Filled with so much pain, love, and loss, I thought of Nick, how we had suffered for years, and now were reunited. Was there a link, a connection?

I couldn't wrap my head around it, Arthur and Anya's ill-fated love. Their sin and separation. The referenced rebirth. What could that mean? I wanted to digest what I read before asking Nick.

Although I had several pages left to read, I snapped the journal shut. The cottage smelled of gloom, and I had to shake it off before Calla and Nick returned for lunch.

Trying to keep busy, I set a skillet on the stove top. Over the course of the last few days, I'd tried several different recipes, each one a bigger flop than the last. Yet, Nick smiled through every bite.

Earlier in the week, Nick took Calla grocery shopping, making a point of hand picking their items and paying at the cash register. While it was okay for him, a seasoned god, to create tangible goods with his mind, our young goddess needed to be kept rooted among the mortals until she had the maturity to use her power wisely.

Stirring seasoning into the butter and vegetables, it occurred to me that my station, whatever it may be, remained in its infancy. Nick had sensed some innate need to nurture, but we chalked that up to Calla returning, my motherly instinct recognizing she was coming back to us.

Calla created flowers and plants, and Nicholas led mortals to victory. How did I fit together in this unknown puzzle? This bizarre plan?

Whatever my station is, it certainly doesn't have a thing to do with cooking, I mused, wrinkling my nose. The stench of burnt garlic wafted from the pan. Scraping the contents of the skillet into the garbage, I looked up to find two familiar shadows passing the window. The door flew open.

"Mama! Can we go back to my garden? Please? Daddy said we can go after lunch. Will you come with us?" Calla's excitement fizzled as she sniffed the air. "Ew, what's that stinky smell?"

Nick followed suit, plugging his nose for dramatics. "Maybe we can get lunch at the diner, Cal. What do you say, Mira?"

"Well, I could make something else?" I suggested, drying the pan off with a towel.

"No!" Calla and Nick simultaneously shouted, each waving their hands and inching back toward the door.

FOLLOWING lunch at the inn's diner, we bundled in rain gear and set out for a walk into the forest. Dampness cooled the afternoon sun. Calla skipped ahead of Nick and me, stopping every few steps to touch a leaf or a wildflower. Her fingers lifted the plants, as if they recognized their goddess, eagerly drinking in her magic. Nick made it clear he didn't want her using her powers, but she seemed in control.

"I am not the best teacher, but I plan to bring Calla here throughout our stay. I want her to learn how to nurture, not manipulate, nature. She got very upset this morning when we came upon a broken tree branch. I felt her mind working to mend it, and I had to explain that plants die to make room for new life. I don't know how good of a job I did, but she let the tree go." Nick shrugged.

"Yep." I smiled. "I remember the tears and tantrums when she came with me to the conservatory for cleanup. She wanted to take the dead plants and leaves home instead of dumping them. She even used to name her plants and talk to them like they were her friends." I shook my head at the fond memories. It seemed so long ago, when she was a normal little girl who simply had a passion for plants. Now she was a goddess, destined to grow gardens.

Again, I wondered about my station, my destiny. "What's my purpose?"

"Purpose? What do you mean?" He stopped walking.

"Well, if Calla is a nature goddess and you're the God of Victory, shouldn't I have a title, or a station? Whatever you call it."

"Is the journal prompting this curiosity?"

"Well, maybe," I sighed. "But, also, you said perhaps you couldn't feel my energy because I wasn't nurtured. How can we nurture whatever it is that needs to be nurtured if we don't even know what it is that needs to be nurtured?" The statement sounded as cumbersome as I felt.

I was the child of a scribe and an ex-goddess. I married a

god and birthed a goddess. We were being sent on a wild goose chase to fulfill some unknown plan that seemed to keep changing. There was too much ambiguity. I needed answers.

Nick laughed, and I frowned. "I'm sorry, I'm sorry. That is just a whole lot of nurturing." He grabbed my hands and pulled me into a light embrace. "We'll figure it out, Mira. It may come slowly, but being around Calla and me will prompt something in you. You're obviously growing. I sensed something before, in Milwaukee, and you created the brush. It's quite a feat to make something concrete here in the mortal world."

"Can I make these little guys grow up?" Calla interrupted. She stood over an empty patch of dirt.

With Nick's nod of approval, Calla brushed her fingers over the soil, her face gleaming. Little buds sprouted, opening slowly, and then blooming into a colorful patch of wildflowers. Violets, foxgloves, daisies, bluebells—each stroke of her hand brought another row of flowers. She giggled, delicately running her fingers over the tops of her creation.

As Calla moved down the path, lilies sprouted next, erupting into perfect, white trumpets. We followed her trail, and nature continued to burst to life with her every step. Ivy wrapped along the trees, hugging their trunks with sweeping vines. Country roses speckled the bushes in soft shades of pink. A breathtaking canvas of colors came alive, almost as vibrant and unearthly as the park in the Land.

From all her hard work, Calla's energy started to wane, and the sun began its descent. We turned around before finding the stream that Aric, the innkeeper, had mentioned lay deep in the woods.

With our daughter between us, hand-in-hand, we

walked back along a freshly budded, colorful path of flowers. Nick glanced over Calla's head, his eyes relaying a million thoughts. Happiness, bliss, contentment. Everything around us was perfect.

Life was as it should be.

THE FOLLOWING day we took another recommendation from Aric. He told Nick of a larger opening to the stream, about three miles away, where trout and pike were plentiful. Too far to walk, we'd need to drive to this secret fishing spot.

Calla helped me pack a picnic lunch, placing three chocolate chip cookies in a baggie.

"And maybe an extra for Leo? He's excited to fish too!" She held up her stuffed friend, wiggling him.

I recalled the other Leo, the little boy from the cove.

"Leo? Is that Leon's new nickname? Like your friend at the cove?" I asked casually. "The little boy you wanted me to meet?"

Calla looked adoringly at the animal. "Leo? Yes, he's my best friend! He's just like me too!"

"What do you mean?"

"Leo is a god like me. He can make people feel strong and tough like a lion!" Calla waved Leon around making animal sounds.

"Like Leon the lion?" I nodded toward the well-loved stuffy.

"Yes, Mama! You know he's been my best friend since I was a baby. When Daddy took me to Grandpa Jake's house, I wasn't even shy because Leo was right there. We get to play every day at Grandpa's, and he takes me to all the fun parks and playgrounds and swimming pools. I never jumped into a lake before, but I wasn't even scared. Leo helped me go from way up high." Her big eyes were round, and her arms waved emphatically in the air. "And when Grandpa Jake said I needed to come back, Leo told me not to be scared because he would be here. And he was right there when I woke up, just like he promised."

The little stuffed animal that Novalee had gifted Calla as a baby now acted as a personal protector.

Oh Novalee, I wish you'd email me. Even if I couldn't divulge the details of the last few weeks, I desperately wished for the connection with my best friend.

AFTER UNLOADING THE CAR, Calla and I found a flat spot in the grass to set up our blanket while Nick scouted the river's edge. He clutched the pole Aric lent him, while a bucket of bait lay near his feet.

"We'll have fish for dinner—I'll cook!" Nick winked to Calla, then grinned at me.

"Let me try first!" Calla's hands dipped into the bucket. "Ew, these are slimy!"

Nick and Calla passed the afternoon fishing. Moments of excitement were followed by long stretches of serene silence. We ate our picnic lunch, and enjoyed the simplicity of the day.

As the afternoon wore on, Nick's attempts at catching a fish continued unsuccessfully. Calla grew fidgety and bored.

"Mama, can I go in the river?"

"It's kind of cold out to swim," I answered, pulling my sweater around my shoulders.

"I don't want to swim, I just want to put my toes in," Calla insisted. She crossed her arms over her chest and jutted her chin. "It's *so* boring here. In the Land I get to swim every day. I want to go home."

Home. The Land. Calla lived in Milwaukee her whole life. The Land, with Leo, Jake, and its magic, had already become home to her. I hoped I adjusted as quickly, if and when we returned.

"Fine. You can put your feet in, but only to your ankles. It's way too cold." I rolled her pants to her shins, then patted her head.

Calla grinned triumphantly to Leo. She gingerly stepped barefoot over twigs and bristly grass before stopping at the water's edge. Cautiously, she dipped a toe in. A gentle ripple of water swirled at her feet. She again looked to Leo, making sure her stuffed friend watched her bravery, and stepped further into the river.

"That's too far, Cal!" I called from my spot on the blanket.

Calla's eyes snapped shut, and her lids twitched, as if she were dreaming in rapid thought. A gust of wind stung my cheeks. I stood frozen, paralyzed. The current picked up, smacking against Calla's legs.

Finally finding my voice, I screamed, "Nick!" The ground trembled with urgency.

Another surge of water crashed into Calla's body. This time, as it rolled in, the force sent her tumbling. Nick rushed from the shore to grasp her, but as his feet hit the water, the waves abruptly stopped. Calla sat up, shaking water off her face.

"Mama, I saw all the fishies. And snails! And little froggies!" Calla squealed, clambering to her feet. "And lots of fluffy seaweed and floating vines!"

Confusion crossed both Nick's and my face. The tumble into the lake should've resulted in tears. I shook out the picnic blanket and wrapped it around her shivering body. Calla shrugged it off.

"You're soaking wet. You're going to freeze!" I again attempted to wrap the blanket over her, but Calla took a step backwards. "Are you okay? Take off your clothes."

"Everyone will see me naked!" she protested, although we were alone in the woods. I stripped off her pants and shirt.

"Nick, feel her." I rubbed my hands over her body. Rolling waves of heat emitted from her skin, like a hair dryer set on low. "She's completely dry."

As Nick reached for Calla, she bolted from my hold. Her little legs pumped fast and swift, taking her back into the river. She stopped shin deep, her arms extended above her head, her legs bent. In slow motion, she catapulted several feet into the air before arching into a perfect dive. Another ripple vibrated through the river's surface, permeating the air with a poof. Nick and I stumbled back, wind knocking our footing. Calla's body disappeared into the water.

A second later, her head bobbed to the surface. Dazed and confused, she looked frantically around before sinking back in.

"Calla! Oh my God," I screamed, breaking from the trance. Nick and I rushed rushing to the water's edge.

He leapt in, diving below before popping to the surface with Calla in tow. They came to shore, both shivering and soaked head-to-toe.

"You're okay. You're okay now." I pressed my face into her dripping hair. She calmed in my arms, and her skin again blazed and radiated with heat.

I set her down, studying her face and body before rubbing my hands over her arms and legs, checking to make sure she wasn't hurt. She wiggled free of the blanket. Nick leaned against a nearby tree, catching his breath. Water dripped from his soaked hair and clothes, but Calla's had already dried. He wordlessly stripped, taking the crumpled blanket to cover himself, eyes glued on our daughter.

We abandoned the picnic, forgetting the bucket of bait, and hastily returned to the car. The curious event hung in the air on the drive home, but none of us spoke of it. We didn't say much of anything. Nick turned on the radio and hummed along to a song while I sat with my head leaned against the window. Just one more oddity added to an already strange new existence.

I hoped no one noticed as our naked child streaked from the car to the cottage, followed by Nick, covered only by a blanket.

~

LATER THAT EVENING, when the events of the day were a fresh, peculiar memory, Nick and I collapsed on the couch. I watched Calla as she slept soundly on the cot set up next to my bed.

"What was that?" I whispered to Nick. "I can't believe it. Did you see her run? It was like she was possessed. And that jump. I don't know how it's even possible for a body so small to get that much air." Nick raised his eyebrows in deliberate meaning. *We are gods, anything is possible.* "It's just weird. Besides the cove, she hasn't really been swimming. She never really liked it, not even baths."

Nick's eyes shifted from Calla to a blank space on the

wall. He ran his palms through his hair. "Was there anything in the journal?"

I crossed my legs under me, and picked at the hem of my shirt, desperately wishing I could speak with Arthur before talking about my parents' story with Nick. The cottage didn't offer Wi-Fi, but I continued to check my email daily at the inn's business office. I couldn't keep secrets from Nick, not when it affected Calla. He'd done it for years, resulting in disaster. We needed complete honesty moving forward.

"Well, there's nothing too amazing... except my mom was a goddess too. And my parents apparently did something bad, a sin that led them to both being reborn, but they found each other again. I only read about half of the story, but that kind of sums it up to my birth."

I looked to the duffel, now upset I hadn't read more. "I should probably finish it. What could they have done that would cause them to be reborn?" I couldn't imagine my mild-mannered parents doing anything morally wrong.

"Well there are rules, kind of like the Commandments. If you break a rule, you face the consequences. The degree of punishment depends on the severity of the sin. To be reborn is a pretty harsh punishment."

"Like having a walking god?"

"Yes, that can be cause for rebirth or losing your godly station. But they had you."

"Okay?"

"Then you'd be a walking god. And Calla." Nick assessed my face as I recalled his words on the walking gods, the powerful gods that walk among all domains. "They may have abused their powers on mortals."

"Like 'bend the rules'?" I asked.

"More than bend the rules. It would have to be mali-

cious behavior, like making a mortal kill on their behalf or
—"

"No, there's *no* way either of my parents could do
anything like that. They're good people." My eyes filled
with tears and I leaned into the couch, as if it could offer a
hug or some semblance of support.

"I'm sorry, you're right. Let's wait until we see them and
can ask them ourselves."

"That seems kind of personal," I replied flatly. When
we finally caught up to them, introducing my sort-of
husband and asking about sins of the past wasn't quite the
reunion I envisioned.

Nick nodded toward Calla. "If it might affect our child,
it gives us the right to ask."

"Really? Their sins can affect her? That doesn't seem
fair?"

"Sometimes consequences aren't fair," Nick stopped,
sensing I was on edge, tired and emotional from the events
of the day. The wind rattling the windowpane proved it.
"Let's leave it for now, but we should avoid the river. That
was pretty insane today." Nick slumped against the sofa.
Exhaustion clouded his eyes.

"You want the bed tonight? I can take the couch." He'd
given me the bed so I could be close to Calla's cot.

"I'd love the bed tonight. You know what else I'd love?
You in the bed with me," he whispered, leaning in. His
breath hit my lips.

Like a moth to a flame, I moved closer until my mouth
hovered centimeters from his. Thoughts from the day evaporated, and the only thing I could think of was his lips on
mine.

I felt them, although neither of us had moved. Soft lips
landing and pulling back, only to land again. The brush of a

tongue, a sweet sample followed by another taste, and another. The morsels teasing my appetite.

"I'll wait, Mira," Nick's voice soothed, and my eyes popped open, my fingers flying to my lips. "I can wait however long it takes."

TWENTY-TWO

Dropping off into a night of restless sleep, I dreamt of Calla and a red-haired mermaid. From the shore, I watched as the two swam a synchronized dance. Sunshine feathered my shoulders, and gentle waves rolled over my legs. Calla and the mermaid glided through crystal-clear water, their hair and body sparkling like diamonds under the sun. Calla's face lit with delight, just as it did when she created flowers. She spotted me at the shoreline, giving a wave before grasping the mermaid's hand and swimming away from me and my dream.

I woke to find Nick and Calla gone. They left a note, set under a to-go coffee cup from the inn's café. Calla doodled little flowers along the edges of the paper, while Nick's scrawling handwriting laid out their plans for the day. He was taking Calla grocery shopping, and then for a drive to find a playground.

I took it as an opportunity to finish Arthur's journal. Curling up in bed with the coffee in hand, I began reading our story again.

You were a joyful baby. Beautiful, sweet, and calm. You had my dark looks and your mother's lovely disposition. The first couple years of your life were bliss as we watched you grow from a precious newborn to a precocious toddler with a kind, nurturing personality. Your mother was in awe of you. She spent hours watching you, holding you, loving you. Her devotion made me forget the years of pain our marriage suffered.

With you, we were complete. Our greatest desires had been fulfilled. The sins of the past were erased in this new life, and our precious family was solidified by you—our child. Your mother repeated the words every evening when she put you down for the night, "Though one may be overpowered, two can defend themselves. A cord of three strands is not quickly broken." You were the third strand that bound our cord. I was certain you were redemption for the pain of the past.

Soon after we settled in a new routine as a family of three, the sea began to grow rough and angry. Your mother turned fearful. Why would the sea react with such force and urgency? Waves smashed against the cliff's edge. She stopped taking you to the shore. Instead, she would sit high above the cliff and look down, consumed with despair. Where peace once filled our cottage, dread began to seep in. What did the sea want? The same sea that delivered you to us, our most precious miracle, was now demanding something in return, but we did not know what.

After rediscovering one another in our new lives, we truly believed we'd been given a second chance. Your mother had been stripped of her station, born anew. We thought we'd paid our harsh penance, but it became clear that the past was not forgotten.

We were fearful. Was it a test? Were we given another chance, only to fail again?

You remained unaware of the storm that brewed around us, the sea that swelled in rage as it beat against the cliff's edge. We no longer were safe in our home. We needed to leave.

The night before our departure, your mother stood at the edge of the cliff and begged for guidance. That night, a protector came to Anya, speaking to her in a dream. We were to leave the salt of the sea and raise you among the mortals. When it was time, we would need to allow you to follow your own path and fulfill your destiny. The protector told us she would come to us again.

We booked the first available flight to the States. As we were carried across the ocean to our new home in America, the sea below roared in anger, somehow aware that we were leaving her. Once in the States, we drove until we found a place that called to us. Your mother wished to be near water, and thankfully freshwater lakes and rivers were no concern, as long as we remained far from the salt of the sea. We settled in what you know as your childhood home—the home that holds some of our most cherished memories.

While mortals could not see it, as your parents we knew something divine lived within your soul. I could not nurture you until we were advised by the protector, but I knew you were destined for great things.

Life was calm, peaceful, and happy, but away from the sea and saltwater, Anya's health slowly deteriorated. Regardless, her love for you and zest for life only strengthened. Over the years, she continued to grow very weak, and we again begged for guidance. Your mother needed the sea, but until we heard from the protector, we would not take you back.

We grew anxious about our uncertain future but knew it was beyond our control. And while we wished to tell you about our divine past, we feared how you—a young goddess raised among mortals—would interpret that knowledge. What if it piqued your interest? What if you explored the divinity that lived within you? Your curiosity could perpetuate your energy. Raising a god among mortals is difficult at best. We couldn't chance it. We'd wait for the protector.

Years passed, and shortly before your eighteenth birthday, the protector came to us again. She told us it was time for Anya to return to the sea, to gain her strength for the years to come.

Anya grew strong again once we settled along the coast of Florida. Years shed as she fed off the energy of the ocean. Life for us settled into a new harmony as I continued my writings, and your mom meditated by the sea. We'd almost forgotten that life was destined to be disrupted yet again.

It was quite unexpected when we learned that you had a new life growing within. Like a flower, you bloomed as motherhood swept you up, fostering your natural tendency to nurture. Your love of life flowed so deeply and extended to Calla like roots growing firmly in place. She was your new bud, a new flower waiting to blossom.

Dearest child, I cannot give you the answers, for I do not know them myself. What I do know is that the sins of your parents have set in motion the train that now tumbles down this track. For this, we shall always repent, but we are the gods chosen to carry out this most critical mission. A divine plan that is still being written. Until then, know that you are bound by the strength of three.

Though one may be overpowered, two can defend themselves. A cord of three strands is not quickly broken.

THE DOOR swung open to a struggling Nick. Several bags of groceries dangled from his free hand, while Calla plopped on the sidewalk and ripped open a package of chalk.

"Heard from Aric there are storms in the forecast, so I stocked up. Maybe I'll start doing some of the cooking." Nick grinned. "Calla's idea, not mine."

"Have at it," I replied, waving toward the kitchen counter, which I had wiped down after finishing the journal. "Although, I have a sneaking suspicion you may have a slight advantage over me."

I pulled my hair back, twisting it into a bun before releasing it again. I blew out a long breath. Some things were better left in the past, but maybe if I opened up to him, we could start to truly heal and put those years behind us.

"After you left on that deployment, I signed up for a culinary class. I wanted to learn to cook. They always say the way to a man's heart is through his stomach, and I could barely hard-boil an egg. I wanted to do something special for you when you got back."

Nick stopped mid-step.

"I fantasized about how life would be when you returned. We'd start up right where we left off. I'd take you up on all those promises you made. When I found out you died, well—" Tears caught in my throat, stinging my nostrils. I glanced to the open door, making sure Calla was occupied and out of earshot. "Everything kind of stopped. Life stopped. At least, the life I'd been living."

Nick watched intently as I spoke, his eyes focused on my lips. He reached over and stroked my arms. His gaze shifted, meeting my eyes as he massaged my muscles. Six years' worth of tension slipped by in a series of lists, sticky notes, schedules and routines. The hectic juggling of life as a single parent. Some of the moments were lived mechanically, going through the steps, while others were laden with emotions.

Leaning in, he rested his cheek next to mine and spoke with a confidence that can only come from the God of Victory. "I will never fail you again."

~

AFTER WE ATE LUNCH, Calla laid down for a rest, which gave me the opportunity to discuss my father's words with Nick. I told him about the angry sea, the protector who came to my parents in a dream, and the pregnancy they didn't expect.

Nick offered clarification on protectors, or walking gods. The powerful, forbidden love child of Land and Sky who were taken to be raised by the angels and saints, praying for all life, and sent to aid gods on critical missions.

"That's what Dad wrote. In the journal, he said we're the chosen ones to carry out this critical mission. A divine plan that's still being written."

"I was afraid of that," Nick said. "An unwritten plan is like going into battle unprepared. Unknowns are an enemy."

"I didn't think you were ever afraid." I half teased. Nick's confidence lent him a formidable, fierce presence. He always seemed to move and act with assurance. Though, I supposed the last few weeks were enough to test anyone, even the God of Victory. "So, what's this mean?"

He shrugged, holding his hands up before planting his

palms on the kitchen table. "I don't know, Mir, but we're in it together. I'm not leaving your side. I'm making good on those failed promises. This is my redemption, our second chance."

I felt truth in his words, I saw it in his eyes, but my stomach sunk as the familiar sentiment echoed in my head. Arthur said almost the same thing about his reunion with Anya.

"My dad mentioned again that it's their sin that started this," I said, although I wasn't sure what *this* meant. Calla's near death? Our sort of nuptials? The wild goose chase to Ireland? "I just can't imagine what they could've done?"

"Let's not speculate. We'll connect with them at some point. Have you checked your email lately?" I shook my head no. "Maybe you should go now. Looks like that storm Aric warned me about is heading our way. When you get back, perhaps I can give you a cooking lesson?"

AS I SUSPECTED, there were no messages from Arthur. While online, I shot Novalee a quick, benign message. The heavy stuff would come soon enough.

"Getting ugly out there," Aric said, peering over my shoulder. The burly innkeeper had a deep voice that didn't quite match his playful, blue eyes. "Already told your husband, but you might want to get your groceries now. Never know how them roads'll fair. Skippett was washed out for a week after our last storm."

Your husband... Our marriage didn't seem real yet. Hearing the reference to Nick as my husband made me blush.

Rain drizzled from puffy grey clouds as I made the short

walk from the inn back to the cottage. Calla was up from her rest and munching on a snack in front of a gentle fire. It felt familiar, like we were back in the Land, cozy and safe in our small home. Nick sat on the sofa, carefully watching Calla.

I plopped next to him, resting my feet on the coffee table. I almost leaned my head against his chest, the urge so natural, but I caught myself.

"There's nothing in my email," I whispered. The light crackling of the fire hummed in the background, and I yawned. "It's getting pretty nasty outside."

"Was the café open?" Nick asked as he swept back a lock of hair that had fallen over his brow. I itched to do it myself.

"Yeah. The inn's booked this week with the start of summer break, so Aric's keeping the café open extended hours." I somehow managed to get the words out without giving in to the urge to snuggle into him. Maybe sitting on my hands would help. The need to touch him was almost overwhelming.

"Mama, I'm finished!" Calla stood up, stretching her arms above her head with a little yawn.

"Want to watch a movie?" I smiled at her, then back to Nick, unsure whether I was happy for the interruption.

"Yes! Can we watch *The Little Mermaid*, please, please, *please*?" Calla begged. The fists above her head swept into praying, pleading hands. "I want to see Ariel!"

My dream. Calla swimming together with a red-haired mermaid. Could it be coincidence?

"We'll have to see what's on cable, Cal," Nick explained, his eyes still locked on mine. Thoughts of my dream fell away, and all I could think of were his lips on mine.

Maybe if we kissed, just an innocent, quick kiss, maybe I could get through a conversation without my pulse going crazy and my mouth stumbling over words.

Maybe, just maybe, I'd put my theory to the test.

TWENTY-THREE

I woke the next morning to rumbling thunder. Calla slept on the cot next to my side of the bed. I glanced around the one-room cottage and spotted Nick, sitting in the kitchen, engrossed in a newspaper. Two take-away coffees from the café sat atop the table. I slipped into the bathroom to freshen up before joining him.

Looking in the mirror, I noted the bags under my eyes were less pronounced. Several nights of sound sleep were like a miracle cream for my complexion, although my rosy cheeks could be chalked up to Nick. Just a glance at him got my blood pumping.

Feeling playful, I tiptoed out of the bathroom and snuck behind Nick, whose nose was still stuck in the paper.

"Boo!" I whispered into his ear.

He swung around while simultaneously pulling me into his lap. I looked up, stunned. It was supposed to be *me* startling *him*. His playful eyes darkened.

Now was my chance, my lips already parted with an "O" of surprise, our mouths only inches apart. But I froze, enchanted by his jawline, which was set firm and solid.

"Nice try. I can feel you coming from a mile away." Nick breathed the words into my parted lips. "Trust me, Mira, I am well aware of where you are every second of every minute."

The yearning in his voice stroked my cheek. I wished it to be his hands, but if they started there, I feared I wouldn't let them stop until they traveled quite a bit lower.

A crash of thunder vibrated through the cottage, jostling me from Nick's lap, and waking Calla.

"Mama?" she called out, her eyes fluttering open and shut.

"Over here, baby." I stood up, grabbing the to-go cup and bringing it to my lips, feeling like I almost got caught doing something bad.

"I dreamed I was swimming with Grandma in the ocean! Remember you said we can go? Now that you're not afraid to fly, can we go? Please, Mama!" Calla sat up, clasping her hands together. "I could swim just like the fish! And I was sparkly all over like a mermaid! I want to find the mermaids!"

Calla's earlier request for the movie and now dreams of mermaids. Just a coincidence or yet another piece added to this strange puzzle? I glanced at Nick, eying him wearily.

"Mama, I want to go to the ocean so bad! Grandma said she's waiting for us!" Calla's voice turned up an octave. "She said we need to come soon. Can we go today? Please, Mama? Daddy?" She looked to each of us.

"Grandma said she's waiting for us?" I took a step back, bumping into the wall behind me. My grip on the cup tightened.

"Yes, she said we have to come soon because it's getting too rough!" Calla's eyes grew wide. "It'll be too scary to swim if we don't go soon. There's a storm coming." Proving her point, the sky shuddered with lightning.

I looked to Nick. "What is this? Can my parents go to her in a dream? Why wouldn't they just email me? Instead they pull Calla into this weird, twisted game?"

Nick stood from the table and reached for my arm. "Didn't your dad say they had sporadic access to the internet? Now that your phone's not getting service, maybe a dream is the only way they can contact us."

"Then why wouldn't they come to me?" Calla watched in confusion as I questioned Nick, anger pitching in my voice. Rain pinged off the windows. "Why not tell me, the *adult*, instead of going through Calla? I mean, haven't they put us through enough? They're what caused this in the first place!"

"Mama! No!" Calla lifted her chin. "Grandma loves us. She can't wait to see me. She said to come before it's too rough, and now look, it's storming, and we'll never get to go!" A glittery tear slipped from Calla's wide eyes, leaving a shimmery trail as it traveled down her cheek.

More tears fell, and Calla's face went aglow, sparkling like diamonds under a spotlight. My jaw dropped and I blinked, then looked to Nick, who appeared as stunned.

"Nick?" I whispered.

"I don't know," he said under his breath.

Calla cocked her head, calming from our silence. As her tears dried, the glitter quickly faded, and her cheeks returned to a normal, rosy complexion.

"Come here, Cal, I want to talk to you," I called. She obediently climbed off her cot and padded to the kitchenette. I lifted her chin, studying her cheeks and eyes. Normal. No glitter, no sparkles. "You feel okay?"

She nodded. "Yes, Mama, but I'm mad you made it

rain."

"I didn't make it rain." She pointed to the window. The rough rain from a few seconds ago lightened to a sprinkle. "Okay, Calla, you're right. Mama will try not to make the sky angry, okay?" Calla again nodded. "Can you tell me where Grandma is, from your dream?"

"She's in the ocean, Mama! Like a mermaid!" Calla did a little wiggle, mimicking the glide of a fish. "Grandpa can't swim, but it's okay. He likes to watch from way up high!"

"Were Mama and Daddy there?" Nick asked.

"Yes, I think so." Calla squinted, trying to remember the details from her dream. "But you were super-duper far away on a big rock! A big *cliff* like the cove, but even bigger!"

The cliff. Of course, my parents were in County Cork. "Was there anything else special you remember from your dream?"

"No, Mama, but do we get to go?" She began to bounce up and down, fingers clasped together. "Do I get to swim in the ocean?"

"Yes, sweetheart. We'll go soon. Daddy and I need to do a little more work here first though, okay? But it'll be soon. Go potty and then we can have breakfast."

We watched her disappear into the bathroom. As the door clicked behind her, I exhaled. "We need to find that stupid cliff in County Cork. Maybe Aric is familiar with the area?"

"I asked him about it. We don't have much to go on. It's the biggest county in Ireland, and there's a lot of coastline. Honestly, I'm not sure where we should even start."

"Well, maybe we should just drive. Maybe as we get closer, we'll know? Something may pop out." I gave a slight, hopeful smile. "We need to do something."

A bolt of lightning flashed outside, illuminating the

room with a menacing silver haze. My smile quickly faded.

Something besides the forecasted storm was brewing. Something beyond our control.

WE ATE breakfast while the rain continued to pummel the cottage. Nick started a fire, trying to recreate the serene feeling of the previous night. We all stood on edge. I had to remind myself that rain was in the forecast. I couldn't infer a simple storm was a prelude to something more sinister.

Calla looked out the window and watched the grey clouds light up to another round of thunder and lightning.

"Oh no!" she exclaimed. "Where's Leo?" She ran to her little cot and lifted the covers, looking for her stuffed lion. "I left him at the river!" Calla's eyes glistened with tears. "I left him at the river, and he's getting all wet!" She ran to me, her eyes pearly and streaked with glitter. "Mama, we gotta get him! He's gonna be so scared!"

I brought a finger to her cheek, running it through the tears. Diamonds swirled with my touch.

"Daddy? Mama? Can we go, please?"

Nick eyed me, giving a nod as he hoisted himself up from the couch. "We'll go now before the storm gets worse."

We stepped into the rain, Nick and I both staring at Calla's face and hands to see if the rainwater would set her skin sparkling. It had no effect.

"We'll talk about it later," Nick said under his breath as we climbed into the car.

Nick drove to the river in record time. He pulled off the road and instructed us to wait in the car while he searched for Leo. Minutes later, he returned with the grimy, soaked, but rescued lion.

Calla hugged tightly to her friend. "He wasn't scared. He's so brave. Even in the dark!"

I wasn't keen on traveling out in the storm but was relieved Nick found Leon. Or Leo. I wasn't sure what he went by these days.

As Nick piloted back to the inn, our car rolled to a stop in front of a branch blocking the road. It must've just snapped from the wind.

Nick looked to me with a little smile. "What's the use of having a nature goddess if we can't take advantage?" He put the car in park and turned to Calla. "Sweetheart, you know how Daddy said you have to be careful and have control when you use your gift?" Calla nodded. "Well, do you think you can show Mama how you can make the tree whole again?" Calla again nodded. She squeezed Leo, and looked at the branch.

Her eyes narrowed as her mind worked to mend the tree.

Nothing happened.

Calla scrunched her face, focusing hard.

The tree still lay split across the road.

"Daddy, it's not working."

"It's okay, sweetheart. Close your eyes and picture the tree whole. Just relax and think of how it would look if the tree were to lift his big branch up like an arm reaching for the sky."

Still nothing happened.

Calla's brows twisted in concern. She dropped Leo and unbuckled herself. "Let me touch him."

Nick cut the engine. The wind howled as the two exited the car and crouched next to the broken limb. Calla gently ran her hands over it. Nothing.

They remained in that position, hovering for several

more minutes, before Nick finally picked up the branch and chucked it to the side of the road.

∾

WHEN WE ARRIVED at the cottage, I instructed Calla to strip off her rain-soaked clothes. She shivered, cold and upset that she couldn't fix the tree's branch, or as she referred to it, her friend's arm. Her hands clutched Leo, as if trying to squeeze out some bravery.

"Leo needs a bath. How about you both pretend to be little fishies in the tub," I suggested, trying to divert Calla's attention.

Water filled the basin, and Calla climbed in after setting Leo on the toilet beside the tub. I added a dab of shampoo. Pearly bubbles popped along the surface but had no effect on her skin. Unlike her tears.

Salty, warm tears.

Dreams of the sea. Salt of the sea.

"Nick!" I nearly screamed.

He stopped under the doorframe with a kitchen towel in hand.

"Stop there," I directed, holding my hands up. "Before you change out of those wet clothes, can you run to the café? Ask for some salt packets or a shaker. Just bring back salt, okay?"

My idea must've registered in his mind, because he left without question. I refocused my attention on Calla. Her small frame sagged, seemingly wiped of energy from her unsuccessful attempt to revitalize the tree.

"Warm enough?" My overly chipper tone sounded fake to my own ears.

She wiggled her toes and scooped water over her legs

and belly. "Can you fill it up more, Mama? And more bubbles, please!"

"Sure thing, buddy. Does that feel good?" Her smile answered my question.

"I got it," Nick called from the door. "Here."

I breathed in, preparing for what might happen with this little experiment. "Hold up your arm, baby." Calla lifted a hand above the surface, and I sprinkled the shaker over it.

Thousands of little diamonds danced in her palm. Calla held a finger closer for a better look, gazing wide-eyed at the dazzling kaleidoscope of colors. I sprinkled more salt along her arm, and it glimmered like the sleeve of an ice skater's shimmery, chiffon costume.

"Does that hurt?" I whispered.

Calla shook her head. "More, Mama," she quietly requested, still holding her arm above the water. I opened the lid of the shaker and let half its contents flow into the bath. The water glowed from her radiating body, projecting a prism along the ceiling and walls. As Calla moved her limbs, rays bounced in synchronization.

Nick clasped my hand, giving it a squeeze.

"I'm a mermaid! Look at me!" Calla dunked under. Her eyes closed, but we could see twitching beneath the lids.

A minute passed, and Calla remained under the water. Her chest moved up and down, as if she were breathing beneath the surface.

Just as I grew concerned that she hadn't come up for air, Calla's eyes popped open. Ivory pearls peered back at us, and glossy lips twitched into a giant smile. She sat up.

"Mama! Is that what the ocean's like?" She held up her glittering arms. "Am I really a real mermaid?" She dunked back under before either Nick or I could answer.

TWENTY-FOUR

We stood outside the bathroom door, watching as Calla continued to play in the bath.

"What is this?" I whispered.

"I don't know." He looked to the ground. "I've never seen a god take on a different station, but Calla's still very young. It's pretty unique for a child god to have lived among mortals for a majority of their life. Something here is prompting a new energy in her. Maybe it's as simple as the three of us together. We're empowering her?"

"We need to find the cliff." I rubbed my eyes. Was it just that morning I had stared in the mirror, feeling rejuvenated? I lost concept of time, no longer seeing the past, only the weight of whatever was to come.

"We can't hide out here indefinitely," I sighed.

We agreed to leave in the morning if the weather cooperated. I got Calla out of the bath, while Nick ran to the main building to return the saltshaker and check the forecast again. He needed to let Aric know we'd be checking out, and he wanted to ask about alternate routes should we run into washed out roads or closures.

After Calla was dressed and content with a coloring book in front of the fireplace, I moved to the kitchen, needing to keep busy. I fished through the cupboard, taking inventory of what groceries were left. I didn't feel like cooking, but Nick had it stocked.

"Hey, want to grab dinner at the café?" I suggested when he came through the front door minutes later.

"Not tonight." He smiled, the edge of his lip twisting playfully upward and dimpling his cheek. "Tonight, I'm giving you that cooking lesson I promised." A large cardboard box balanced on Nick's knee as he struggled to remove the key from the knob.

"What's that?" I asked, nodding toward the box.

"This," Nick said with a wide grin, "is a little surprise for Calla." He set the box down on the coffee table. Calla leapt from the floor.

"For me?" she asked, clasping her hands together.

Nick plucked a DVD from the box. "Mr. Aric lent you this." He flashed the cover, then handed it to her.

"*The Little Mermaid!*" Calla squealed. She bounced up and down, hugging the DVD like a teddy bear.

Looking to me over Calla's head, his grin widened. "She can watch it during our cooking date. The rest of the stuff in here is our ingredients." He patted the box.

Cooking with Nick sounded oddly intimate, especially since he referred to it as a date.

A date. I hadn't been on one in years. Butterflies danced in my stomach, and I swallowed hard, suddenly warm and shy, and feeling way too nervous by the mere idea of a date with the man who was my kind-of husband.

I pulled a pan from the cupboard and filled it with water for buttered noodles—Calla's favorite and one of the few meals I could make without fail. My skin grew warmer as the water boiled. Silently, I watched the time tick down until the noodles were ready to be drained. Steam wafted from the pan, bringing more heat to my cheeks.

I hadn't felt this wound up for a date since high school, when Adam Aikens, the captain of our football team, took me to prom. *That night ended with a kiss... would tonight?* I fanned my cheeks, then brushed way strands of hair that clung to the back of my neck.

Nick already had the movie started and a blanket set out for Calla's picnic dinner. I set her bowl of noodles down, then moved to the high-top table, watching Nick's muscles tense and relax as he pulled packages from the box and reached for pans in the cupboard. Somehow, he made the simple task look sexy.

"What're we making?" I asked, my voice lower than intended.

"Chicken alfredo." Nick glanced over to Calla, then met my eyes. His cheek dimpled. "With a little something special I picked up for dessert."

"Okay, what can I do?" I brushed off any hidden innuendo and slid from the chair.

"Can you rinse and chop these?" He pointed to a container of mushrooms. I wrinkled my nose. "Oh, you don't like mushrooms?" His eyebrow shot up, and I shook my head. "Noted. Can you measure out some butter and milk?"

"Yes, Nick. And I can boil water." I laughed. "I'm not a complete failure in the kitchen."

The compact cooking area shrank with our two bodies sharing the space. We couldn't seem to turn or step without brushing elbows.

"Pass the heavy cream." He nodded to the carton.

I grabbed it, pivoting from the stove to the counter and

back. Only he'd taken a step in that split second, and I ended up colliding with his chest.

"Oh," I said into his shirt, smelling his unique combination of woodsy aftershave and sweat. I lifted my eyes. "Nick."

"Yes?" he whispered. His chin skimmed my forehead.

Just kiss me already, I silently pleaded, tilting my face to his. My nose swept along his jawline. My lower lip dropped, willing him. Nick's hand cupped my face, and his thumb stroked my cheek.

Then I heard it, the song *Kiss the Girl.* Sebastian and friends singing to Eric and Ariel, so convincing, it could've been us they were urging on.

Nick's lips lingered over mine, brushing so slowly, so gently, I wasn't sure if it was real or yet another figment of my imagination. But then I felt it. Our connection, his touch and taste. The softness of his lips over mine. Sweet and subtle, until it turned eager and desperate, to gentle again, to a fluttering graze against my mouth.

I floated away, swept up by his touch. All doubt dissipated, like clouds clearing to a sunny day, and a realization came so strong, I pushed back, gasping for air.

Nick blinked, and then focused on my lips.

"I..." There was no way to explain it. The link was no longer relevant.

This was real.

TWENTY-FIVE

According to the weather report, the storm wasn't to let up for several more days, but when I woke the following morning, sunshine peeked through a crack in the blinds. I crept from bed to pull open the shade, my hands fumbling to shield my eyes as light flooded the cottage.

Palpable eagerness jarred the room. Nick rolled over from the couch, and looked to me with a smile spreading over his face. "You feel good this morning, huh?"

Good was an understatement. I hadn't floated down since our kiss the night before. I returned his smile and nodded toward the window. "It's a sign, Nick."

Someone, or some *god*, was pleased with our decision.

We were on the road by mid-morning. Calla's forehead pressed against the back-seat window, gazing glossy-eyed at the sun-soaked terrain. She'd barely touched her cereal bar at breakfast, which now sat in a baggie on her lap, nor had she questioned our abrupt departure. Her usual curiosity was replaced with quiet contentment.

The atmosphere of the car tingled with my excitement. Every small detail, from the white marshmallow clouds in the sky to the bright blossoming wildflowers on the ground, led me to believe it was nature's signal. We were traveling the right path.

I studied the county map Aric had given Nick. It'd only take us so far as we'd soon be departing Kilkenny. County Cork was a large, sprawling area occupying the southern-most part of Ireland. We'd travel through Waterford next, and then hug the coast until hitting Cork.

It wasn't long before we saw signs welcoming us. I folded Aric's map, his part in this journey now over.

"*Failte go Co. Chorcai*; Welcome to County Waterford." The words rolled off Nick's tongue in an authentic brogue.

"Impressive." I smiled and glanced to Nick, taking the moment to admire my sort-of husband, and realized we had so much yet to learn about one another. For instance, he didn't know I despised mushrooms, and this sexy Irish brogue was news to me.

Did he speak any other languages? Did they come inherently to gods? Spanish class was my only B in high school, so maybe not.

I looked forward to a time when we could learn every-thing about one another. And perhaps, have the carefree experience of newlyweds that we hadn't been afforded. Romantic walks, talks, and nights of passion.

Especially the nights of passion.

I reached over to place my hand on Nick's thigh. He peered down, looking a bit surprised at my bold gesture.

After our kiss, I'd come to a firm resolution; linked or not, I *wanted* Nick. But for Calla's sake, I needed to stay level-minded while we sought answers. Finishing this plan, whatever it may be, took priority.

Maybe it was my hand, now gripping Nick's thigh, that grounded me, because the weight of what was to come, the unknown, didn't faze me. Knowing he was mine, my god, my husband, the father to my child, and possibly more children. That was enough.

More children. I hadn't thought of having another baby. Life as a single parent was difficult. Now, with Nick by my side, the idea drifted in and out of my mind. I stared blankly out the window to nature's canvas. The rain made everything crisper, a stark contrast to my head, which fogged with ideas.

Nick pointed out a patch of wildflowers to Calla, but she didn't respond. Glancing to the backseat, I realized she was asleep. Her small head lolled with the bumps in the road. Leo sat at attention on her lap, as if keeping watch of his charge.

"Nick," I said softly, not wanting to disturb Calla. "She's asleep. It's so peaceful right now, such a strange feeling." I placed my hand over my heart. "There is so much we still don't know, but everything seems... okay?" I shrugged, clueless as to how anything could seem okay after the last few weeks, yet feeling calm.

He smiled, looking quickly to me before returning his focus to the road. "That's good, Mira. Just remember, whatever happens, we're together. This is our second chance. We'll get through it."

"Whatever *this* is," I whispered, but didn't question Nick further. None of it made sense, but he was right, we were in it together, and with the God of Victory by my side, we had to succeed.

The drive continued in content silence. Rolling hills and fields of waving tall grass passed in the distance. Lulled by nature's grace, I slipped into a light sleep.

A little girl with inky black hair filled my dreams. Wind whistled around her, blowing the girl's hair so I couldn't see her face. Maybe it was Calla, spinning and twirling in her pink, floaty dress. She danced with a joy I recognized, surrounded by emerald green grass. But then the wind picked up, rustling the trees, spinning the little girl, twisting her faster until her dress became a pink blur.

"Stop!" I called out, startling myself awake.

Nick hit the brakes. The car jerked, and my head nearly smacked the dash.

"Mira! What's wrong?" He glanced in my direction, then to the rearview mirror.

Calla stirred in the backseat. My voice and energy shifted the composure of the car, making the air thick and tense. I took a breath, trying to settle my pounding pulse.

"Can we stop?" My fingers shook as they pressed against my temple. "I need caffeine, coffee. I, um, can't seem to keep my eyes open."

Nick pulled off the highway at the next exit and turned onto the frontage road leading to a gas station. He maneuvered into an open space next to a vintage pick-up truck. As he cut the engine, I looked over to admire the classic. Arthur used to take me to car shows, and this truck was in pristine condition. A brawny, bearded man with a curly crop of hair winked at me from the front seat, then tipped his head, as if nodding goodbye. The truck groaned to life and crept from its parking space. My eyes fell to the circular writing under the driver side window.

Three Seas Services, Baltimore, West Cork.

I gasped, again startling Nick. This time when Nick asked what was going on, I knew. *I knew.*

Almost laughing, I pointed to the truck, which was now rumbling out of the lot, and whispered, "Baltimore."

"Who?" Nick squinted in the direction of my window. "What?"

A small, disbelieving smile crept along my lips. "My parents didn't lie. I was born in Baltimore, but Baltimore's here, in Ireland." Nick cocked his head in confusion. "The truck listed services for Three Seas in Baltimore, West Cork. I can't believe it. I think we've found the cliff. Can you run inside and see if the clerk can give us directions?"

NICK and I huddled over the map trying to locate Baltimore. The clerk couldn't help. Hundreds of little towns and villages speckled the southern coastline of Ireland, making for a tedious search, and the clusters of islands off the shore didn't help.

"Let's get moving." Nick gestured to the window, where grey clouds started to form above the gas station. He navigated to the highway while I continued the futile search for Baltimore.

Calla snacked on the cereal bar with her forehead still pressed against the window.

"We'll be to the ocean soon, baby," I said to her, twisting in my seat to look back.

"Okay, Mama," she said with a yawn. Too many days of highs and lows must have caught up with her.

We followed signs toward Waterford, another county hugging the coast. I pictured their namesake crystal. Anya kept a set of their goblets in her hutch. When I was a kid, on special occasions—New Year's Eve or my birthday—she'd let me drink juice from them and pretend it was wine. They were precious to her, one of the few belongings she'd brought from Ireland.

The salt of the sea had once sent my parents fleeing this land, now it summoned us back.

The highway wound sharply, edging along the coastline as bits and pieces of the ocean peaked in and out of view. Giddy energy bubbled from my belly, tingling through my limbs and swelling into my fingertips. I poked a finger to Nick's side, testing if I'd physically turned electric. A little shock sparked between us, and he flinched.

"Sorry, I couldn't help myself." I squeezed my hands into fists, then settled them on my lap. "This is right. I can feel it."

As we got closer to the coast, my fingers felt so plump I could hardly clench them. I opened the window and let my hand wave in the wind, sending currents of pent-up energy crackling with the breeze. I wiggled my fingers until they drained.

Sighing deeply, I rested my arm against the windowsill. Sunshine and salty air filtered over the fuzzy hairs on my forearm. I watched them dance in the breeze.

We continued on the highway, cutting through an expanse of tall, swaying grass. Once again, I was lulled by nature's grace and the briny scent of the sea. I needn't close my eyes this time when the little girl from earlier returned to my daydream.

Now, she twirled among the same golden grass we'd just passed. Swirling like the little hairs on my arm.

"Mama, Daddy, look!" Calla exclaimed, snapping me back to reality. She pointed to a wave forming out at sea.

Nick slowed the car. We watched as the ocean's wall of power swept across the surface, surging to a tower nearly three stories high. The monster wave roared to shore and crashed against a bed of rocks. Water exploded through the air, falling like tiny Waterford crystals back to the sea.

Nick's hands grasped the wheel. Three deep lines etched his forehead. The car careened forward. Parts of the road hugged so close to the edge that I feared a sneeze would send us over. Calla perched alert with her nose pressed to the window, eyes sparkling like the crystal waters that sprayed with each crashing wave.

As we glided down a particularly steep hill, a patch of land, sea and sky illuminated on the horizon, the sun's rays painting an arrow, like an X on a map. I grasped the edge of my seat, sucking in a breath.

"This is it," I murmured.

Nick let his foot up from the gas and allowed the car to coast until it came to a stop. I recognized the field that lay before us. Tall blades of green grass blanketed the ground, while lush trees and overgrown bushes lined the horizon. Across the field, a small cottage was barely discernible, shielded from the road by a circle of tall shrubs.

Just past that, at the spot where the dazzling sun met land and sea, was my mother's beloved cliff.

"Home."

My declaration was nothing more than a whisper.

TWENTY-SIX

Nick and Calla climbed from the car while I sat frozen in the front seat. Memories crowded my head as the little girl with inky-black hair appeared yet again.

She slipped out of the stone cottage to run barefoot through the field. Mother called out, but the warnings didn't stop her. She wanted to dance in the rain. She loved to feel the tall grass blades tickling her legs, the moist dirt rubbing between her toes.

"Mira?" Nick called out. "You okay?"

"Sorry, yes." Warm air hugged me as I stepped out. This was *home*. And I knew that answers lay in the distance. We walked slowly into the familiar field. I grasped Calla and Nick's hands, linking us in a chain. *A cord of three.*

Just as it had years ago, tall grass blades brushed against my legs. "This is it."

The warm air thickened, turning sticky, feeding off our excitement. Humidity steamed from the grass and mixed with the ocean's salty breeze. Land and sea were at play, mingling in the air like two lovers in a dance.

I looked to Calla. Her face glowed, not with diamonds or glitter, but with life.

"Mama, can I go there?" She pulled away, pointing toward the cottage. Ungroomed trees and overgrown shrubs partially covered it, yet I recognized the solid stone structure from my childhood.

I could picture it vividly, as it had been in its prime, built with chunky stones that made the cottage an impenetrable, strong fortress in my childlike eyes. Its thick, wooden front door was the barrier between me and the perils of the outdoors. I wasn't supposed to go outside alone, but I didn't always listen. One day in particular, long, long ago, when I desperately wanted to dance in the rain, I slipped away without permission.

But I couldn't dance. I couldn't even see. Angry black clouds spit out fat raindrops, making my pink dress sticky against my body. I cried out for Mommy and Daddy, but the wind howled, and the waves beat against the cliff. My pleas were lost. I shielded my eyes as I ran blindly back toward the cottage, stumbling along the muddied way. Tears, rain, and wind stung my cheeks. Why had I left my fortress? Why did I leave Mommy and Daddy?

"Sweetheart, stay by us. Hold our hands." Nick's voice broke the spell cast by my memory. He pulled Calla close to him. She reached for my hand, again linking us in a chain.

We continued to walk through the golden grass, but as we neared the cottage, menacing clouds dotted the horizon. With each step, the sky became darker. Light drops of rain hit my cheeks. I hesitated. Was it a warning? It was too familiar, too similar to the memory that had just played in my head. Nature seemed to be urging caution as each step brought us closer to the cottage and the cliff's edge.

Nick sensed it too. He picked up Calla and held her tightly to him. She rested her flushed face against his chest.

The rain fell harder, but we trudged forward, stopping just steps away from the abandoned cottage. Moss grew dense along the stone walls and covered the front door. I held my hand up to Nick, indicating for him to stop and wait.

The thick wooden door was guarding something. Secrets. Truth. I breathed heavily as I lifted my hand to the tarnished knob.

I was floating, swimming, running, but I wasn't moving. I was crying, laughing, scared, excited. Feeling everything and nothing, I didn't know what to do. What could I do? Mommy! Daddy! I was drowning, but I was on land. Mud, water, and air. I tasted it. Wind and waves. I felt it. The land and sky and sea colliding.

Slowly, I turned the knob and pushed. The rusted hinges groaned as the door creaked open. I hesitated, preparing myself for what I may find.

My security blanket stroked at my cheek, comforting me from my nightmare. I lay safe in my bed. Mommy and Daddy were just outside the door. I could see them, sitting at the table. The fire hugged us, reassuring us. Mommy and Daddy were so worried, but it would be okay. I was safe. They always protected me.

Stepping inside, emptiness greeted me. Much like Jake's home, a big hearth was situated beyond the foyer. A compact kitchen and great room were on one side, while doors lined the other. Furniture and other personal affects had been cleared. Only dust and grime remained.

I walked toward the wide fireplace mantle and let my hand glide over the smooth wood. The center of our haven had provided years of warmth and protection. Now it stood abandoned.

Mommy's face looked scared and I wanted to give her a hug. I snuck from bed, but as I got to the door, the fire roared like a monster.

A spark crackled, and I stumbled back. Fresh ashes floated from the blackened fireplace while a puff of smoke burned my nostrils. I turned on my heels, fleeing the cottage and the memory.

"No one's here. It's empty," I panted, stopping in front of Calla and Nick.

"Look!" Calla exclaimed. "There!" She pointed to a clearing in the trees. The ocean peeked through, where land, sea, and sky met at the cliff's edge.

Nick moved to me, pulling me close with one arm while Calla remained tucked into him with the support of his other. He rested his chin on my head. The rain had stopped, yet the clouds above us remained an ominous shade of grey, and the smell of ash hung in the air. I pressed my face into Nick's arm, breathing in his scent.

Nick. My husband, my chosen one. *Though one may be overpowered, two can defend themselves. A cord of three strands is not quickly broken.* I placed my hand over Calla's small fingers. Our little girl, our legacy, the third strand that bound us.

The air changed yet again, becoming so heavy with sea-salt that I could taste it on my tongue. A thick breeze rippled along the treetops, carrying a strong, familiar scent.

Mother.

"Mirabel. Niko." Our heads swiveled toward the direction of her voice just as her slight frame appeared through the clearing.

The woman before us was indeed my mother, but she

was changed. Her skin shone porcelain white, her eyes icy blue. Red hair floated around her head as she moved fluidly toward us.

Nick kept his hold on Calla and me, but his grip loosened in recognition.

"*Mother*," he said, bowing his head slightly.

"Mother?" I whispered, jerking away from Nick, confused by his salutation.

"Don't be afraid." Mom's voice rolled over us, calming like the sound of waves. Then, my father came into view, stepping out from the shadows of the trees.

"Mom?" I asked again, looking from Nick to my mom, and then to my father. "Dad?"

"Let's go in," Arthur said evenly, extending his arm toward the cottage.

I wasn't scared, yet I began to shake. Slow, fat tears escaped my eyes, flowing down my cheeks and into the corners of my lips. I licked them unwillingly. Salty like the sea, comforting me like the nipple to a baby. I shook my head, trying to shake away the taste that tied me to the sea. It was pulling me, undeniably moving something deep within. Nick reached out again, shielding Calla and me with his strong arms, again connecting our family.

My sobs subsided beneath Nick's hold. His touch—our divine link—overpowered my misgivings, and I relaxed.

Pulling slightly back, I swiped my face. My hand glimmered like a disco ball. The sea was in me, running through me like the blood that flowed through my veins. I knew it then. I felt it so strongly that I fell against Nick.

A crack of lightning lit the sky.

"Dad?" I looked to Arthur. Streaks of grey mussed his glistening black hair.

"Mira," Anya breathed, sending another wave of calm through the air.

"Mira," Arthur spoke next, his voice cool yet not as effective as Anya's. "It's okay. It's our destiny. It's part of the plan."

"No!" My composure shattered, and the sky roared along with me. I was a child again, stomping my foot, but now it caused the ground to tremble. The wind picked up, rustling our hair and stinging our cheeks. I looked up to the clouds, dark with fury. *My fury, my anger.* I stomped my foot again. "No. Nothing is okay! What is going on?"

The air shuddered, and Nick stumbled, encumbered by Calla. My anger startled us both, and Nick's eyes locked on mine, grounding me once again. *Control. Control yourself.* But it was too late. The sea raged with my anger, beating against the cliff's edge like a giant awakened from its nap.

Concern flashed in Anya and Arthur's eyes as they moved toward me. Dad reached for my hand, but I jerked away, slipping on a slick patch of mud and tumbling backward to the ground.

Again, I was the little girl with inky-black hair and a sticky, rain-soaked dress, swirling and twirling as my world heaved out of control.

The sky opened, another giant awakening. I grasped at chunks of sludge as fat drops pelted my face. The instant storm hissed, roaring over my head like a train running off its track, steam blowing and metal screeching, colliding before my eyes.

And as the train exploded, the sky burst with the fiery crack of lightning.

The vibrations settled to an eerie silence. Anya and Arthur moved away. I assumed they were allowing me space, but quickly realized they were shielding something.

Or someone.

Remorseful eyes locked on mine as they each took a deliberate step in opposite directions, unblocking the view of the trail's mouth. Coming quite purposely up the path was the last piece of the puzzle.

"What?" The words choked from my throat. Nick's eyes widened with shock, then softened from recognition.

A trifecta of deceit stole my breath as my dearest and closest friend aligned with my parents, forming a jagged triangle.

"Novalee?" I whispered. "Novalee?" Unbelieving, I shook my head. I looked from her to my mother, to my father, and finally to my husband.

"A protector." Nick's face gentled.

"Hello, Mira." Novalee's voice floated through the air. The woman before me radiated with an unearthly beauty. My friend, but changed.

Who was this creature?

I stared back dumbly, unable to find words to return her salutation.

"Mira, I've missed you. And Calla too," Novalee soothed. She extended an arm to me, beyond my reach, yet I felt her touch. I pushed away the heavy air and clamored to my feet. Her warmth did not waiver, her smile genuine and pure. "We have a lot of catching up to do."

Indeed.

Novalee again reached for me, and I grasped for Nick, leaving a trail of mud down his shirt. She stepped back but her aura—her being—still emanated comfort and familiarity, and I recognized her efforts. She was desperately exerting her god-given powers to make me feel her, remember her, trust her. But I also realized I was becoming a strong goddess myself. My defenses shielded me from her energy.

"Please, Mira... *feel* me," she pleaded. I looked to Nick for his assurance. He pulled me closer into his hold. Calla, fast asleep, remained safely nuzzled against his chest.

Novalee closed her eyes, breathing in and out with yoga-inspired breaths until she entered my thoughts. Pieces of our shared past jumbled in my head.

"You must be Mira? Looks like we're destined to be best friends!" Her chipper voice from adolescence echoed. The vivid image of us as college freshmen flashed in my head, a snapshot of the first time I met Novalee at eighteen, when she had eagerly swept me into our new dorm room. I felt now, as I did that day, stunned by her charisma and beauty.

Faster, more snippets spun in the space between us. *"Mira, she's beautiful!"* Novalee's adoring eyes gazed at the new life I had just delivered, the new life *she* had helped me deliver into the world.

Novalee was by my side during every major life-defining moment, including Calla's birth. We had grown together, from the innocence of college to the harsh reality of adulthood. She lifted me at my darkest moments and cheered alongside me at my very best. The many tears, the deep-belly laughs, the heartbreaks and adventures. All the experiences, good and bad. Regardless of the future, we would forever be bound by the past, and I could not deny her.

Just as I had forgiven Nick when I learned of his betrayal, I would also absolve Novalee. There was no use fighting it.

As my defenses caved to the memories, I saw a vision of her as the protector. Embracing me, guiding me, loving me. Beauty and grace. Peace and understanding. Love and conviction. Truth and strength. She embodied the very essence of good. I could not fear her words, nor could I fear her touch.

Dubious minutes passed before the atmosphere calmed. The dark clouds dissipated to blue skies. I sighed, then gave a slight nod of my head. "Okay."

"Let's go inside, shall we? We'll set the fire and have some tea." Arthur gestured toward the cottage. "Are you hungry?" His benign question lent normalcy to the bizarre situation.

Words seemed stuck in my throat, but I was hungry, and a fire did sound good. Nick sensed my ease and nodded toward Arthur. I followed their lead.

Inside, I discovered the cottage had changed. A gentle fire crackled in the hearth. A wooden table was set with fruit, cheese, bread, and chocolates. Life had filled it in the few minutes since we first arrived.

Anya led us to a bedroom. Hand-carved, wooden furniture adorned the small room. I recognized the sweet flower embroidery along the edges of the bedspread. The same soft security blanket from my childhood now welcomed Calla. Nick laid her down. She didn't wake, but her brows scrunched.

"Leo!" I whispered to Nick. "He's in the car. Can you get him?" Calla may have my childhood security blanket, but she needed the security of her fierce friend.

Nick slipped from the room to retrieve Leo.

I cradled Calla until Nick returned from the car. A smile played at her lips as we tucked the little lion under her arm. I brushed a kiss on her cheek before leaving the room to face the inevitable.

For anyone looking in from the outside, they'd see a cozy scene from a family holiday. My parents sat at the table with steaming cups of tea set before them. The fire cast a warm glow around the great room.

I washed my hands at the kitchen sink, then splashed cold water over my cheeks. Nick stayed within arm's reach of me at all times. I set a hand towel over the drying rack, before spinning to meet my parents' watchful eyes.

Arthur gestured to the two seats across from him. I stiffened, hesitating, but Nick took my arm and guided me to the table. We sat with our backs to the fireplace, yet it enveloped us, warming my bones until I felt mushy and soft. Nick poured tea and offered me a plate.

"Where are we?" I questioned after forcing down a strawberry.

Anya leaned back. "This is where you were born. Well, right below here, past the edge of that cliff." She hitched her thumb toward the window. "A gateway sent from *Him*. The Almighty."

"A gateway?" Nick asked.

"Yes, Niko," Anya answered.

Mother. I remembered Nick's greeting. "Nick, is she your mother?"

They chuckled, and the mood instantly shifted.

"Oh no, dear child," Anya said, her hand reaching out to touch mine. I didn't pull back this time. "But Niko," she continued, looking from him to me, and back to him. "I am no longer Anna, Mother in the Land."

Jake's counterpart who had not been seen in decades—who was perhaps sent on a critical mission. My mother... was *the* Mother.

"Jake's sister in the Land, although they aren't biological siblings. No blood relation," Nick clarified, even though I already pieced it together. "You were stripped?"

"We have a lot to tell you." Sadness flashed in Anya's

eyes. "The sea is angry, Mira. Will you come with me? Novalee needs you."

Her hand still held to mine, and Dad placed his on top. Our skin tingled as we connected, a tiny jolt of electricity. *A cord of three.*

From inside the cottage, we could hear relentless waves beating against the cliff. The ground vibrated from its fury. The sea was calling me, and I could no longer deny it.

∼

NOVALEE STOOD at the mouth of the trail with her back toward us. Her eyes remained locked on the horizon as she addressed me. "The sea feels your worry."

My legs unwillingly brought me to her side. She waited until I stopped before reaching out to grasp my hand. All air momentarily left my lungs, and as it did, the world around us went absolutely still. Not a single wave rolled, or blade of grass moved. The sky turned eerily quiet.

It couldn't have been more than a few seconds that passed, yet it felt like an eternity. Suddenly aware of my emptied lungs, I gasped and greedily sucked in air as if I'd been holding my breath for minutes. I dropped Novalee's hand and leaned over, setting my trembling palms on my thighs, and panting heavily. As my breathing slowly evened, nature returned to normal. The wind and waves picked up to an amicable current.

I straightened, lifting my hands in front of my face to study my fingers. They'd sucked anxiety and worry from Nick over the last few weeks, but now, with Novalee's help, they'd sucked the fury right from the sea.

Novalee brushed her hands over her pants and then glanced my way, shyly meeting my eyes.

"Who are you?" I asked her quietly.

"I'll explain everything later. For now, we need to focus on Calla."

"Calla? What does she have to do with this?" It was *me* in the vision, swirling in the storm. I was the reason we left the cliff.

Calla brought life to the land; she created flowers and gardens. What could this have to do with her? The wind picked up, sensing my confusion.

Novalee's posture stiffened as my thoughts pinged off her. "Let's go inside. It's safe now." She peered over the edge of the cliff before turning her back on it.

I glanced over too. A sandy white beach sat below us. I recognized it. Like another home from childhood, the place of my birth. The path, steps from where I stood, was the one my parents had taken every day to appease the sea during my mother's pregnancy. The sea had given me to them.

My miracle. Mira, my miracle. My miracle of the sea.

It had to be me.

I CAUTIOUSLY FOLLOWED Novalee to the cottage. Nick, Anya, and Arthur had moved to the living room, each looking formidable in their own way as they watched us enter. Two couches faced one another with a coffee table positioned between them. I slumped into the space beside Nick, while Novalee pulled up a kitchen chair. Like a judge at a hearing, she stood ready to mitigate, personifying the lawyer I knew.

I leaned my head against the couch, closing my eyes. Minutes of uncomfortable silence passed before Anya spoke.

"Niko, I didn't know it was you."

I snapped upright. "So you know each other?"

Nick was looking at my mom, but he spoke to me. "Your mother was Anna, Mother to the Land. Everyone knows her."

"And Niko, he is a great warrior." She smiled, seeming pleased. "The God of Victory. It makes perfect sense."

"No, it doesn't." I shook my head. "Nothing makes sense." I looked at my mom, studying the face I knew like the back of my hand. Her skin was pearly, almost iridescent. I never noticed how bright her eyes were, bluer than sapphires.

"Let me explain," Novalee began. Although she'd come in from the raging sea, she looked perfectly mani-cured. Every hair still in place, and her clothes laid crisp against her athletic body. She stood stiff and resolute, like she was in court, mediating this bizarre debate. "The Almighty has a plan, and we are the ones chosen to fulfill it. It is to be done." She spoke neatly and without further explanation. Her hands were clasped on her lap. To her, it was a simple proclamation. She was the judge and gave us the sentence.

"What do you mean?" Nick asked. His grip on my hand tightened.

"Niko, you know how we were created, but for Mira, I shall start from the beginning. Back many eons ago, when original sin tempted mankind. The Almighty created the gods, giving us dominion for the betterment of humanity, but he also gave free will, free choice. Human reasoning, human will. And some—gods and mortals—chose evil over good." Novalee shook her head and her cheeks flushed. "It was so easy for them to fall into temptation, choosing sin over salvation. The Almighty was furious, and in turn, he chose to rid his earth of the unfaithful, cleanse it of sin. He unleashed the fury of the sky."

"This sounds a little like Noah's Ark," I stated dubiously.

"The Bible, the Qur'an, the Vedas, mythology—there are truths and embellishments to all recorded history." Novalee brushed a stray lock of hair off her forehead. "The seas continued to swell, raging out of control until floods nearly destroyed everything. That is when the Almighty realized that the waters seethed with an *evil* that he did not create." Novalee spat the word evil, just as Nick had back when he explained the ways of the gods in the Land.

"How?" My voice was a whisper. I leaned into Nick, thankful for the link that kept me grounded.

"Evil sought dominion over the Almighty's creation. When their armies found a broken link—the sea—their leader used it to plant his seed. The gods desperately tried to swipe it away, but his disease was too strong. The Sky had dominion over the heavens and the Land over earth, but the seas were defenseless."

"Wouldn't the Land protect the water? Aren't the oceans on earth?" I asked.

"Creation was in its infancy. The waters were an expansive space that separated the heavens and earth." Novalee earnestly explained a history I could hardly imagine as truth, yet I somehow could not deny its veracity. "The Almighty repented for his actions. He wanted to do better for his creation. So, he called for a new army of gods to be born. And they will have dominion over the waters."

"What exactly does that mean?" Nick asked, still gripping my hand.

"He looked to that great vastness known as the ocean, and called out, *'Though one may be overpowered, two may defend themselves. A cord of three shall not be broken.'* The Land, Sky, and new gods of the Sea. A cord of three. The Land was to continue protecting the sea until the day came when the prophecy would be complete." Novalee paused. "That day has come."

"You're not answering the question." Nick's jaw clenched.

"The Land and Sea will now separate, and the gods of the Sea shall rise to their proper station, with the true God of the Sea as their leader."

"True god?" I squeaked.

"Yes."

"What *exactly* does that mean? For my family?" Nick's hand crushed mine.

The Land and Sea will now separate.

"Niko, it is our destiny," Anya said gently. She averted her eyes from us.

"I don't care!" Nick boomed, leaping up from his chair. The fire in the hearth sparked and then fizzled.

I realized I was holding my breath. As I slowly released it, cool white puffs floated from my lips like smoke.

Novalee, Anya, and Arthur stood steadfast.

"I will not have my family torn apart," Nick's voice warned. Frost crept along the glass of the windows.

Novalee stood up to him, a floating cloud. "Niko, it will be done."

TWENTY-SEVEN

We were motionless. Nick towered over my mother, father, and Novalee. He was fierce, in battle mode. The air stiffened, turning wintery cold.

"Why, Mom?" I asked through chattering teeth. "Why us? Why now?"

Arthur took Anya's hand. He looked at Nick. "You know Anna, but you do not know me. I was a young scribe, foolish and undisciplined. I lacked passion or reason. I wandered aimlessly. Nothing piqued my creativity. Nothing captivated me. I was an artist with no canvas, no paint, no picture. And then I met Anna. She held unearthly beauty, igniting every divine sensation within me. We were among the mortals, but when I looked to her, she was heaven. I could not resist, nor could she. It was perfect love, pure and simple. The most innocent yet provocative encounter, beyond the bliss and ecstasy I had only read about. We fit together. Two broken pieces of a mold that united and became one. Before we knew... before we knew... it was done."

"What was done?" I whispered.

"We committed the most severe of sins," Anya answered. Her eyes blazed.

"*What* exactly happened?" I was finished with secrecy and cryptic explanations.

Hail pinged against the windows, either my anxiety or Nick's anger.

"We had a child," they answered in unison.

"Me?"

"No, our firstborn." Sparkling tears filled Anya's eyes. They fell like crystals into her lap. "We didn't know," she sighed, looking around the room. "I didn't know your father was from the Sky, and he didn't know I was of the Land."

Nick gasped, shaking his head with pure disbelief. "A scribe of the heavens? How? How can that be?"

"Niko, I had left the Land many, many decades ago. I was Mother, *the Mother*, but I couldn't bear children of my own. It began to burn in me, the desire to have my own child, to experience pregnancy, labor, and the bond of one's own blood. I begged. I pleaded. I was angry. A cruel irony, the Mother who could not have children." She shook her head.

Anya continued, although the pain and shame to do so was palpable. "I needed to leave the Land; I despised it. Children clung to me, sought me for comfort, but they weren't mine. I thought among the mortals I could escape my divine intention. I ran away. I couldn't do my duties, so I ran away to live with the mortals. Among them, I found Arthur. We found each other. It was fate. No matter the consequences, we were destined. There is no other explanation for how or why."

Anya was caught in her past. She closed her eyes and continued. "We did not know... we could not feel each other as gods from another domain. We should have—I should have sensed Arthur, just as he should have sensed me. But it was not until it was too late that we discovered the cruel twist of fate. What sparked Arthur's divine intention and what completed my divine station—our child—was forbidden. How does that make sense?" Anya's voice grew louder. "I still do not understand."

Arthur patted her leg, trying to comfort her as she struggled for composure. He continued, letting my mother take a break from the pain of the past. "Anna, the Mother, who had longed for a child of her own, could not bear children of the Land. Then she met me, Arthur, the scribe of the Sky, *me*, who could not write anything worthy of the heavens. I was able to give her a child, and she was able to give me my words." He shook his head. "We do not know why. There *is* no explanation."

We sat in silence, absorbing their story, the raw truth, and aching honesty. A forbidden union with the direst consequences. Like many painful love stories, there was no happy ending. Or was there?

"What happened?" I asked. "To the baby?"

"We don't know." Mom's eyes were glassy. "Hunters took Arthur before our child was born. Then they came for me. I never heard my baby boy's first cry." She paused. "Anna died during childbirth. I, Anya, was reborn unto the sea below this cliff. My station as Mother was stripped, but divine blood still runs through my veins."

I vaguely remembered Nick's explanation of the hunters' role. Like the police or bounty hunters of the divine, they find gods who've defied their fate, refuted orders, or abused their powers.

Again, silence choked the room. The ending to Anna and Arthur's love was tragic. I closed my eyes at the pure heartbreak of their loss. Nick sat again, leaning into me. The mere touch of him filled me with comfort, our link working its magic.

But a new revelation struck.

"Nick." I took his hands and looked to him. "Us... you couldn't feel me, but you should have. We... Calla." I shook my head. It couldn't be true.

I rushed from my seat, four sets of eyes watching as I hurried into Calla's room. She was there, sleeping peacefully, Leo still tucked beneath her arm. I lay beside her, pressing her into my body. Her heart was beating, she was breathing, and she was here with me.

Nick filled the doorway. Concern replaced his anger.

"She's okay," I whispered, stroking her hair. "She's okay."

Calla's eyes flickered open for the briefest moment as she whispered, "I'm sleepy, Mama. Let me sleep."

"Why is she so tired?" A sick feeling pitted my stomach.

"I don't know," Nick answered, raising his eyebrows, "but your parents may."

We left Calla and returned to my parents, who now stood at the long picture window. Anya's gaze fixated out toward the edge of the land. Trees blocked our view of the water, but we could hear its presence.

"Tell us what's going on," Nick demanded.

Mother turned, sadness in her eyes, and choked, "She's going."

"Going?" Nick and I asked in unison, but his voice overpowered mine. "Going where?"

"To the sea," Anya whispered.

"For God's sake, Mother! Stop! Stop with the half answers and half stories. *What the hell is going on?*" My voice shook the floor and echoed off the walls. Nick looked at me with a warning, but I teetered on edge. "I will not be calm until they tell me what the hell is going on!"

A bolt of lightning lit the sky. Anya and Arthur shrank away, while Nick squinted at me with odd uncertainty. I swelled with immense anger. I could feel it thickening my blood, roiling through my veins. The sheer mass of emotion terrified me, but somehow, being *out* of control gave me a sense of control.

"Tell me!" The wide window behind my parents shattered. Splinters of glass sailed over the lawn outside, and lightning flashed against the shards.

Nick moved to me, palms held up. "Mira, try to calm down."

"No!" I shrieked again, and the window above the kitchen sink exploded. "*What* is happening to my daughter?"

Electricity sizzled in the clouds, unleashing golf ball-sized hail. Chunks landed at our feet, rolling over the carpet like a putting green. My outburst released only a fraction of pent-up anger, and my hands began to shake uncontrollably with the balance. I staggered backwards, now fearing the rest of my fury would burst by the slightest fuse.

Calla's cry broke through the cottage.

"Mama! Daddy!" She wailed. "It's raining so hard! I can't see!"

We rushed to the bedroom. Water cascaded from the ceiling, soaking over Calla, and flowing into a puddle on the floor. She stumbled to her feet, hands held up to shield her face.

"It's okay, baby." Nick pulled her into his arms. "We're here. We're here."

Appalled, I stumbled back. Had I caused this? My anger? I panted with heavy breaths.

Calla peered around the room, her fear palpably disintegrating as she took in our faces. "Grandma! Grandpa!" She held open arms to my parents, but I blocked them out.

"You're awake, baby." I sniffled into her wet hair, whisking her from Nick and out of the storm-drenched bedroom. We sunk onto the sofa. "You've been asleep for so long. I was scared."

"You made the sky angry again. You keep making the sky angry." A drowsy smile played on her lips.

"You're okay?"

"Yes, Mama, but I'm so sleepy." Calla yawned, as if to prove her point. "I'm so sleepy, and when I close my eyes, I can swim in the ocean." She rested her wet head against my shoulder. From her steady breathing, I could tell she was fast asleep again.

I looked at my parents, this time with control. "What is going on?"

"It's time, Mira." Novalee's voice reverberated through the room. "Please, let me try to explain." She came from the front door. "You were chosen for a reason, all of you. Anna, the barren mother of the Land, destined to bring forth the true God of the Sea." Novalee looked at my dad. "And Arthur, the scribe destined to not only write the history of this divine plan, but also be a part of its creation. Together, you bore Mirabel, a walking god, born into the Sea from Land and Sky. Now, Calla completes the cord." Novalee stroked Calla's hair. "Niko, our God of Victory, you've ensured this plan is victorious." Novalee eyed Nick. "It is to be done." As she whispered the words, Calla stiffened in my arms.

"What's happening?" I clutched her closer, feeling a chill sweep over her body. "Mom? Nick? Help me!"

Anya scrambled to my side, half pulling Calla into her

lap, and using the rest of her strength to grasp me. As our skin connected, an energy radiated between our bodies, so strong that Calla's limp frame lifted from my lap. *A cord of three.*

My breath left my chest, and I was filled with something else. Something so strong, more than a memory, it engulfed my entire being.

Rain and salt. Mud and air. Wind and waves. Clouds and dust. Flying, swimming, running. Land, sky, sea.

I stood motionless, consumed by excited, jumbled thoughts. *Calla's thoughts.* A child trying to make sense of it. Flowers, vines, and trees. Seed, soil, and rain. A plant growing and reaching to the sky. Climbing past the clouds to heaven. The bright sun, fading to white.

I peered down, and we were spinning. Twirling on the shore. Sea, salt, and sand. Calla whirled and twirled, spinning and spinning until I felt her giddiness.

She was happy. She was home.

Now I was a little girl again, twirling in the grass, my hair fanning my face as I spun in the field, getting dizzy, so dizzy I was going to fall. My stomach heaved. I was wilting, the grass between my toes turning crunchy. Something was sucking the moisture from the land beneath me.

Calla.

A flower drinking from the soil, she was sucking the sea from me.

My eyes flew open, and I gasped for air, clutching my mother and daughter so tightly we were one. *A cord of three.*

Calla turned hard under our touch. I looked down, and her skin glittered, blinding my eyes with thousands of crystals.

Salt. She was a flower that had sucked the sea from me,

but too much salt will kill any plant. She became still. Her body hardened like a rock. I screamed, breaking the cord.

I screamed over and over.

Novalee was the only one seemingly able to move. She grabbed Calla's stiff body and carried her out of the room and out of the cottage. The rest of us were too bewildered to do anything but follow, too shocked to do anything but watch as Novalee jetted to the edge of the cliff and held Calla like an offering.

We couldn't move, we didn't do anything to stop her. Instead, we froze in place as the scene played out. Novalee, rooted at the edge, her mouth moving in a silent prayer. Time stood still, everything stood still, until finally the spell was broken by one swift movement—Novalee's arms extending while simultaneously releasing my baby.

Calla soared over the edge, disappearing into the crashing waves below.

TWENTY-EIGHT

"You felt her, Mira," Nick coaxed. He guided me onto the sofa. "She's okay."

After Novalee had tossed Calla into the sea, Arthur, Anya, and Nick had to physically restrain me from jumping over myself. Using their supernatural charm, they sedated me enough to lead me down the long, winding trail to the beach below. There, Calla's calming presence whispered in the waves, soothing my devastated nerves.

Now, back in the cottage, I teetered on edge again.

Sitting stiffly at the edge of the couch cushion, I shot back at Nick, "She may be okay, but I am not."

Novalee cleared her throat in an effort to get our attention. She hovered in the doorway, waiting for Nick to give her the nod before entering. She wasn't the only one walking on eggshells. Arthur and Anya already escaped to the village to give me space.

"I need to explain," Novalee said, moving to the hearth. "It wasn't meant to happen like that. But when Anya, Calla, and you connected, the final phase of the prophecy was set into motion. *A cord of three.* You drank from one another, absorbing the divinity that runs in your veins."

"None of this makes sense." I shook my head as tears sprouted in my eyes. "How could you do that to Calla? You're like a sister to me!"

"I know I have a lot to explain, but please know our friendship is true. It remains."

"No. It was built on lies." I pointed an accusing finger at her.

"It wasn't. I'm a protector. It's my divine calling."

"A protector? Novalee, you were always gone! How did you protect us? You were gone when Calla was hit by that car. Where *were* you?"

Novalee flinched. "They call us protectors, as if we are trained to be bodyguards or the secret service." The fire illuminated above her head like an angel's halo. She sighed and rubbed her eyes. "I was a very young god when I was sent here, sent to you. My mortal existence began when we first met. The 'end of the innocence' they call it. Among the angels, I only knew beauty and goodness. With the mortals, I felt everything. I *wanted* to feel everything. That's my sin, and I'm sorry. But mortal emotion... it's beautiful. Overwhelming, but beautiful."

"How did I not know? I should have sensed you," Nick interrupted as he took a seat beside me. He scooched close enough so our elbows, knees—any bare skin—touched, constantly feeding me his energy. His soul working overtime.

"My energy was set aside before I came. It had to be, otherwise I could have empowered Mira. Can you imagine, two walking gods as college roommates?" Novalee gave a limp smile. "Mira, our friendship is real. I was sent without power, sent to complete this most important mission without the ability to use divine intervention. I was given free choice and free will. Please understand, over the years, everything we experienced together was real."

"Why didn't you prepare me for this?" My eyes darted to the window, signaling my sweet Calla, whose body had just been sacrificed to the sea.

"Sometimes when a protector is called upon, we're given a new light, or new life, to assimilate into our role among the mortals. Some of my memories were masked. That is, they were masked until Nick took Calla to the Land. Then the sea turned angry, creating currents and cyclones so strong that I felt it. I felt it in my blood. And like a bolt of lightning striking my soul, my energy returned. She is the true, pure child of the Sea, and she will complete the prophecy. She's not gone, Mira, she's waiting to return."

Novalee watched me intently. Her face relaxed, and she breathed in and out, releasing a wave of calm and peace that enveloped my emotion-wrecked body.

"This is the true trial of my time as your protector, to help you through this final phase. I won't fail you, Mira. Calla will return."

"So, what now? How do we get her back?" Nick asked, his jaw twitching. The God of Victory couldn't sit idly by.

Novalee sunk into the sofa opposite of us. She shifted uncomfortably, picking at the hem of her shirt. "Well, now you two..." She looked up with a wide grin, then wiggled her eyebrows suggestively. "You know." Smooching noises followed, which I never thought I'd hear come from Novalee's lips.

"You mean," Nick hesitated, looking from Novalee, to me, "Calla will be reborn, not to the Sea, but to us? I don't understand. Won't she be a walking god?"

"The Land and Sea will inevitably be connected,

always. It's the way it was created. Calla will be of the Sea, but she will always have ties to the Land. Don't fear, she's now your miracle of the Sea." Novalee's face tensed with urgency as she pushed from the sofa. "I'm not sure what may happen to me once I complete my divine calling, so I must tell you this now." She stared at the ceiling, her voice low and soft as if she were sharing a secret. "Anna was reborn to the Sea, becoming Anya, and you were delivered into the sea. When Calla is reborn, she completes the trinity. Three gods, three generations—*a cord of three*—washed, cleansed, and reborn, delivered into the Sea. The past, present and future. The prophecy. Land, Sea, and Sky. It all ran through your veins, but you took from one another. You drank each other's energy until Calla was filled with the sea, Anya with the Sky, and you with the Land. Calla brings upon a new era of gods. When the time comes, she will lead the Sea. She's destined to do great things."

"Who will raise her?" My voice shook. I wasn't sure I wanted to hear the answer.

"Well, *you*—and Nick, of course. The ocean is a powerful force, and it provides the most basic of necessities for all creatures to survive, *water*. Like the tree of life that drinks from the sacred waters, the Land and Sea will remain united. For the sake of humanity, Calla is destined to be a Commander of the Sea, building an army to ensure evil never again curses the bloodline of life. Soldiers of the Sea will train with the soldiers of the Land, and Calla will learn from Nick how to be victorious. From you, she'll learn how to be Mother."

"*Mother?*"

"Yes, my dear friend, you've inherited your mother's prior station. When you return to the Land, you will be Mother, and Calla—when she is of age and body—will bear forth the new generation of gods, becoming Mother to the Sea."

"What about my mom?"

"Anya absorbed the Sky from Calla and you. She'll now walk with your father in the heavens. And Arthur, well, he's done his part in rewriting history. Maybe he'll retire." Novalee smiled, relaxing as the tension eased. "You'll always have here, among the mortals, to connect with your parents."

My energy drained as all the pieces of the puzzle we'd been searching for finally settled into a picture. Arthur and Anya will finally have redemption, and Calla will not be torn from us. Our family would not be ripped apart.

And I will be Mother. The weight of it added to my already heavy shoulders.

"There's only one problem," Nick interrupted, exhaling as he lifted his hand from my thigh. He looked to the ceiling, fixating on a random speck. "We haven't consummated the marriage."

"Um, you're married?" Novalee's eyes lit. She rushed to my side, squeezing me in a bear hug. "I can't believe I missed it, Mir. I can't believe I missed my best friend getting married! We definitely need some girlfriend time. You gotta tell me—" She cocked her head in confusion. "Wait. You haven't consummated, as in, you haven't done *it*? What? Why?"

He looked me straight in the eye. "Because we can't. I can't."

TWENTY-NINE

"This is a lot like the Hark," Novalee said without looking up. She sat in the sand with her chin resting on her knees.

I'd come from the cottage to find her, unsure where she'd gone after leaving to give Nick and me privacy to talk. "The Hark?"

"Where I grew up." She still didn't look at me. "I have a brother. Haven't seen him in almost fifteen years."

"And here I thought you were an only child from Chicago."

"I'm sorry, Mira."

Another apology. Why did everyone that I loved lie to me? My parents, Nick, Novalee. The events of the last few weeks nagged in my thoughts like a migraine. I worried if I didn't start getting some of it out of my system, I'd explode. And while we were lucky to have powers that could mend broken windows and clean up flooded bedrooms, I figured operating with a level head was the more mature route. I was the Mother, after all.

I sat next to her, tucking my legs under my butt. We

stared blankly at the waves. I'd planned to confront her, but she looked young and vulnerable sitting in the sand—how Calla looked after being scolded or sent to time out.

There'd be no need for confrontation. I understood. As difficult as the last several weeks had been, I wasn't the only one suffering.

"Do you know why you forgive so easily?" Novalee asked. She could always read me like a book. Maybe it was the protector in her.

I shook my head. Before Calla's accident, I had no reason to offer unconditional forgiveness.

"A mother's love is one of the most powerful kinds of love." Novalee glanced my way. "A perfect love."

And now I was *the* Mother.

"You have free will, free choice, of course." She closed her eyes. "But I know your heart."

We sat silently with our eyes fixated on the rolling ocean waves. Serenity engulfed us. I closed my eyes, waiting to feel Calla's presence. The only way to connect to her now was here, on the beach at the Almighty's gateway.

"What's it like?" I asked, stretching my legs out in front of me. The heels of my feet sunk into wet sand. "The Hark?"

"Beautiful," Novalee whispered. Glancing over, I saw a single tear roll down her perfect complexion.

In the fifteen years I'd known Novalee, I had never seen her cry. Not a single tear. I was the emotional one, having cried enough tears over the course of our long friendship to cover for the both of us.

I figured it would be rude, and definitely not the appropriate time, to point it out. But as the tear traveled toward her chin, she carefully scooped it up with her index finger.

"We don't cry." Novalee studied the tiny droplet for a

second before rubbing it between her thumb and index finger. "We hear the prayers and cries of the mortals, yet we only know goodness and love in the Hark."

A world without all the bad, messy stuff sounded pretty good to me.

"Did you know the first time I felt pain was when we got our tattoos?" Her eyes were clear and refocused.

"Our sisters knot," I stated with a smile playing at my lips.

"Forever bound, forever sisters."

I FOUND Nick sitting in the kitchen with his elbows propped on the table, chin in hand. An untouched beer sat in front of him. He heard me enter. I knew by the slight jerk of his head as the door clicked behind me.

"We need to talk," I said, still standing in the foyer. "Want to go for a walk?"

Nick's head bobbed a yes. Before moving to me, he picked up the beer and tipped it back, draining it in one fluid gulp. Setting the bottle down, he turned and gave a resolute nod.

"When in Ireland, do as the Irish?" I shrugged.

Nick wordlessly took my elbow and guided me out of the cottage. We stood under the hot sun, each looking in opposite directions.

"Let's go this way." I gestured toward the eastern path. It shared an opening to the trail that led down to the beach. I knew Novalee was still down there. The gateway fed her the additional energy that'd be needed in the days to come.

It wasn't until we were thick into the woods that Nick stopped, taking both my arms, and twisting me to face him.

"I wish there was another way," he said, looking more forlorn than I thought possible. "But I made a vow to you, to both of us, that we'd bind the marriage once the link was severed, once you came to me of your own intention. I cannot fail. Do you understand?"

I itched to touch him, to reach over and brush off the flop of hair that seemed to always make its way over his brow, but there was no use now. Soon, all those urges to comfort, the emotions, the constant awareness of one another, all of it would be swiped away. It was the only way Nick could keep his vow, a vow that the God of Victory couldn't fail.

"I know we can get through this. It's just one more step, Mira. One more challenge."

Instead of replying, I hung my head down and willed away my tears.

"Mira, can you look at me?" he pled.

I met his eyes, then wished I hadn't. So much pain, sadness, and regret weighed heavy on his face. This time, I didn't hold back. My hand flew to cup his cheek, and I forced a smile.

"I get it, I do," I said softly, "but I'm scared."

He leaned over, brushing a kiss on my cheek. *"Be not fearful. There is no fear in love, but perfect love casts out fear*. I know your heart will lead you back to me."

"Can we go now?" I whispered. "Let's get this over with before I change my mind."

Nick nodded, taking my elbow and leading me silently back to the opening of the trail where we switched course, swinging to the left to take the steep, winding path to the beach.

As we descended, I felt it again, as I did when the elevator first opened to the trauma center, the day when grief had transported me straight out of my skin. An imminent sense of desperation and fear. My breath caught in my chest, and my legs trembled as we neared the bottom.

Novalee stood in the distance, her presence instantly calming me—like Nick's energy, only more encompassing and surreal. With the sun glistening over her blonde hair and the waves swooshing in the distance, she emitted an innocence, a purity, that could only be described as angelic. My feet moved on their own, taking me to Novalee without thought or resistance, even knowing what was to come.

"Are you ready for this?" Novalee said to me. She smiled brightly, yet it barely reached her eyes.

"If breaking my link to the divine is the only way, I guess this is it."

"Mira, it's going to hurt, it will. You'll be human, mortal, until your heart, your soul, chooses its path. Human emotion, human reasoning—without the assurance of the divine, without the link to Nick, without help from me—it'll be overwhelming. It'll set you on an emotional rollercoaster, from pain and anger to sadness and loneliness. You'll have to let it in, and then let it go. Let go of that which you cannot control. Have faith, have hope. I know your heart will lead you back to Nick." Novalee took my hand, and I flinched. "Not yet, I want to explain something to you first. You'll know when I'm ready. First, just feel her. Calla's out there, and in the days to come, I'll be here. I promise I will always be here. Waiting for you to return, for everything to return."

The current picked up, seemingly understanding the immensity of her words. I closed my eyes, willing myself to feel Calla's presence one last time before it was taken away. Like a faint mist that could not only be felt but also seen and heard, her sweet essence stroked my cheeks and brushed against my lips.

"Once I sever your link to the divine, you will feel that loss intensely, but as you remember, as you let it back in, that hole, that emptiness, will be filled again. Once you are able to put the pieces together, once your heart leads you back to Nick, the link will return. It'll return as swiftly as it's being severed. Be strong, Mira. I know you can be strong."

Now it was Nick taking my hand, murmuring words that stroked my cheek, the light feathery touch that had calmed me so often. "I'm sorry, Mira, but I made a vow to you, and this is the only way. You coming to me of free choice, free will, without the link."

"Let's get this done." I averted my eyes, which were again filling with tears.

"One last thing," Novalee said, our three sets of hands now connected to form a circle. "Remember, some things are beyond our control. There's no fault, no blame. Once you come to realize that, you will know your path." She squeezed my fingers, giving a faint smile before closing her eyes.

As if moving backward in time, living life in reverse, each event over the course of the last few weeks played in high speed rewind. From Nick and me on the path just a few minutes ago, to the second I spotted him in the Land when our two sets of stunned eyes connected in the unearthly park. Each minute plucked away, pulled like a page from a notebook, leaving the memory, but stripping the attached emotion.

My stomach filled with despair and doubt, fear and confusion. And then it was gone. Emptied.

Novalee gasped, then released our hands. "It's done,"

she whispered, stumbling backwards as she caught her breath.

I saw it in Nick's eyes, the way they widened as his chin tilted to the side. Something was terribly wrong. He moved to touch my cheek, but I jerked away, stepping in the opposite direction. Novalee, Nick, and I formed a defensive, jagged triangle.

"Oh no," I whispered, yanking my hand away and pressing it against my stomach. "What have we done?"

Nick didn't respond. Instead, he looked to the waves.

"What have we done?" Louder, I repeated the question. But the void refilled with emotion, so intense, I knew the answer. *Calla was gone.* Nick had taken her. He'd set this series of events in motion, and unless I submitted to him, she'd be lost, gone from me forever.

Deafening silence. Aching loneliness. Gut-wrenching grief.

I could hardly stomach looking at Nick, but I wanted him to know. I needed him to know.

I'd never forgive him. Deceiving me, taking our child, and now forcing my hand. If I didn't return to him, I'd never see Calla again.

No, I couldn't bear to look at him, let alone allow him to touch me.

We'd never consummate. *Never.*

THIRTY

Nick looked into my eyes, his face pleading as he raised a hand, reaching for me. I stumbled back, no longer feeling any semblance of comfort from his efforts. All of it gone, stripped, leaving only a big blanket of anger and resentment. I shivered, feeling so cold it could be snowing in summer.

"Mira? Look at me, sissy," Novalee implored, still panting from the exercise—from stripping the divine link. Her brows scrunched as fresh concern hardened her face.

Still I felt nothing. Her power as my protector... gone.

"Where is she?" I didn't recognize my voice, filled with so much loathing and disgust. It churned in my stomach like sour milk, and suddenly I was bent, heaving and puking onto the sand. Novalee rushed to my side, rubbing my back until the quakes subsided.

"Here, sit." She guided me to the water's edge, her hand hot on my back. My elbows dug into the sand, and I sunk further as waves splashed over my legs. My shorts were drenched, and I shivered from the frigid water, but the weight of the world was too heavy for me to move.

"I want him gone," I muttered through a clenched jaw, not bothering to look at either Nick or Novalee. Then I sobbed, the wretched howl of mourning, of a loss so deep, so profound. I wished the waves would sweep me away, carry me off so I didn't have to feel any of it.

"I know, sissy, I know. You're revisiting the memories, Calla's accident." She didn't touch me, instead, she sat next to me in the water, allowing it to lap her up as well. I almost felt bad. Novalee, who always looked so poised, so perfect, now sat immersed in sand and seawater, uneasy and anxious.

We sat for hours, silently watching the sea as I traveled on a rollercoaster of emotions. Stages of anger, grief, and loneliness ebbed and flowed as I relived each day since the accident, attaching new feelings to the memories using human emotion and reasoning.

Loneliness is where I remained as the sun set. Each person I loved had failed me—my parents, Nick, and Novalee.

"Let's go up," Novalee suggested. The moon peeked over the horizon. We'd scooted back as the tide rolled in, our backs almost touching the boulders that buttressed the cliff. "You can come back in the morning."

I had no energy left to speak, let alone argue. I let Novalee guide me up the trail—the same trail that Arthur and Anya had taken so many times in her attempts to appease the sea. Now I knew that in the end, there was no appeasing the sea.

The cottage lent no comfort, even knowing it was the place of my birth, the strong fortress that had kept me safe from the perils of the great outdoors. Nature had won, sweeping away my daughter and holding her prisoner.

Novalee led me inside where a fire radiated through the

great room. Nick sat at the sofa, perking up as we entered. The ire from earlier had simmered, and I was left with a hole, an emptiness so wide and vast that when I looked at him, I felt nothing. Not an ounce of anger, but also not an ounce of love.

"Mira," he spoke my name, his eyes hopeful.

"Hey, Nick," Novalee offered when I didn't answer. "She's okay."

Was I? I looked down to my feet and legs, caked in sand and dripping from the ocean. I felt nothing. Stripped, barren, empty. Maybe it was better this way, better than the grief and pain that threatened to consume me earlier.

"I've got to shower," I mumbled before walking away.

The shower didn't do anything. It couldn't wash off this unnerving feeling, not like before, when I could see the distress drip off my body and swirl down the drain. Without the link to the divine, I felt no such comfort.

Regardless, I stepped under the head and let cold water chill my already frozen bones. *Think, Mira, think,* I commanded and turned the water to hot. Maybe it'd get my blood and thoughts pumping.

But my poor Calla was drowning in that cold sea. How could I feel warmth when my baby was freezing?

She isn't freezing. Remember. A blip of Calla, soft and sweet. It came and went. Tears slipped from my eyes, falling over my cheeks. *Calla is safe, she's out there, waiting for us.*

But the great gloom took over, and once again I felt her loss.

Stepping from the shower, I didn't bother with a towel. Still dripping wet, I plodded to the adjoining bedroom and dropped onto the mattress, allowing the hole, the despair, to swallow me up into darkness.

THIRTY-ONE

The screech of tires. The smell of burning rubber.

Each morning I'd awaken from the same nightmare, with my eyes popping open and my head twisting side to side, searching for Calla. Then I'd remember, and the emotions would come crashing back.

Immeasurable days passed, mashing together into a blur of misery, until one morning when I rose to find Nick's large frame filling my bedroom's window frame.

"Nick," I mumbled, pulling the comforter tightly to my chin. He swiveled around, wide-eyed, like a child who'd been caught sneaking candy.

"Hey, sorry," he hesitated, then moved from the window to the door. "I didn't mean to... I just wanted to check on you. I'll leave, give you space."

"Wait," I said, fumbling to sit. Nick perked up, his shoulders straightening before he came to my side, his hand on my back as he helped support me.

Those hands... the hands that calmed me, caressed me, touched me with love and longing.

Again, a memory came and went, but all I was left with

was a hole, knowing Nick should be there, but not able to fit him in. Inadvertent tears fell from my eyes.

"Oh, Nick," I cried. "What have we done?"

"You haven't done anything, baby." His voice soothed, yet unlike before, it didn't feed my soul.

"It's not back, Nick. The link is not back."

"I know, baby. It takes time. It'll come."

"But it hurts so bad. I go from feeling nothing to feeling everything. It hurts, Nick." I sobbed now, back on the roller-coaster as my emotions ebbed out of control.

"I wish I could take it away," he whispered into my hair.

I nodded and swiped away the tears. "Just go. Please, just go." I rolled over and closed my eyes. I couldn't talk to him anymore. There was no use. The only thing that mattered was the vast void. The great nothingness. If I went there, I didn't feel the pain.

I heard the door shut. I don't know where he went, but I mustered whatever energy remained in my spent muscles and shuffled to the living room. Glancing around, I checked for signs of life. Everyone should be gone. Anya and Arthur were staying in the village, and Novalee at the beach. But who knows? Maybe they lied. I wouldn't put it past them. They all lied. That's simply what gods were, liars.

The wave of anger rapidly passed. After several seconds of silence, I gave a confirming nod. I was alone. With them gone, maybe I could think. But first I'd eat. Bread, fruit, whatever. It didn't matter. I just needed something to sustain me.

At least they'd stocked the refrigerator. It was the least they could do. I grabbed a brick of cheese and a sleeve of crackers. Good enough for me.

I shoved them in my mouth, gnawing with newfound hunger until tremors started in my belly, and I hunched over, heaving until my nervous stomach was empty again. I tossed the crackers behind me, not looking or caring to see where they landed. It didn't matter. Nothing did—Calla was gone.

I closed my eyes as the next wave drowned me. The loss of Calla. With the link severed, I couldn't feel her essence in the ocean's breeze. Panic gripped my throat.

She's out there, drowning in the sea, and I can't feel her. But they can. After all they'd done, all the lies. They've taken everything, stripped me of it all.

The emotional whiplash turned fresh anger toward Novalee. The one who'd taken the link, setting it aside until I go to Nick on my own, until I choose him without divine influence.

So now here we were, waiting for some strike of lightning to shoot those feelings created by a divine link back into my human soul. Until then, I was alone, so very alone. And I couldn't hear Calla.

Renewed anger lent some strength to my muscles. I moved to the fireplace and ran a finger along its edge. Nick kept it lit, the stone cottage's interior damp and chilly even with June's humidity. A vase of wildflowers was set at the corner of the mantle. Anya had picked them for me before returning to the village.

"I spotted calla lilies, but they haven't bloomed yet," she trailed off as she noted my watery eyes.

Where was Anya now? Having a second honeymoon at some cutesy bed and breakfast in town. If anyone were to blame, it was my parents. *Their* sin. The path *they* paved. Now they get to walk together, all forgiven, while I am left all alone.

"I don't even like daisies," I said through gritted teeth, then I swatted Anya's vase. It went flying, shattering against the wall. I walked over the shards and dirty water, feeling as crumpled as the petals.

The cottage was closing in on me—damp, dark, and hopeless. Without bothering to locate shoes, I bounded out the door, and down the gravel path to the trail at the cliff's edge, traveling the same path Nick and I had taken before the link was severed.

"The days ahead may test you, your strength, your beliefs. But faith, hope, and love will guide you. Even if you don't understand, they'll lead your heart on the right path." Jake's guidance, the lecture from the scorched farce of a wedding ceremony, stopped me in my tracks.

I brushed off his words, continuing with renewed vigor to get as far from the cottage as possible. The pebbles that bit into the soles of my feet didn't slow me down. No, the pain only propelled me further.

"There may be storms and sunny skies that delay or propel you." Now it was Arthur's words from the journal humming in my head. *"Understand we are part of something beyond ourselves, our own wants and needs. We are on our way to complete a most important plan."* I covered my ears, not wanting to hear any more, not from them. It was their fault anyways.

"Some things are beyond our control. There's no fault, no blame. Once you come to realize that, you will know your path." Novalee's voice echoed her last divine guidance before she stripped me of the link.

"Get out of my head!" I yelled to the trees.

"This needs to be your decision. I need you to come to me on your own, without that influence." Nick's vow to me.

"Then get out of my head," I whispered, still clutching my ears. I spun around, lost in thoughts I couldn't control, as the trees continued to rustle and whisper with moments of the past. They rushed over me like the crashing waves that consumed my baby.

Next, I was running. Running so fast, I made it back to the cottage, but I didn't stop there. I continued through the field. The grass scratched against my legs and rocks tore into my bare feet. The pain only drove me faster. I kept running, even as my lungs burned and my calves ached, until I made it clear across the lawn to the gravel road.

Our rental car, the one we'd gotten in Dublin, sat abandoned in the shoulder. I stopped to catch my breath, heaving as I grabbed the hood for support. I gave a frustrated groan before standing straight again.

And then I saw *it*. In the ditch across the road. It shouldn't be there. Maybe my eyes were playing tricks on me. I gingerly stepped over gravel, my feet bloodied and bruised. Bending to touch it, to confirm its tangible truth, I studied it, and then plucked it.

A perfect, lone calla lily. I placed it behind my ear.

Calla, my lily. Calla, my life. My life in the Land.

I was running again. Running so fast I thought my legs would lift off the ground. I kept going, past the cottage yet again, my feet only pushing harder as I came to the opening of the path, pumping and pumping, until I no longer hit the ground. I spiraled over the edge, soaring like Calla, plummeting into the sea below.

THIRTY-TWO

Water bubbled into my mouth and stung my nostrils, filling me as I sunk deeper, choking and gagging on algae and seaweed particles.

No, no, no. My eyes darted toward the fractured sunlight that skimmed the surface. I flapped my arms, trying to propel myself above water. The current sucked me back, rolling me over and over, until I jutted into the seabed. From there, it shot me upward like a ping-pong ball, rejecting me, and spitting me out. My head bobbed to the surface, and I flailed my limbs, struggling to stay afloat.

The rocky beach where Novalee was staked out was too low to spot, but the rugged boulders of my mother's beloved cliff towered in the distance. I dunked under, trying with all my might to paddle closer to shore—close enough where someone could hear my cries. The waves picked up and crashed over my head, pushing me back under.

Help me! I attempted to call out, but my words gurgled into the water. *Nick, help me! I need you!* Each movement of my lips only brought more water into my belly, and I tasted the briny flavor of the ocean. Like the nipple to a baby—like a mother's milk—it calmed me, and I no longer could fight. I allowed the ocean to embrace me, consume me.

Drowning, dying, but no longer afraid.

"Be not fearful. There is no fear in love, but perfect love casts out fear."

I closed my eyes, succumbing to the sea, and sinking further. Slowly now, like a bloated anchor drifting to the bottom of the ocean. My arms floated above my head as my legs dangled beneath my torso, no longer feeling like a part of my body. Instead, they were weights floating away and freeing me from the past.

As they slipped away, I felt the release. My confessions, guilt, sins, and regrets. Everything clearing from my conscious, each piece of my life that had beleaguered me since before my birth.

"Let go of that which you cannot control. Have faith. I know your heart will lead you back."

I wasn't giving up. I was letting go, allowing the sea to free me of the control I guarded so closely, cleanse me of the doubts and fears, every misgiving that held me from having faith that my heart would lead me back. They floated away, lifting in layers until I was stripped bare, my life whittled down to its essence, where I could finally see its truths.

My child, born of the gods, destined to lead a new era.

My parents, sinners like me, given redemption.

My husband, my chosen one, holding me in his victorious arms.

My eyes popped open, but at the bottom of the sea, I couldn't see anything, and I couldn't move. It was too late.

The sea had stripped away everything, including my life.

No, Nick. It can't end like this, not after all we've been through. It isn't over. Not until I tell you. Not until I say it.

I love you.

THIRTY-THREE

"You're okay. You're okay." Nick's hand stroked my cheek. I bolted upright, heaving and spitting up saltwater.

"Mira!" Novalee rushed from the shoreline. "Mira!"

Nick leaned in, cupping my face, his thumbs brushing over my lips. "Can you hear me?"

Still sputtering, I nodded, and relief passed over his face.

"It's back!" Novalee exclaimed, leaning in and hugging me. "Stay still. Don't try to move." She lay next to me on the beach and ran her hands over my body, sucking up the sea that had bloated my system.

"Better?" She grinned, wiggling her hands.

I nodded again and sat up, feeling more normal than humanly possible after a brush with death. *But I'm not just human.* Now I grinned, feeling the divine, the link that not only bound me to Nick, but transcended nature's two planes. *Divine and human.*

"I'm more than okay. I'm alive!" My voice came out surprisingly light and airy.

Nick shook his head in amazement, his eyes widening with relief. "You're back. *It's* back," he whispered.

I nodded, grinning ear to ear, as Nick lifted me from the sand, and hugged me, spinning around with a joy I felt deep in my soul. Our link was back.

Nick's arms remained around me as we started up the trail. Novalee followed a few paces behind, her breath labored.

"You okay?" Nick turned back to check on her.

"Yeah. That was intense," she puffed out, smiling brightly.

"You're telling me." I laughed, then stopped to link hands with Novalee, Nick on my other side. "But, we did it. The first step at least."

"Maybe I should leave you two alone, you know, for the next step." Novalee's eyebrows shot up, and then she giggled as she winked suggestively. "But seriously, I really should stay at the beach. I'll be recharged in no time."

The gateway could help her recover much faster than food or drink. She squeezed my hand before leaving, and I knew then, she'd come into her own. She'd become the protector she was destined to be.

ONCE ALONE WITH NICK, a new shyness arose as I became keenly aware of him. His mind, body, soul. He emanated with pleasure, longing, happiness, excitement... every and any good thought bounced off him and hit me in waves of pure bliss.

"Maybe lunch can wait," I whispered, looking up from under my eyelashes, "but I definitely need a shower."

Nick's eyes swept my face, his desire already stroking me. "While you hop in the shower, I'll make you a plate."

After showering away sea and sand, I took care in combing my hair, rubbing lotion over my body and pinching my cheeks into a rosy glow. And then I tried it—mind control to create something sexy. Closing my eyes, my face scrunched with concentration. I reopened them, looked down, and giggled. A filmy, white negligee, erotic yet feminine, covered my skin.

I stepped out of the bathroom, catching my breath as I peered around the adjoining bedroom. Long, sheer curtains waved from an open window, and a lacy blanket with pink rosebuds stitched along its edges adorned the bed. Delicate bouquets of white roses and calla lilies covered every open space. The same room Nick had created for me at his home in the Land now stood before me.

Nick waited near the window, his eyes turning dark with desire as they met mine. I was in his arms in two steps, kissing him, stroking his hair and face. My hands desperately traveled along his shoulders and over his chest, then back up to his face, cupping his cheeks.

"Do you know what brought it back?" I whispered, looking into his eyes. His head shook slightly. "The thought that I'd never get to say it. That I'd die, and you would never hear it." Nick tilted his head. "I love you. I *love* you, Nick."

His mouth crushed mine, confirming my words. I was in his arms and on the bed in one swift motion. Nick's lips were back on mine, while his fingers traced over my arms, hips, belly, absorbing each curve, as they peeled away the filmy gown. Glorious minutes passed as he caressed every inch of my body, his hands moving by memory.

When our bodies joined for the first time as husband and wife, I saw Nick. All of him. The sum of his existence flashed in a second. Every smile and tear, each laugh and cry. Victories, the good and bad. Stunned, I looked into his eyes, and saw my life flash just as quickly. Fleeting memories, there and gone before we had a chance to absorb them.

Our eyes remained locked, our bodies connected. My skin again seared with Nick's touch, but as we rocked, his touch—this new touch—ignited into a fire, smoldering like the sun. Over and over, little fires erupted between us, dying out, then reigniting until our two bodies and our two souls melded into one.

THIRTY-FOUR

"Good morning." Nick sat on the edge of the bed. Sunlight streamed over his sandy hair. My limbs were heavy as I struggled to sit up, exhausted from a day and night filled with lovemaking.

A wave of nausea passed over me, and I clutched my mouth. Bolting from the bed, I ran to the bathroom, heaving and gagging into the toilet. Nick came behind me, patting my back and holding my hair from my face. My fingers clenched the toilet, and I shuddered as nausea rolled over my body.

Alarm filled his face, but as he looked from the toilet to me, his eyes lit up. "You're pregnant!"

Pregnant? Already? How could it even be possible?

The thought was confirmed by another wave of hormones that bowled through my stomach. Along with the queasiness, I felt her there now. My sweet Calla, safely back within me. I closed my eyes, still grasping the edge of the bowl.

A flickering light—the heartbeat of life.

I snatched my hands from the toilet and brought them

over my belly. Coarse laughter turned to sobs as I wrapped my arms around him.

"She's here, Nick. She's here."

∼

CALLA SEEMED to grow bigger by the hour. Within a day, my belly extended well past the waistline of my pants. I had to change into a forgiving dress as my body quickly filled out. By the second day, I felt kicks. She grew at an alarming, unnatural speed. During the third day, I swelled from pregnancy.

Arthur and Anya returned from the village and joined us in the cottage, which had magically sprouted more rooms, to await Calla's rebirth. Our home buzzed with activity as we harmoniously prepared for her imminent arrival. Novalee and Anya worked feverishly, setting up a nursery in my old childhood room, using both their minds and hands to create an homage to the sea. Little fish and octopus hung from Calla's mobile, and an aqua-blue baby quilt hung over the crib.

Toward the end of the third day, my back ached with an intensity I could only describe as early labor pains. Sorely uncomfortable, I begged Novalee to walk with me down to the sea.

"It's calling me," I told her through gritted teeth. "It's calling me." But Novalee insisted it wasn't time, and the walk down the steep cliff was too dangerous with my swollen belly. So instead, I took a long bath filled with seawater. It soothed my aching back, but wasn't enough.

During that last restless night of pregnancy, I rolled out of bed. Sleep was futile. The pain in my back had intensified to the point that I knew Calla would be arriving soon. My stomach bulged like a balloon ready to pop.

Grabbing my robe and padding to the kitchen, I planned to warm up milk. As a pang ripped from my tailbone to my legs, I set the empty mug down with shaking hands and stumbled to the window. Soft waves echoed in the distance.

Before I knew it, I found myself on the trail leading to the beach. My belly bobbed as I slowly trekked barefoot down the path. The moon provided the only light, and the air was eerily quiet. Each step closer to the shore brought a calmness I hadn't felt in days.

Making it safely to the bottom, I buried my feet in the cool, wet sand. A gust of wind disrupted the quiet as my heels sunk in. Happy shivers shot through my body. *Yes, this is right.*

Sitting down, I looked to the dark horizon above rolling waves. Calla sensed the sea. Her body swooshed and danced within my belly.

"Slow down, naughty girl," I chided, and then lifted my nightgown to rub sand over the spot where her feet lay. She slowly pressed toward it. I watched in wonder as my belly extended with the form of her foot. "It's almost time, baby."

Periods of rest were followed by moments of intense pain. Time moved so slowly that I barely noticed the sun beginning its ascent in the early dawn of morning.

The first real contraction stabbed in my back just as warm rays hit the surface of the sea. Doubling over, I panted through the pain. Tears blurred my vision as I looked toward the cliff above me. I shouldn't have come down the trail alone. It was too early in the morning for Nick to wake and notice I was gone, and the contractions were rapidly intensifying.

Breathe, breathe, one... two... three... I repeated in my head. *Breathe.* I inhaled and exhaled through each ripping ache.

Moving to my knees, I groaned and grasped at sand as another contraction rolled over me. After it passed, I gathered what energy I could muster to call out into the silent air.

"Nick! Mom! Novalee!" Clouds formed as I uttered each name, blocking the sun's dim light. "I'm down here!" A tear slipped down my cheek as rain started to sprinkle my heated skin. "Nick..." It came out as a choked whisper. There was no way they could possibly hear me.

A low, primal groan echoed through the air as I bucked at the pain. The sky reacted with a rumble of thunder, as if we were in agony together, weeping along with me.

Panting heavily, I crawled into the water. My nightgown dragged from the weight of rain and sea. I moved on all fours, scooting further from shore, until my entire belly was immersed in the icy waters. The wind howled, and waves crashed over my cumbersome body. Lightning blinded the sky, and I shook along with the land and sea.

I'm going to drown. I can't do this alone. I'm going to drown.

The sea continued her assault, and I became certain the waves would swallow me before I could deliver Calla. I had no energy left to face the pain. I groaned to the sky, and prayed, calling to Novalee, my protector.

Where are you? I need you!

Over and over in my head I repeated my plea until, miraculously, I saw flashlights through the rain.

As Nick, my parents, and Novalee treaded down the muddied path, relief flooded my body just as another wave crashed overhead. The sea was turning rough. She was ready.

Nick and Arthur's arms were laden with blankets and flashlights. Novalee and Anya hurried to me, their legs swishing in the water as they rushed by my side.

"This way, Mira," Anya directed as Novalee placed a firm hand under my armpit. They helped me crawl back toward the shore.

Unable to vocalize my gratitude, I looked to them with love and hope. Just like Calla's first delivery, Novalee and my mother stood on either side of me. Their presence lent renewed strength just as another strong contraction crept from my tailbone to the very core of me. I thrust my head back and moaned. Novalee positioned her hand under one leg, and Anya grabbed the other. They coached me through the next contraction while Nick and Dad remained behind us, helpless to ease my pain.

As the tightening in my belly heightened, I could no longer acknowledge any of them. I was being torn open, my vision blurring to a stinging light. The world around me spun, white and bright, twirling beyond recognition.

"I found her out here, by herself!" a man's voice exclaimed. "Where's the midwife?"

A firm hand clutched the woman's arms, hoisting her from where she rocked on all fours, screaming in agony, "The baby's coming!" She was led to the shore, where she sunk back into wet sand.

The bright sun shone above, and the scent of antiseptic from a midwife's freshly cleansed hands stung her nostrils. Confusion and chaos choked the air as a crowd formed.

Tears, sweat, blood. Dripping in distress. Pleas and cries.

"She's bleeding. There's so much blood!" Desperate voices.

"She's coming!" Novalee and Mom's arms held steady as they coaxed me through the final phase. "She's coming. Push, push, you're almost there!"

"Push, push, you're almost there!" The midwife ordered. "It's almost over, puuush!"

"I see her head, Mira, you can do it. One more push! It's almost over. Puuush!" Novalee commanded.

Her head bent back, her face contorted in agony.

We shrieked together, the primitive sounds of birth, screams of pain and life. I felt my baby pass through me just as I felt another life, distant but familiar, being born. We cried together, the young mother and me, with joy and relief as our children were delivered into the world.

The blinding pain had ceased but a new pain was building in me. I waited for the first cry. I closed my eyes feeling blindly as I struggled to reach for Calla

"It's a boy!" a voice exclaimed.

She reached for her baby but was too weak. Her head fell back. "Why isn't he crying?" she choked out. "Where is he?"

Frantic commands, yelling, screaming.

Her chest tightened. "Where..." She again reached to feel for her baby, but the space went black.

"Why isn't she crying?" I heard my own voice. "Where is she?" I grasped air, reaching for my baby. As I searched frantically, my wild eyes rested on Novalee who was calmly holding a wide-eyed Calla. They gazed at one another. Tears slid down Novalee's cheek, falling over Calla. She brushed a gentle kiss, and then delivered my daughter to me.

"Welcome back, little one," Nick whispered, resting his arms over my shoulders. Calla blinked, her eyes lighting in recognition.

The waves picked up, splashing against my swollen

body. Arthur took Calla from my arms, while Nick and Anya helped me move further up the beach onto a blanket. I looked out to the waves where Novalee still waded. The sun had returned and was showering over her, a golden halo.

She's an angel.

"Novalee," I whispered. Her posture stiffened as she turned toward me, a slight smile lighting her face. But as a gentle wave rolled over her shins, she stumbled, and then crumbled into the sea. "Novalee!" I cried, scrambling to get up.

Anya was already splashing into the water, moving to pull Novalee's lifeless body to shore. I reached beside to help. As I touched Novalee's ashen face, a jolt of energy passed through us, flowing from me to Novalee to my mom.

We connected by more than the touch of skin, we were united. *A cord of three.*

Novalee's eyes remained closed, but I felt her mind working fervently as she silently spoke to us in images.

A baby whose first cry went unheard. He was born and delivered home, followed shortly by a twin sister. Warmth and love, clouds and music. They sat among the angels. Bathed in gold, her dress was pearls and his playground was arches and waterfalls. They danced in the clouds and sang in the sun.

A little girl swirling and singing, her white hair fanned like a halo. Angels watched as a symphony of music floated in sunshine. Her face radiated with pure joy. Safe and secure, blanketed in perfect love, she was home.

The little girl looked to us; a child, yet we recognized her. With sparkling blue eyes that shined like sapphires, she stopped singing to smile. She floated closer, igniting into a divine ray of light.

She was home.

The images dissipated, and Novalee remained limp in our arms.

"Nick! Help us!" I screamed.

Nick picked Novalee up in his arms and carried her to the blanket on the sand. He looked back to me, shaking his head.

"No! Help her!" I was shaking, and the sand beneath my feet trembled with my pleas. "Dad! Help her!" Arthur took over, handing Calla to Nick, who then came to me as sobs racked my body.

My mother, shocked by the scene unfolding, stood frozen. Tears streamed from her sorrowful blue eyes.

Sparkling blue eyes that shined like sapphires. A baby whose first cry went unheard.

"Twins, Mom, they were *twins!*" I exploded, sending Nick stumbling back. Confusion and desperation suffocated me. I could barely choke out words. "Mom, Dad, help her."

They came together, realization settling over my parents like a wall of wind, hitting them so hard the sky shook. Anya fell to her knees, sobbing as she reached to hold onto my dad and Novalee.

It was their tears dropping from the clouds above as they held their daughter for the first time.

THIRTY-FIVE

Long after Novalee left us, we remained on the beach. Her mortal body lay peaceful in final rest, her skin white like clouds in a clear sky.

Anya was wracked with grief. For years the protector had come to them, and they had not known she was their child. Perhaps Novalee herself did not know. Now it was too late for answers.

Afternoon turned to evening as we continued to quietly mourn. My dad came to Nick and me, encouraging us to return to the cottage. Hormones from birth roiled my body. I needed to mourn my best friend, *my sister*, but I had just gone through a taxing delivery.

Nick cared for Calla while I took a long, hot shower to cleanse my body of sand, salt, sweat, and tears. I watched them swirl down the drain and wished I could rinse away the memories of the last several hours—the final moments before Novalee crumbled into the sea.

Novalee's ashen face and snow-white skin. My mother's stricken cries. I feared the images would haunt me forever.

Fresh tears formed in my eyes. I lifted my face to the

water, trying to wash away my sorrow. How could she be gone?

As I soaped my body, I felt the spot above my hip, where our tattoo would be an eternal reminder of our sisterhood.

Forever bound, forever sisters. Somehow, the sentiment calmed me, and I managed to mindlessly dry myself off, slip into pajamas, and fall into a dreamless sleep, not waking until the following morning.

The other side of the bed and the bassinette were empty, but Nick's voice carried from the kitchen below as he hummed a song to Calla. I pushed myself up from plush pillows and felt my stomach. It was surprisingly tight following childbirth. I healed quickly following Calla's first birth, but the taut tummy under my touch was as unnatural as the pregnancy.

Downstairs, Nick worked his way around the kitchen with Calla in his arms. Coffee perked in the pot, biscuits browned before my eyes, and eggs sizzled on the stovetop. I watched from the stairs as he looked to the sink, and water spouted into a cup. Multitasking with a little bend of the rules; I couldn't help but smile.

"There you are, dear wife." He looked up, quickly coming to me.

I pulled Calla from Nick and held her tight in my arms. Her eyes popped open, and she stared up at me with an unusual alertness for a newborn. "Will she grow faster during this rebirth?"

"Hmm?" he asked over his shoulder, now using his hands to pour another cup of coffee.

"Will she grow up faster?" Calla's eyes widened as I spoke. She broke away from my gaze and gave a toothless, gummy grin.

Nick peered over my shoulder, looking down into Calla's tiny face. The familiar crop of dark hair and sparkling eyes from her first infancy stared back at us. She peeked from Nick to me, as if also waiting for his answer. "My pregnancy breezed by in days. Is the concept of time different for gods?"

As he considered my question, he brushed a finger along Calla's cheek. "Time in the mortal world follows clocks and calendars. When we return, you'll learn more about the ways of the gods."

When we return. Of course, we'd go back to our home in the Land. The Sea and Land now separate, but forever connected. We'd return to our home, a place where Calla could be taught the ways of the gods.

She giggled, as if taking in Nick's words. Her little body wiggled with excitement.

"Does she understand us? Does she remember everything from her previous life?"

"Not now, but in time she will." Nick's finger rolled from Calla's cheek down my arm. His touch shot shivers down my spine. "At least, I think she will. Arthur remembered his past life and eventually Anna—Anya—did after her rebirth."

"Will Novalee be reborn?"

He smiled gently. "She's completed her divine task. She's earned her wings, a home among the angels. I know you are sad, heartbroken, but Mira, it's the ultimate reward to sit among the angels and saints, to earn the glory of the Kingdom—the heaven of heavens. You will understand in time, but she is *home.*"

"Will we see her again?" I read the answer in his eyes. "Never?"

"Angels in the divine world are much like saints.

They're supreme beings, purely divine. She no longer can transcend the border. I'm sorry, baby. I really am. Please know, as an angel, Novalee will only know love and peace. She'll never again feel pain or sadness. She'll never again experience the impurities of humanity."

A part of me did understand. I saw her memories; I felt them. An intense love. *A perfect love.* Her world was filled with the purest beauty and grace.

I had to accept that she was home, yet I wished I could thank her and say goodbye. *Not as a friend, but as my sister.*

Calla fell asleep in my arms. I didn't want to put her down. Her little body offered me the greatest comfort in dealing with Novalee's loss, but I grew restless sitting on the couch in silence, unable to shake my sorrow. I noticed a television that I was certain hadn't been there before, set on top of an entertainment center.

"What's with the TV?" I called, trying to keep my voice low enough to not disturb Calla.

Nick grabbed the remote and flipped it on. "I got a little bored during the night when Calla woke." He looked sheepish. "I know, I know. I shouldn't bend the rules. But while I'm confessing, I tapped into my favorite American stations." His eyebrows wiggled mischievously. "I don't know what's come of TV, but all I could find in the night were those ridiculous reality shows."

"Well, what's the use of being a god, unless we can bend the rules every so often?" I shrugged, and leaned into a cushion. "I kind of miss the normalcy of television."

Nick's face faltered, and I followed his eyes to the screen.

"Breaking News... Alert... Breaking News..." scrolled along the bottom. Nick turned up the volume, and we listened to the news anchor's solemn voice.

"We're still getting updates on a raid that occurred early yesterday morning at a compound in Constanta, Romania, located along the coast of the Black Sea. Internal sources close to the operation tell us that mass amounts of an unspecified chemical were discovered within the compound that would have had a catastrophic effect on millions of Europeans should the region's water resources, including the Black Sea, have been poisoned in an unprecedented bio-terrorism attack. We'll keep viewers updated as we learn more. In other news, category five hurricane Lily has pushed further off track from original projections..."

Nick leaned back and closed his eyes. "I don't think that's a coincidence."

~

SETTLING Calla in the nursery that had been staged in my childhood bedroom, I absorbed the memories of the last several days when we had prepared in haste for her arrival. Created as a tribute to the Sea, the only animal of the Land was Leo. I smiled at the little stuffed lion that Novalee, the protector, had given to Calla as a baby. He was to be hers again, forever her best and most courageous friend. Her personal protector.

I ran a finger over Leo's plush body, again thinking of my best friend—my sister. My eyes filled with tears, but I quickly brushed them away as I heard Nick's voice call out. Arthur and Anya had returned. I gave Leo a little squeeze, hoping he'd extend some strength to me as I faced my parents.

We sat around the fireplace as they told us vaguely of the events from the last twenty-four hours. A sense of serenity settled over them, and it was apparent they did not want to interrupt the peace that had been restored following their devastating revelation.

Arthur's tranquil tone soothed as he spoke of Novalee's death. I wondered if it was purposeful. Was he, as a scribe, saying the words in such a way to maintain our calm? Anya sat poised and resolute while my dad described the beauty that unfolded in the sky.

I smiled as his words replaced the images in my head. No longer could I envision my friend's—*my sister's*—crumpled body being consumed by the waves or her ashen face as she left us. I no longer heard my mother's cries when she realized the profound truth.

I only saw the picture painted by my father—Novalee's soul in all its beauty and glory being delivered home. She basked in the sun's golden rays, filled with pure warmth and perfect love as her spirit lifted ever so gently toward the sky. She was gone with the clouds, dispersing into the air, leaving nothing but bright blue skies in her wake.

EPILOGUE

Arthur scribbled frantically in the journal. He'd been holed up in a makeshift office on the second floor of the cottage for hours. Something was happening, something he did not yet understand. He let his hands take over as the words flowed, writing so quickly he could barely decipher the thoughts that erupted from within his soul and poured onto the paper.

Sun filtered into the room, choking the air. Arthur's eyes darted from the journal to the window. Beads of perspiration formed around his hairline. The temperature peaked, almost unbearably, but he couldn't stop writing. Drops of sweat fell freely from his face, dripping over the paper and smudging his words.

Like a dying star, a supernova, she will burst with one final explosion before fading.

Arthur was burning out, drained by the heat and the intense energy of the room. The sun shone so brightly he had to shield his eyes as he feverishly finished the last sentence. His eyes welled up, and soon tears mixed with sweat fell over the journal like a baptism. He wept and his hand trembled.

The final page of her story was complete, but he realized with hope, it was just the beginning. He reread the last line, a sob escaping as he absorbed the words.

She will reignite, a new star lighting the sky. She is destined to shine brighter than ever.

He shut the book and wrote in large, block letters on the cover: *To Nova, Light of the Sky.*

ALSO BY GINA STURINO

Of the Gods

Fruit of the Land (Book One)

Light of the Sky (Book Two) Coming January 2021

ABOUT THE AUTHOR

Gina Sturino has been devouring romance novels since her teenage years. After marrying her very own Prince Charming, she found the inspiration to write her debut novel. While her husband isn't a god (like Nick in Fruit of the Land), he's pretty darn close (he may or may not have told her to write that), and helped inspire the character. They've lived in cities coast-to-coast and have settled in their hometown outside of Madison, Wisconsin, where they are raising their daughter.

You can find author Gina Sturino at:
www.ginasturino.com
Sign up for her super exciting newsletter at:
https://ginasturino.com/newsletter/
Gina loves to hear from readers! Email her at:
gina@ginasturino.com

facebook.com/ginasturino
instagram.com/ginasturino

ACKNOWLEDGMENTS

When my husband and I married, he said it'd be a "funky adventure". I can honestly say he has delivered. Thank you Hubbin' for helping me realize each and every dream, including writing this book.

I am extremely fortunate to have a close-knit, loving family. There's never a dull moment at our get-togethers, from dance parties to pie-eating contests. Much love and gratitude to you all - your support and encouragement means the world to me!

To my parents, thanks for your love and guidance. You're perfect role models in parenthood, marriage, life, and love.

To my O-Monster, thanks for bringing me so much joy, and for always telling me you're proud of your mama.

I've made many amazing friendships over the years, but one of my oldest, dearest friends provided the inspiration for Novalee. Like Mira and Novalee, we were college room-mates turned "real-life" roommates, and many of my favorite memories include her. Cheers to you, BRE!

To my Milwaukee crew, UW, DeFo, and military

friends, you guys are the best! I treasure the crazy memories made and look forward to creating many more!

Special thanks to my workout buddy – sorry for all the texts! I'm so grateful for our friendship!

Finally, my sincerest gratitude to the wonderful friends I've made in the writing community, including my incredible editor Jessica Fraser, publishing mentor Amy Briggs, and fabulous beta readers.

Made in the USA
Monee, IL
09 September 2021